Kensington books by Jodi Thomas

Honey Creek Novels

Breakfast at the Honey Creek Café

Picnic in Someday Valley

Dinner on Primrose Hill

Sunday at the Sunflower Inn

Historical Romance

Beneath the Texas Sky

Anthologies:

The Wishing Quilt

A Texas Kind of Christmas

The Cowboy Who Saved Christmas

Be My Texas Valentine

Give Me a Cowboy

Give Me a Texan

Give Me a Texas Outlaw

Give Me a Texas Ranger

One Texas Night

A Texas Christmas

SUNDAY
at the
SUNFLOWER INN

JODI THOMAS

ZEBRA BOOKS
Kensington Publishing Corp.
www.kensingtonbooks.com

ZEBRA BOOKS are published by

Kensington Publishing Corp.
119 West 40th Street
New York, NY 10018

All Kensington titles, imprints, and distributed lines are available at special quantity discounts for bulk purchases for sales promotion, premiums, fund-raising, and educational or institutional use.

Special book excerpts or customized printings can also be created to fit specific needs. For details, write or phone the office of the Kensington Sales Manager: Kensington Publishing Corp., 119 West 40th Street, New York, NY 10018. Attn. Sales Department. Phone: 1-800-221-2647.

Zebra and the Z logo Reg. U.S. Pat. & TM Off.

First Printing: April 2023
ISBN-13: 978-1-4201-5138-1
ISBN-13: 978-1-4201-5139-8 (eBook)

10 9 8 7 6 5 4 3 2 1

Printed in the United States of America

For my beautiful grandchildren

Chapter 1

The Lost McCoy

Friday, February 14
Houston, Texas

McCoy Mason leaned his crutches next to his duffel bag and sat down on the bench just outside Houston Methodist Hospital's main exit.

If a cab came by, he might get in.

If he had any idea where he was going.

If he had enough money to get there.

Three "ifs" seemed a long shot. He decided to sit on the bench until a few of his brain cells thawed. After three weeks in the hospital, his mind had slipped to the IQ of a frog.

On the bright side, the sun was shining and the wind was low. Except for the fact he was headed nowhere, life wasn't all bad. Maybe he was just confused, maybe mixed up and disoriented. Definitely broken. Homeless. Alone.

McCoy decided to stop thinking. He was running out of adjectives.

"I'm not lost, just nowhere to go," he said aloud. "Not brain dead, just wounded." He looked down at his cast. The tip of a sock covered his toes. He had a boot on the other foot, but one cowboy boot wouldn't be much use once he got the cast off.

Maybe he could go to the beach. Then he wouldn't need even one boot. He could just be a beach bum until his money ran out.

He almost smiled remembering what his crazy dad used to say when his mom suggested a vacation. "It don't cost nothin' to go nowhere."

Maybe he should stay here and save what little money he had left.

McCoy shrugged. Nowhere seemed about as good as anywhere to go right now.

Mom must have disagreed with Dad. One night she left with all their savings and never came back from her vacation. Dad got up the next morning and went to work and never mentioned her again.

McCoy looked down at his new Wranglers. The nurse had to cut through the denim to get one pant leg over the cast. He'd considered yelling at her to cut off the plaster instead. After all, he could hop around on one leg, but he only owned one pair of jeans. But before he could put words to his thoughts, the damage was done.

Right now, the break just below his knee was the least of his troubles. One broken bone seemed no big deal, considering his other problems. He'd had a head injury everyone thought would kill him after he'd totaled his Mustang on Interstate 45. He lived, but the car died.

Breanna Bell, his fiancée, stopped coming around after three days. She'd said that staring at his bruised, broken body was too much to bear.

She should have seen it from his side of the fence.

Two days later, his new boss called and told him he'd lost the job that had brought him to Houston. A week later, his landlord texted that the apartment he'd signed a lease on was no longer available.

Last, Breanna left town, taking everything but the duffel bag with his work clothes stuffed in the bottom and the outfit he'd bought the day of the accident. Jeans, a western shirt, and a Stetson hat—his first western outfit. After all, he was in Texas now.

Breanna had talked him into getting hundred-dollar tickets to a rodeo the night of his crash and clothes to go with the date so he'd fit in with the crowd. But he'd never made it home to change. Now he felt like an imposter dressed up as a cowboy.

The one time he'd been awake enough to talk to Breanna on the hospital phone, she'd been mad about him standing her up. She also mentioned the moving van with all their junk would be on its way back to Georgia and she planned to ride along.

She didn't have time to unpack and pick all his stuff out, so if he wanted anything, he could collect it the next time he was in Georgia. She'd shopped for most of the household essentials, so she considered everything more hers than his. Just before she'd hung up, his fiancée said she'd stuffed her engagement ring in the chest pocket of his work overalls.

He must have decided to go back in a coma about then because days later when he opened his eyes, he couldn't remember much else of what she'd said.

If the hospital hadn't saved his wallet and phone when they cut off his bloody clothes, she probably would have taken them as well. His cell was dead, but a few hundred dollars were still in his wallet.

He was in too much pain to think, so he gave up on time and dates completely. Hell, he didn't even care what year it was. The facts he thought he knew: He was twenty-nine, single, had no kin he wanted to call. Oh, and he loved the hospital ice cream and hated the Jell-O.

Now and then, one of the nurses would wake him up and ask him what his name was. If he got that right, they'd move on to, "Do you know the date?" like it was some kind of trick question.

How could he explain that he didn't know or care? The last construction site he'd worked on had relocated inside his brain, and the noise was blocking everything out.

As the sun started to set behind the buildings of downtown Houston, McCoy frowned, trying to recall Breanna part by part. Her hair was soft. Her breasts were rounded. Her mouth was always moving.

He smiled, remembering another one of his dad's sayings. "Son, the right girl for you is the one who says yes. Don't build up your hopes on more."

Night was moving across the huge parking lot, and McCoy didn't bother to care. He didn't have enough money in his pocket to start over, and no one was picking him up. He'd inherited being a loner from his dad. "No sense making friends you'll just leave behind, son."

McCoy considered sitting on this bench until he starved to death. If he took the painkillers in his pocket, he probably wouldn't notice hunger or cold. Three weeks ago, he'd had a smoking hot girlfriend, a new direction, and a great car. The job he'd moved halfway across the country for promised to lead him toward the future he'd always wanted. He would have been the boss of this building site. Not bad considering he wasn't yet thirty.

Somehow one wreck washed away all of his chalkboard dreams.

The janitor who had cleaned his hospital room walked by. "Evening, Mr. Mason." The short man grinned like they were old friends. "You finally getting out of this place, or did one of them nurses just leave you out here by accident? I swear if you stay still around this place, they think you're a potted plant."

McCoy smiled. "Evening, Roberto. I'm going to miss your great jokes. Most days you were the only one who talked to me other than the nurses asking questions."

Roberto set a lunch box on the bench as he zipped a gray jacket that matched his uniform. As always, he seemed to have time to talk. "That pretty, long-legged blonde picking you up? I wouldn't mind hanging around to see her."

"No, she's gone. Moved back to Georgia. She left me with a bag of old clothes and what I'm wearing."

The janitor laughed as if he thought McCoy was joking.

"You got family around?" Roberto might be short and forty pounds overweight, but he was one of the heroes in this life. He cared. "Friends picking you up?"

"Nope. My dad lives in Alaska. He told me I've got a grandfather in some little town called Honey Creek. I couldn't even find the place on a map when I looked years ago."

"I know where that is." Roberto smiled. "My *primo* lives there. Runs a garage across from the bus stop." He pushed his chest out. "I've got cousins in half the towns in Texas."

"Must be nice," McCoy lied.

Roberto asked a few more questions and then seemed to take over McCoy's life. "If you don't know where to go, you should head up to meet your *abuelo*. He'd probably be glad to see you. He's kin. He can't turn you away."

"I doubt that's a rule for my relatives. My family tree is more like a fence post."

"My cousin says the folks in Honey Creek are friendly. While you're healing you should look him up."

"I don't know about that."

"With that leg, what else you gonna do? There's a bus

that heads that way around midnight. I could drop you off at the station. It's not far."

To McCoy's surprise, Roberto picked up the duffel bag. "Wait here, I'll get my truck and take you. You'll be in Honey Creek by dawn. You got forty-three bucks for the ride?"

McCoy hesitated, then nodded once.

Roberto stared at McCoy. "You got any better place to be?"

"Nope." His head hurt too bad to argue. He could starve there as fast as he could here. "Maybe the bus will be warm and I can sleep. The fare is probably cheaper than a hotel."

A few minutes later, Roberto helped him into an old Chevy pickup truck and told McCoy that his cousin would meet the bus and help him find his kin in Honey Creek.

It crossed McCoy's mind that this could be the plot of a kidnapping movie. But what else could they do to him? Sell him into the sex trade? There couldn't be much demand for a scraped-up fool with one working leg and no memory of what day it was. Plus, he considered he might not be that great in bed if Breanna only took three days to forget him.

On the bright side, his always-absent grandpa might let him sleep on the couch for a few nights. That had to be better than a shelter.

Long after dark, McCoy climbed into the bus heading north. He stretched out on the back seat and tried not to breathe in too deeply. The air smelled of whiskey and piss. He guessed the couple falling in love on the seat in front of him were the origin of the smells. They were deep into slapping tongues. The sight made him want to forget even thinking about sex or eating.

He had no future, no love life, no job, and no relatives

except Grandpa Sadler Mason, whom his dad had mentioned a few times in passing. Dad had said he didn't remember ever having a mother, and when he was seventeen, he told his father he was leaving, and Sadler Mason simply said, "So long. The land will be here waiting if you ever want to come home."

That one line from a grandfather he'd never met gave him a spark of hope.

McCoy closed his eyes as his head pounded, keeping time to the throbbing in his leg. It didn't matter where in the hell he was heading. Forget the pills in his pocket. He'd take the pain. It was the only thing reminding him he was alive.

He told himself he wasn't a quitter; he was simply tired.

If Sadler turned him away, he'd find a place to lie down and sleep off this nightmare.

Chapter 2

Melody's Journey

Melody Avendale slipped into the upstairs bathroom, locked the door, and pulled her phone from her backpack.

6:15 P.M.: SEE YOU TOMORROW. WE'LL HAVE ALL
    DAY. PARENTS IN AN ALL DAY MEETING.
    CLIFTON LIBRARY 9:00. LOV, MEL

6:16 P.M.: CAN'T WAIT. HAPPY VALENTINE'S DAY,
    LOVE MICHAEL

"Melody, supper's ready. We need to hurry up and eat. Your father and I have a great deal to do before tomorrow's presentation."

Mom was still yelling when Melody rounded the stairs into the kitchen. As usual her mother didn't give her time to speak. "Are you sure you want to stay in the library in Clifton? We could drop you off at your grandmother's in the morning."

"No, I've got lots to do and the Clifton Library is much better than the high school library. Okay if I walk over and get lunch at the student center at noon?"

"Of course, dear. But don't bother to try to talk to anyone. College students don't like to talk to high school kids."

Melody's parents had been warning against the world since they first let her walk across the street. The two professors had been micromanaging their only child's life since she was born and Melody had never thought to rebel.

Until now. Until she was three months away from her eighteenth birthday.

Until she met Private Michael Alderton.

Until she fell in love.

> 11:15 P.M: GOOD NIGHT, MELODY. DON'T FORGET. HIDE THE PHONE. IT IS MY ONLY LIFELINE TO YOU.
>
> 11:16 P.M.: GOOD NIGHT MICHAEL. CAN'T WAIT FOR TOMORROW.

She shoved her phone into the tiny pocket at the side of her backpack. Her parents had given her the cellphone on her thirteenth birthday but had told her it was only for emergencies. Which meant their calls. She used it so rarely in front of them, Melody guessed they'd forgotten about it.

But since she met Michael, she'd found a great use for it. It was like they were connected by a thread even if they were a hundred miles apart.

The fear that the thread might be broken haunted both of them.

Chapter 3

Honey Creek, Texas
Almost Midnight

Jessica Ann Mackenzie, "Jam" for short, sat near the bend in the Brazos River where hundred-year-old cottonwoods lined the shore for endless miles. Her tall, thin frame blended with the trees' shadows, making her invisible to anyone on the water or at the café looming behind her.

Not that it mattered. No one would be either place after midnight.

She'd worked late. Every couple wanted their Valentine's dinner at her place, even if a few looked like the love had been strangled long ago.

She'd heard one couple arguing over money and another complaining about each other's parents. The love songs playing in the background hadn't seemed to reach the couple talking low about divorce. Jam noticed they didn't eat much and never seemed to look directly at the other. When she'd offered to box the meal, they'd both said no at the same time. Apparently, that was all they'd agreed on.

Sometimes Jam swore romance had disappeared with

knights in armor. Love stories were meant for movies and books, too flighty to survive real life.

As she'd cleaned up after all the couples left, the love songs still playing had simply made her sad.

By the time she'd prepped for the breakfast run at dawn, it was too late to bother driving the few miles to her family's small farm, Sunflower Lane, where her hideaway home waited. She decided to stay upstairs above her café in a room she'd turned into a bedroom. With the huge number of Mackenzies, there was often a relative who needed a place to stay and Jam was often too tired even to make the short drive home.

Someday she'd remodel that farmhouse and make it hers.

But for now there was no time for "someday." She was too busy with today.

The farm, where her clothes and books lived, was becoming more of a getaway place, and the sea captain's old house, turned restaurant, had become her life.

Somehow, being alone upstairs always made her uneasy, but exhaustion let her sleep. Stories of ghosts haunting the place never seemed to die. They were as much a part of the café as the studs and tile.

The house by the water had been built over a hundred years ago by a sea captain. He'd had three wives who gave him four homely daughters. It was said all the wives died in childbirth. Then the captain gave up on marriage and hired a housekeeper to run the place until the girls were grown and he retired from the sea.

As the story goes, the housekeeper left one morning without even saying goodbye and it was almost six months before the captain came home.

He stayed, but some said he never smiled again.

The few men brave enough to come courting the captain's daughters were turned away. As the years passed, sorrow

Jodi Thomas

seemed to frequent the family. Two daughters died of a fever while still in their teens, the oldest daughter drowned in the river, and the last daughter just disappeared one night. Rumor has it she took her life, but a few believed she ran off. The captain put up her marker beside her mother's grave and lived his remaining years alone in his huge house by the Brazos River.

There were some who said it was the moans of the dead man that whispered in the night. Jam told herself it was just the wind in the trees. The old café was hers now. No longer a home. Just a café.

Tonight, no more than thirty feet from her café, Jam felt like she was the last human alive. Not even the wind moved across the land still sleeping in winter. She'd bought the house in her twenties and spent every waking hour turning it into the best café around. Only now, after ten years, she felt she might be like the captain. She'd grow old and die here, alone.

When moving amid all the couples having candlelight dinners tonight, she tried to remember how long it had been since she'd even been kissed. Really kissed. First date kisses didn't count and neither did drunk ones.

In her teens she'd been pretty, in college she'd usually been friends with guys she met. By twenty-five the dates were casual, then after thirty the few dates she had were "settling dates." No passion, no chase, just men who saw her as a good, hardworking woman to settle for.

She felt lonely all the way to her bones.

No one would kiss her good night on this Valentine's Day. No one would call her "sweetheart."

At thirty-two she'd achieved her dream of owning the best restaurant for miles around. The Honey Creek Café was successful. Her finances were solid. The whole town seemed to be her friend. But Jam had no lover to hold her in the night.

Looking back, she'd dreamed too small. Somewhere between making bread every dawn and polishing off the accounts after dark, she'd lost herself.

Lowering her head to her knees, tears fell unchecked. No one would hear her. While building a business, she'd lost all her other goals. She'd learned to work, but she'd forgotten to live.

The river splashed against the shore as if demanding attention.

Jam often sat near the water to think, to plan, to rest, but never to cry. Tonight, she felt like she'd lost a lover she'd never taken the time to meet. She'd given up everything for one dream. The huge old house held a fine café that would never love her back.

Another splash came, louder, closer.

Jam raised her head listening in the night, trying to see across the river, but it was impossible. All she saw was the black flow of the water a few feet away.

Another splash and a shadow seemed to plop onto the bank. It landed a few feet from her with a hard thump, as bits of water sprinkled along her side.

Jam didn't move. Her first thought was of Old Henry. The catfish, which locals claimed was as big as a man, must have jumped onto the bank.

No, not possible.

An alligator was her next thought. She'd never heard of one this far north. "Not likely," she mumbled as she made out two long powerful legs. Maybe she'd wished herself an imaginary date.

Then she heard cussing. That couldn't be part of her fantasy.

No fish. Definitely a man rose from the mud.

As he stood, she noticed he was fully dressed down to his boots. Army style, not cowboy boots. T-shirt, khaki pants.

Jam knew she should be afraid, but this was too strange. This had to be more of a joke than an invasion.

The impossible sight made her smile. "You know, mister, most folks swim in trunks or even skinny-dip. You're a bit overdressed in that uniform."

He didn't look at her, so she reasoned he was just a figment of her imagination. She must have had too much wine. No one crawls out of the river dressed like a soldier. The nearest fort was hundreds of miles away.

Jam decided to keep talking to the vision. "The water flows too fast around this bend to be safe, but it calms a few miles down. You must be from out of town if you think you can swim here."

He slung his head, splashing water over her.

She couldn't make out his face as he began to strip off his clothes. The lines of his body were sketched against the moonlight. She decided he looked as good as she could have possibly conjured up. Wide shoulders. Slim hips. Muscles pretty much everywhere. "You real, mister?"

As he poured water out of his boot, he turned toward her, "Are you? I'm guessing not many people sleep in cottonwoods."

"Nope," she answered without hesitation. "I haven't been real for a long time." When she'd been in her early twenties, she'd always fallen in love with men who walked away like she was no more important than the half sandwich they'd left on their plate. If she wasn't real then, she doubted she'd be now.

The mud man just stared at her. It had to be almost fifty degrees, but he didn't even look like he was cold as he stood in front of her. His clothes were knotted in one hand and his boots in the other.

"I was told never to trust a slender cook, but you are a
[m]aster." He winked at her. "And I am not saying that because
[I']ve been living on army food for a dozen years."

He ate and she watched him enjoy the meal. They didn't
[kn]ow one another well enough to make conversation. She
[f]illed his milk twice, and he thanked her both times.

[As] he finished the plate, the buzzer went off on the
[dry]er. He stood and moved to the shadows under the stairs.
[Wit]h no hesitation, he dropped the towel, pulled out his
[wri]nkled uniform, and began to dress.

[W]ithout hesitation, she watched.

["H]ow can I repay you, lovely cook?" His back was to
[her a]s he buttoned his trousers.

[Jam] stepped closer, almost near enough to touch the
[muscl]es on his back.

[Wh]en he turned, she saw surprise in his eyes, then a
[q]uestion, and then definite interest.

[For o]ne long moment their gazes locked. Two people
[study]ing one another. His words came so low it seemed
[like hea]t passing between them. "Name it, Jam. What's on
[your min]d? Name how I can repay you."

[Closi]ng her eyes, she whispered, "My café was full of
[toni]ght, and I can't even remember the last real kiss

[He fro]wned as if he didn't believe her. "You're sure?"
[He seeme]d to breathe the question in as he halved the
[space betwe]en them.

"

[Lik]e a man approaching a mirage, he moved his
[hand to the s]ide of her face. She felt the warmth of his
[hand. She clos]ed her eyes, pretending he was real. Pretend-
[ing he wanted] her.

[His arm cir]cled her waist and pulled her against him
[as his l]ips brushed her ear, not her mouth.

When she didn't say anything, he finally added, "I was fishing and flipped my boat after a water moccasin crawled in with me. I grew up in this valley, but I've been gone a dozen years, and apparently I've forgotten all I ever knew about fishing."

He sounded angry, not at her but maybe at the world. Jam wished she'd brought out a flashlight so she could see him better and, if needed, to use as a weapon. "What's your name?"

"What do you care?"

"I own this land you flopped up on."

His words were no more friendly than hers. "You want me to jump back in? It seems I'm in hostile territory."

He reminded her of a wild animal. Powerful. Primeval. Ready for battle. She had no doubt he'd dive back in the water if she ordered him off her property.

"No. You can stay. I've got towels in the kitchen. You can borrow a few. I might get arrested for letting you walk back to town naked." Jam couldn't resist looking, just to make sure he was totally naked.

He didn't seem to notice or care. "Thanks. I'm Sergeant Tucson Smith, by the way. My younger brother is getting sworn in as sheriff tomorrow. If you want to file charges on me for trespassing, call him."

She relaxed a bit. Her mud monster was becoming human.

"I know your brother. I'm proud to call Pecos a friend. I'm Jessica Ann Mackenzie. Everyone calls me Jam." She didn't say more. They knew one another's families. That was enough of an introduction.

Jam headed to the house. He followed.

As they reached the porch light's glow, she looked back. Mud man had Pecos Smith's coloring, brown eyes and hair, but this older brother was twice the deputy's weight and looked solid as a tree trunk. Even naked, he marched like a soldier.

"Where are you staying, Sergeant Smith?"

"Nowhere. Pecos said I could borrow the mayor's boat if I wanted to fish, but to tell the truth, I didn't even bother to buy bait. I just wanted to drift on the water for a while. I figured I'd just sleep out here, but I'm guessing my gear and the mayor's boat are both at the bottom of the river."

She opened the back door, reached in, and handed him a towel that barely went halfway around his waist. "Drop your things in the washer under the stairs. You can shower upstairs while you wait for your uniform. I can at least offer that to our new sheriff's brother. He may be young, but most folks in this county look up to him."

"Good to hear," Tucson said as he walked into the shadows of the stairs.

It crossed her mind that he could have gone to the farm where he grew up, but Pecos never talked about his parents. Maybe they'd moved years ago or didn't speak to their sons.

She heard Tucson follow orders. He dropped his clothes in one of the café's washers. "It won't take long," she said.

The only answer was the sound of the washer lid dropping.

Jam forced herself not to look at him as she turned on the prep table's light in the big kitchen. "You hungry? I could scramble you up some eggs and make toast."

Halfway up the stairs, he turned. "I don't want to be a bother. I'll be on my way as soon as my clothes are ready. I got a rental car up the road a few miles. I can sleep in it. Come morning I'll buy something to wear to the ceremony."

She nodded and added, "Shower is the second door on the left. I'll watch your clothes. How many?"

He was on the landing. "How many what?"

"Eggs. I'll have them ready by the time you cl

"A dozen if you've got them." Then wearin towel, he disappeared.

"I've got them," she murmured. It occurred the valentine wish she always made might h come true. A lover for a night with no strin came wrapped in a towel.

Only the soldier seemed about as cuddly and he looked like he never bothered to smi

She made him ranch eggs with sausag then heated several pieces of homemade b and cinnamon sugar on top. By the tim wearing a bigger towel, she'd switched dryer.

Jam handed him the biggest T-shi café's logo on it. It stretched over hi skin.

They sat on stools pulled up to th passed him a heaping plate, he "Thanks, I'm starving."

"I hope it's good."

He grabbed another fork fro her. "Join me."

When he took his first bite

Then he stared at her, and if he were no longer talkin

She reached over and s it while he ate a meal bi

No longer covered i Smith was an attractive to touch him. Some since she'd found hir Valentine's Day.

"If we're going to do this, Jessica Ann Mackenzie, I want to take my time. You may not believe this, but no one's ever asked me for this favor, and I want to do it right."

"Please." She brushed her cheek against his jaw. "One perfect kiss."

"You'll never have to ask me again."

Light kisses glided across her face. She couldn't open her eyes. If this wasn't real, she didn't want to know.

She'd expected a hard kiss, but the soldier was gentle and in no hurry. Slowly he pulled her closer until she felt him press along the length of her body. As his kiss deepened, she seemed to melt into his warmth.

One perfect lover's kiss from a stranger.

His hand moved down over her hip lightly as his free fingers tugged the clamp from her hair and let it fall, straight and midnight beautiful. While her heart pushed against his, the world slipped away, and passion rotated in the night, in his arms, in his kiss.

When she moaned, he lifted her and walked to the stairs. While kissing her throat, he slowly carried her up to the second room on the left.

Jam took a deep breath as dreams and fantasies blended with feelings she'd never let show. For just a few moments she wanted to believe in love. No, more than that. She wanted to believe someone could care for her like a lover would.

Without a word he laid her on the bed and covered her with the bedspread. Leaning down, he kissed her one more time and whispered, "I'll watch over you until you fall asleep and imagine what you might ask me for when you wake."

His hand moved along her body as he held her.

She was independent, strong, but tonight somehow, he sensed her need to be held. He feathered kisses over her cheek then leaned back beside her so close his breath tickled her hair. Just two lonely people needing companionship if only for a few moments, she thought as she relaxed.

Jam drifted to sleep still floating on a dream that almost seemed real. A deep peace welcomed her tired body and mind. She was safe from ghosts tonight. She was in the arms of a dream lover.

He watched over her. The wind rustled the leaves on the old cottonwoods and the river whispered as it moved along, but she simply slept.

In the morning she stretched and decided she'd just had the best dream ever. It filled her thoughts as she showered and changed into a clean white chef coat and black cargo pants. A few brushes of her hair and she was ready to start the breads.

The dream of being kissed drifted in her mind as she rushed down the stairs smiling. "Almost real," she whispered. "Perfection."

She was still half dreaming when she reached the prep table and saw the two stools and one dirty plate with two forks.

Jam froze. It couldn't be true. She'd been exhausted. She'd had too much to drink. The man from the river was only a dream. Yet she could almost feel the warmth of him by her side.

Her employees wandered in. Most had worked the night before and still looked tired. Jam tried to be cheery. She met them with muffins and juice. "We've got a lunch for twenty after the ceremony at the sheriff's office. Other than that, the afternoon-run should be slow. Folks don't usually come in the morning after a big night out."

Her people yawned and shrugged. A light crowd would mean light tips but an early day.

"I've got eight mini red velvet cakes left over, so each

of you can take one home. We should be out of here by two." On weeknights she was always the last one to leave. Being open early on weekdays for breakfast and lunch was enough. Then on weekends it was brunch only.

Her employees might work five days on and two off, but Jam was there when the door was open. Now and then, she took a Sunday off to work in the garden at her folks' old place.

If she could just remember last night's kiss for a while, maybe she could smile and enjoy the day.

Chapter 4

Mr. Winston

Saturday

The old gentleman put on his least tattered tie and looked in the antique mirror hanging on a wall that hadn't been painted in fifty years. Like the house, Charles H. Winston III stood solid against aging.

At sixty-seven he liked the man he saw in his reflection. He lived by the principles he'd set out when he arrived in New York almost fifty years ago. He was honest. Never talked about himself. He was kind and thoughtful. He lived his life by the clock and valued order. His acquaintances called him Mr. Winston and his friends just called him Winston.

He glanced at the tiny note taped to his mirror and whispered the words aloud. "A man is measured by how he lives today, not yesterday."

He smiled thinking in a few hours his world might just change a bit. He was shifting his routine. At half past noon he'd have a lunch date with three lovely ladies at the Honey Creek Café, and he planned to pick up the bill.

Charles considered himself a man much blessed and he would spend a bit of the wealth.

As he brushed his coat, he decided he might purchase a new tie if time permitted. After all, if his plan worked, he'd be proposing marriage soon. It would be an important thing, being engaged. Something he thought would never come in this lifetime.

Chapter 5

McCoy's Homecoming

As McCoy Mason hopped off the bus in Honey Creek, Texas, and fought to balance on his crutches, he saw a short, chubby man who favored Roberto, his friend from Houston, running toward him. The stranger was covered in oil and dirt. He smiled like McCoy was the catch of the day.

"You the cowboy my cousin sent this direction? If you are, I'm Leo, your ride."

McCoy didn't have the energy to explain. "I guess I am since no one else is crawling off that torture chamber on wheels except a girl who probably wasn't out of high school. But I'm no cowboy."

Roberto's clone whispered, "You could have fooled me, cowboy. You look like a young John Wayne except your leg is broken, your eyes are bloodshot, and your hat's on backward."

"No, sir." McCoy removed his Stetson. "I think my head is turned around wrong."

Leo laughed as he opened the rusty door of his Chevy pickup parked a few steps away.

McCoy grabbed his duffel bag and tried to hang on

to it as he moved slowly toward his ride. "Your truck looks almost the same as Roberto's," he commented as he climbed in.

"Yeah," the cousin answered. "We got the same uncle. All he sells are cheap, rundown trucks that will get you where you're going. That's good enough, I figure."

McCoy didn't bother to ask a single question as the Chevy rattled down the main street of Honey Creek, a town too cute to be real. It had a café on the square with a hand-written *special of the day* in the window. An ice cream parlor that looked like it was straight out of a children's book. A bakery. A barber shop. Even a little pool hall with a WELCOME sign over the door. In the middle of a square was a grand courthouse that looked to be a hundred years old.

About the time McCoy decided he was dead and this was heaven, Roberto's cousin started talking.

"I'm Leo, in case my cousin forgot to tell you. Roberto and me figured out where to take you, McCoy Mason. There are a few Masons in this valley, but only one we thought was old enough to be your *abuelo.*"

Leo thought for a moment, then added, "Do you realize you have two last names? Seems that runs in the family, that is, if Sadler Mason is your kin." Leo turned and stared at McCoy for a long moment. "You know, if I wrinkled you up and painted that black hair silver, you'd look like him. Only his whole face got stuck on a frown and his eyebrows went wild."

"Really?" McCoy just looked out the window. "I've never seen even a picture of him."

The mechanic laughed. "I will take you straight to the Mason farm. Your maybe grandpa is old as dust and keeps to himself. I called him and told him you were coming. He said this wasn't a good time for a visit, but you can come."

"What's he like?"

Leo shrugged. "He orders parts from me now and then. He always pays his bills. I've seen him in town a few times. I wave and he waves back. 'Friendly' is not a word I'd stick on him. I hear he's had a bit of trouble with a few guys in Dallas who want to buy his property. They showed up saying they wanted to look at an old stagecoach station that was on his land a hundred years ago. But their gear was more survey equipment than metal detectors to explore. Sadler wouldn't allow them to set foot on his land."

Leo laughed so loud he frightened the birds perched on the last lamp pole leaving town. "Like anyone would leave something valuable in an abandoned stagecoach station that is no more than a pile of rocks. If you ask me, they were trying to trick the old guy but your grandfather is no fool. Since then other strangers have shown up, all wanting to look over Sadler's land. Word is they are some big developers out of Dallas. Some say they've bought up all but Sadler's place. It's vital to a project those city folks are planning."

McCoy didn't care about his grandfather's problems. He just needed a place to crash for a few days. Maybe this whole idea was insane. He'd never had roots. What made him think he'd find them now? He was headed toward a stranger who'd never made any effort to find him, and apparently Sadler Mason had problems of his own.

If McCoy had the money to leave, he would climb right back onto that smelly bus. He'd find work somewhere, even if he was limping.

His dad had been an ironworker and moved around from job to job. He'd always kept three hundred dollars under the driver's seat of his van. Rainy day money, he used to call the stash. McCoy continued the practice, but he kept it in his wallet. That was all he had now. He'd blended his bank account with Breanna's when they'd left Georgia and he guessed she'd closed out the account as soon as she got back.

When he was a kid, wherever his dad stopped for a job, he'd buy a little rundown house to live in and start fixing it up on weekends. By the time they moved to the next job, he'd sold the house for thousands over what he'd paid and put the money away in a bank in Alaska. Dad always said that one day, when McCoy was grown, he'd follow his money up north. And, he did.

His father never tossed a ball with his only child or read him a bedtime story, but McCoy could swing a hammer by the time he was three and replace the pipes in any sink at eight. By the time he started work at sixteen, he could do almost any job on any site.

Dad retired at fifty and moved to Alaska. Last he heard, his dad was building tiny lake houses in the summer and getting fat in the winter. McCoy called him every holiday and got the impression he was bothering his dad.

McCoy always promised to go up north for a visit, but he never seemed to have the time. And now, he had time and no money.

Leo turned the pickup onto an unpaved road and pointed west. "That's the Mason farm. Looks like he unlocked the gate for us. Land out this way ain't worth much, too rocky."

McCoy frowned at the rundown house that looked like it had been built on from every direction and the only thing holding it together was trumpet vines.

His first thought was *How do I get out of here?* Then he got an idea. Maybe he could stay around a few days recovering, then work his board and food off by fixing up the crumbling Tinkertoy shack. Every window and door was painted in a different color and the roof had been patched so many times it looked like a faded quilt.

Several outbuildings were scattered around: chicken coops, barns, a storage locker made from a railroad car, a pole barn with dilapidated farming equipment rusting inside.

As Leo's truck rattled down the bumpy road, McCoy mentally began listing a few things he'd do. From the shape he was in, it was either this place or a homeless shelter.

He'd been homeless the first winter when his dad moved away and the weather had kept him from working. He'd slept in his car before he got a job sacking groceries. It was easy work compared to construction, but the pay was lousy.

"It's a pretty place, don't you think?" Leo said, interrupting McCoy's thoughts. "Some say your grandpa lives with the fairies on this land. When spring comes, wildflowers grow all over his few acres."

"Doesn't he farm?"

"No. He fixes farm equipment and cares for broken-down donkeys."

"Fairies? Donkeys? Really?" McCoy fought down a laugh.

Leo smiled. "The fairies keep him company, and folks say he's a good mechanic. I've tried to get him to help me a few times at the garage, but he says he only works on farm equipment."

McCoy didn't say anything else. Most of the time he didn't believe in himself. How could he believe in fairies? His grandpa must be the only mechanic around who worked on farm equipment. How else could he make a living?

By the time they pulled up in the yard between the little house and a big barn with corrals, a man stood at the door.

He was tall, almost as tall as McCoy. His shoulders were wide but rounded slightly. He wasn't smiling.

McCoy thought of telling Leo to turn around. But he'd come this far—he might as well meet the man who'd raised his father.

Sadler Mason stepped onto the porch but didn't say a word as they pulled up.

McCoy slid out of the truck and used his crutches to maneuver to the steps. Neither man offered to help him.

"I just need a place to rest up for a few days." McCoy wasn't afraid of this stranger over twice his age, but he'd need to know he was welcome before he took another step. He didn't go into a long explanation; either the old guy would let him stay or not.

Sadler's granite gray eyes met McCoy's. "You can stay until you heal. There is no doubt you're kin."

McCoy had a feeling he was staring at himself forty years from now. "Thanks."

Sadler frowned. "I ain't no nurse or cook. Can you take care of yourself?"

"I might need a ride into town next week to see a doc."

The old man nodded. "I go in most every week to pick up supplies. I'll drop you off at the clinic and pick you up in about an hour."

"Fair enough." McCoy turned and thanked Leo, who seemed in a hurry to leave.

Watching Leo drive off, McCoy felt a bit like he'd been abandoned on an iceberg to freeze to death. When he turned back to the porch, his grandpa was already headed to the barn.

McCoy watched him for a while, but the old guy never turned around. Picking up his pack of dirty clothes, McCoy slowly moved up the steps, fought with the screen door, and finally made it into the house.

The place reminded him of army barracks. Only the necessities. One couch, one overstuffed chair, one desk, one dining table with two cheap office chairs on wheels. The only surprise was the books that were stacked everywhere. No shelves, just piled so high they looked like they might fall over any moment.

It appeared McCoy had one thing in common with the old man.

His grandpa didn't have a TV, but he had a library of paperback Westerns. McCoy had read adventure stories in grade school, science fiction through high school, and half a dozen suspense novels a month through his twenties, but he'd never read Westerns. Now might be a good time to start.

Using his last bit of energy, McCoy made it to a bedroom with a note taped to the door. *Settle in. Supper will be on the table at dusk.*

McCoy shoved the door wide open and stumbled in. He found a bed long enough to fit his frame, sheets on top still folded, and an empty dresser. One bottle of water sat on a box that served as a nightstand.

McCoy downed the water and two pain pills, then collapsed atop the folded sheets.

Just a wild guess, but McCoy decided his grandpa probably hadn't studied for a career in the medical field or decorating or cooking.

As exhaustion washed over him, he thought he saw fairies dancing in the hallway. One of them had ginger-colored hair to her waist and a blue sundress that ballooned out as she twirled.

He'd ask questions later. Right now, he needed to sleep. Apparently, he was home.

Chapter 6

Melody

Melody's phone pinged, sounding across the empty Clifton Library.

9:25 A.M.: YOU READY TO HAVE AN ADVENTURE?

Melody almost squealed. She looked up and saw Michael coming through the library door. He was tall, with dark blue eyes and a smile that lit up her world every time she saw it.

Like her, he was shy. The first time they'd sat near each other in the library, neither said a word. Then, he'd passed her a piece of paper with a tic-tac-toe symbol, and they'd smiled as they played. Slowly, one question at a time, they talked.

At lunch she shared her sandwich and he bought their Cokes from a machine. The last thing he said to her when her parents called to say they were waiting outside was, "Next week?"

She nodded once.

That had been almost a year ago since they'd met at the Clifton College library. Michael must have passed half a dozen libraries to get to a quiet library where he could settle in and read all day. He'd said he just wanted to relax, and he didn't mind the hour-long drive from Fort Hood. He claimed he grew up here and all his childhood friends were heroes from books.

The second Saturday, Melody boldly took the seat two spaces down from him and by noon they were talking again. When he offered to buy her lunch, she'd said she'd share her sack lunch with him outside on a bench. Though the fall weather was cool outside, neither noticed.

They were just two lonely kids who loved books. Sometimes they'd cuddle far back in a corner and read to each other. He'd read his favorites and she'd read hers. Once she'd fallen asleep on his shoulder and he'd said the hour she was using him for a pillow was the best hour in his whole life.

She'd known from the first that they'd be good friends. There was no flirting or teasing. Just friends. At exactly five o'clock, when her parents picked her up, Michael would always hold her hand until the last second, then he'd vanish as she walked away.

He'd been a foster kid after his dad kicked him out. The families that took him in were just doing it for the money so he tried to make it easy on them. He took care of himself and they always left food for him. When he finished high school, everyone thought he should sign up with the army and Michael agreed.

Since September they'd spent almost every Saturday together while her parents taught their classes at the little college south from where they lived.

All through October and November, Melody and Michael mostly stayed in the library. Sometimes he'd help her do her school research papers or they'd play chess, but they almost always ate outside together. In the library they talked of books and world events, but outside they talked of their lives and what they wanted for the future.

Then, Thanksgiving came. She felt glued to her parents for the holiday and Michael was alone. He'd been a kid shoved between relatives who didn't want him, then finally dumped him in the system.

Melody's heart hurt all week knowing he was alone. He called late Thanksgiving night and asked her to tell him all about her day. She told him how boring it was and how Mom overcooked the turkey and Grandmother fell asleep before dessert.

Michael said it sounded grand.

They talked the next night but they didn't see each other. Michael figured out a plan. If they were careful, they could stay in touch.

She could call him any time after seven. If he had duty, he'd text "later."

He never called her, but he'd text "talk." If she was alone, she'd call.

As they fine-tuned the signals, they seemed to be constantly in touch. Just a few words at a time, but December passed with her feeling he was always with her. At night, when the house was quiet, they'd talk about everything.

When he'd ask something personal, she'd giggle and he'd whisper, "I swear, Mel, I can hear you blushing. If I was with you, I'd kiss your warm cheeks."

Both decided that was the only bad part of their relationship. They couldn't kiss. A few times behind the stacks. Once in the rain with both under the umbrella.

Neither pushed it; both were shy.

Michael made up one last code. If she called and let it ring once, it was all right to call her. Two calls with only one ring each time meant don't text or call until she called.

Three one-ring calls meant she needed him.

Then, in February, her parents said they'd planned an all-day workshop. Melody couldn't wait to tell Michael. They began to plan a trip. His hometown was only thirty miles from Clifton. With time he'd show her the whole valley. They could eat lunch at the Honey Creek Café or on the dock by the river.

Finally, the Saturday had arrived. Melody watched him walk toward her, smiling as if it was his birthday, Christmas, and the Fourth of July all rolled into one.

They were free for eight hours.

As she gathered up her things, he handed her a box. "Happy Valentine's."

She frowned. "But I didn't get you anything."

"Yes, you did. You showed up." As she opened the box, he said, "It's a camera that takes and prints pictures at the same time. They're not great, but now you'll have pictures of our day to remember."

They ran to his old car that he drove to the Clifton Library every Saturday from Fort Hood so he could see her.

He'd told her he'd bought it because he liked to drive on weekends when he didn't have duty. Driving and libraries were his peace until he met Melody.

Two blocks away from the campus library, he pulled into a parking lot. He offered his hand. She laced her fingers in his like they always did under the table.

"Would you mind if I kissed you? Really kissed you. Not just a fast kiss."

She couldn't stop smiling until his lips touched hers, and she realized he didn't know any more about kissing than she did.

Melody pushed away. "Have you ever kissed a girl?"

"Not really." He straightened, looking away from her.

She laughed. "Me either—never kissed a boy, I mean.

We've got a lot to learn. I think we should practice as often as we can today."

"You know, Mel, you're perfect."

"No, I'm not, but just maybe we're perfect for each other." She leaned back. "Now drive. I have to read the directions to this camera."

Two hours later, on a cloudy day, they were sitting on a dock by the river. He pulled off his sweater and wrapped it around her, swearing he wasn't cold.

Then he pulled off his shoes and claimed he had to at least put a toe in the water.

Michael told her how he used to swim all summer. "I was pretty much a free-range kid in summer, but winters, when I had to stay inside, were the hard times. I learned I was less noticed if I had my head in a book."

"Was it really bad?" She pulled out the lunch they'd stopped to eat. Fries, burgers, and Cokes.

"No, most of the time I was ignored. I learned where the safe places were. Libraries, attics, just being gone until dark in summers. If it got bad, I had a few places I could hide out for a night or two. I'll show you them if you like."

"I'd like to know everything about you."

He grinned. "Would you run away with me, Mel?"

She stood to take a picture of the river with the camera he'd given her. "No. I couldn't run away with you. My parents would have to come along. And, Grandmother would probably come too." She shot the river raging against the wind.

Michael's voice was low. "Would you marry me?"

"I'm not old enough. Three more months. I'll be eighteen and graduated with fifteen hours of college under my belt. Who knows what could happen in three months from now."

"You're killing me, Mel."

She heard a sound as if something hit the dock.

When she turned, Michael was spread out on the dock, his T-shirt covered with ketchup across his heart. "You've broken my heart."

Mel laughed as she shot pictures. In the cloudy day, with his white T-shirt stained red and his eyes closed, he almost looked like a murder victim. Shadows from winter trees darkened his face and his dog tags were spotted with red.

She knelt beside him. "I'd never break your heart. Don't you know? It belongs to me, just like mine belongs to you."

"Always?"

"Always."

Napkins and photos flew in the wind as they grabbed their lunch, his shoes, and ran for the car.

As a light rain spotted the windshield, they cuddled in his old car and talked about their future. Their dreams might seem small to some. A quiet life in a small town, kids, maybe travel to places they could talk about when they grew older, and love, lots of love.

She hadn't said she'd run away with him or marry him someday, but she'd told him he held her heart and that was enough.

Chapter 7

The Café

Jam Mackenzie left the decorated dining room. The long banquet table was set for the new sheriff and his guests. Pecos Smith's mother-in-law made sure the cake was perfect with an icing badge on top that was ten inches across. Some folks claimed she hugged on Pecos like he was her son. Pecos claimed it was more like a chokehold most days.

Jam's staff could handle serving the party. She wanted to wait on the table of four senior citizens who'd asked to dine by the river. She'd set them beneath the gazebo just in case it sprinkled. This lunch was always special to the three old women and one old man who reserved a table every third Saturday.

So, as always, when it ran after hours, Jam took care of her guests, even after the other diners and the staff went home. When they ordered a third round of tea, Jam would bring ginger cookies as well.

She didn't mind. This group of four had been regular customers since she opened ten years ago. They ate together once a month if the weather cooperated.

Today, Mr. Winston, the town's sweetest bachelor, wore

his straw Panama fedora in honor of spring's coming and a suit probably tailor-made for him in the eighties.

Two of the Mackenzie widows, Jam's aunts, both almost seventy, managed to look sweet in matching hats. And then there was Jam's favorite guest, Miss Lilly Lambert, who'd served as the town's only pharmacist's assistant for forty-three years.

The kind lady was willow tall and slender. She'd never married or dated that anyone knew of. She never said an unkind word about anyone and somehow remembered everyone in town by name.

Miss Lamb, children called her, would ask about everyone in her gentle way. She'd say, "Has your little problem passed?" Folks never took offense. They'd tell her their secrets and she'd keep them safe. The doctors in town might come and go but Miss Lamb was always there with her computer to explain every illness or prescription.

The group's leader was Mr. Winston. He insisted on pulling the ladies' chairs out when they arrived, and he always looked out for their needs. He'd say quietly to Jam, "I think Miss Nancy needs another napkin. The wind blew hers away." Or "Miss Lilly could use a bit of hot tea. There is a chill."

Jam always whispered a thank-you because Mr. Winston was taking care of his ladies.

Most of his life he'd served as a butler for a wealthy man from Chicago, who'd once thought he might want to retire in Honey Creek. Mr. Winston handled procuring a fine old home and oversaw the updating. But the rich man never had the time to come to Honey Creek.

For several years Winston came every spring and waited all summer for his boss's arrival. Winston had told Jam once that the house was the rich man's run-away-someday home.

Winston planted a beautiful flower garden and joined

the community while he waited. He, with his slight whisper of an Irish accent and his gentle way of treating everyone like they were a delight to meet, soon fit into the town like a native.

The rumor was that Winston's employer died several years ago, leaving the house to his butler in exchange for a retirement package. Jam knew Winston's social security barely paid the bills and allowed him to have a few fancy lunches at the café each month. But he was happy. He had a fine life, he'd always say.

As Jam served the senior citizens their lunch, the four were debating as soon as they took their seats.

"We started meeting three years ago when Lilly retired," one of the widows said.

"Oh no, that couldn't be the first time," Lilly said. "I was still working when we started. This is our sixth, maybe seventh spring by the river."

Jam grinned as she walked away. She loved the way people talked around the servers as if no one was listening to their conversations.

As she headed back to the café, a man stepped out from the shade of the long eaves. The tall, well-built businessman reminded her of the soldier who'd come out of the river last night. The one she thought was a dream, too good to be true.

The businessman removed his jacket, and she stilled. The white tailored shirt fit tight across his muscular shoulders. Just like the T-shirt once had.

Even without seeing his face, she knew it was Tucson! He was dressed in what looked like brand-new clothes. He'd done what he said he'd do and bought something to wear to his brother's swearing-in ceremony.

Slowly she moved past him. When he raised his gaze,

she met his brown eyes. He winked, then took a seat on the porch bench as if he had nothing else to do.

"Your brother's party has been over for a while," she whispered so no one could overhear.

"I know. It's official, my baby brother is a sheriff."

"So, you're leaving?"

"No," he answered as he seemed to study her. "I was waiting to see you first. Then, I'll head back."

"Me?"

"Yes, you. We have to talk. Last night . . . Last night I . . ."

Surprise, peppered with panic, choked any answer. She'd felt it too last night, but she couldn't put it in words. Talking about how she felt might make the feeling go away.

So, she ran back inside, both afraid this something between them was real and panicked it was not.

When she calmed down enough to step out again to refill the outside party's drinks, the soldier-turned-businessman was in the shade of the porch. He was so still, for all she knew he was asleep.

As she circled by him once more, she set down an extra iced tea on the tiny table beside him and asked, "How long are you planning to wait, Tucson?"

"Until you have time to talk, Jessica. Or should I call you Jam? The nickname fits you. Sweet and a bit complicated."

Again, she walked away. At this rate they'd never finish a conversation. It had been so long since she had a date she'd forgotten how to talk to a man.

Ten minutes later Jam served a second round of cookies and tea to the four guests. They were talking about what they wished they had done in their lives.

She would have thought they would mention places

they'd never gotten to see or adventures they'd been too afraid to try.

But not one of the four named a location or grand quests. They all wished they'd loved more, laughed more, and taken bigger bites out of life.

Aunt Nancy had been married and widowed before forty. She claimed she'd been too petrified of the pain of loss ever to marry again. She swore she'd live in Widows Park, a huge old house, with all the other Mackenzie widows until she died.

Her sister-in-law, Geraldine, had married twice, but neither relationship lasted the seasons round. Since she was a Mackenzie before marriage, she also lived at the huge old estate surrounded by gardens.

But, as Jam listened, it was Lilly Lambert who made her cry. The kind clerk had lived her life alone in one of the apartments above the pharmacy where she worked and never wandered from her safe little neighborhood. Miss Lamb had never known love or heartache. She'd walked between loneliness and safety. No adventures. No danger.

The sun was low over the water when the diners paid their bill, always ten dollars, and walked away. Jam knew Mr. Winston would walk the ladies home, stopping at Widows Park first and then at Miss Lilly's place.

Like Jam, everyone in town had probably watched the ritual. Winston would offer his arm to Lilly when it was just the two of them. He'd walk her all the way up to her apartment above the pharmacy. She'd invite him in for coffee. He'd say no. Then they would both smile and say good night. It would be dark by the time Winston circled back to his two-story Tudor house a block from the town square.

Nothing ever changed in Honey Creek. Jam could almost see every season of life spread out before her.

As she cleared the table, she thought of what the old folks said and pondered if fifty years from now, when she was in her eighties, she would wish she'd traveled more, had more adventures, loved more.

Tears blurred her vision for a moment. There was no more for her, she realized. She'd never known a true love and probably wouldn't. She'd grow old running the café and when she retired, she'd move into Widows Park without ever having been a widow. Her parents had passed away years ago, and none of her dreams for the family farm had come true. Maybe they never would.

Her hideaway farm was not where she lived; it was simply where she hid from life. She'd dreamed of building something grand on Sunflower Lane.

She glanced at the shadows on the porch to see if the soldier who'd switched to dress clothes was really there. How could she have slept so soundly with a stranger in her bed watching over her? How could he have known just how she'd needed to be kissed?

A half-empty glass of tea rested on the bench where he'd been.

Tucson Smith was gone.

If he'd really been there at all. She'd been working way too late, pushing herself. She'd been half-drunk last night. Maybe the man was just something she wished for in her exhausted mind.

Her soldier wearing dress clothes this afternoon was no more than a hangover fantasy.

Jam put the last few dishes in the sink. She didn't have to clean up tonight or prep for the early crowd. The café opened late on Sunday, and now and then she'd let the staff handle the Sunday buffet.

As she removed her apron and flipped off the kitchen lights, she turned toward the door. She'd drive to the farm tonight and sleep as long as she wanted to in the morning. Maybe she'd work in her garden. Maybe she'd clean house. The few Sundays she took off were simply a different kind of workday.

In the last blink of a dying sun, she thought she saw the outline of her soldier by the stairs. The dress clothes had been replaced by a uniform, now clean and pressed.

No fear this time as she smiled. "Are you real, Sergeant Tucson Smith?"

"Not for long. I have to be back tomorrow before dawn and it's a long drive. I just had to say goodbye. I thought we'd have time to talk, but it's late."

He had waited his time away while she worked.

Silence held them for a moment, then he added, "Watching you sleep last night was the best dream I've had in years. I'll remember you wherever I'm posted next. We barely know each other, but wherever I am, I have a feeling I'll be sleeping beside you for a long while." He watched her as if trying to gauge her reaction before he spoke. "You may not believe this but I feel like you're a part that I've been missing all my life."

With a cry she ran toward him. It made no sense, but she felt the same. She was in full flight when he caught and held her against him. Real or fantasy, she didn't care. She would not spend the rest of her life wishing she'd done this one thing. Whether they had a moment or a lifetime, she had to hold him.

She had to pull this one stranger close until his heart pounded against her. She had to believe that for a moment she'd had a chance to be loved.

For a while he just held her. They were two people who were not just attracted to one another; they seemed to match. If they'd met at a bar or a party, or even church, they might have talked, maybe dated for a while. Maybe they'd even eventually gotten married.

If there had been time.

All could-have-beens melted away. All they had was a moment.

One blink. No more.

They lived in different worlds. There was no time or place for them.

"How long?" she whispered against his ear.

"One hour. A minute longer and I'll be late." He moved his arm down her back and lifted her off the ground. "I don't want to talk."

"Me either." She leaned her head against his throat as he climbed the stairs.

One hour, she thought. One hour to run flat out toward life. One hour to build a memory that might last a lifetime.

As he stopped on the landing to kiss her, his cell sounded.

Half a flight up and they would have been lost to passion. But the buzz shattered the mood. She was so close to him she heard every word as he answered.

"Pecos?"

The voice on the other end almost shouted. "You still in town? I got a big problem. I need you, brother."

Tucson slowly lowered Jam as he stared into her eyes. His hurt, his longing reflected back from her blue gaze. The world was rushing in, destroying the one hour they'd thought they might have.

"I am," Tucson said into the phone.

"Then get to my office ASAP," Pecos yelled. "You've got to see this. I need your help, Tucson. I've got pictures of a crime scene scattered all over my desk. Looks like a man was killed."

"Not my beat. I have to head back to the fort. Just ask yourself the standard questions. Who was he? Did it happen around here? You can handle this, Pecos. I can't interfere with local law."

Pecos was silent for a moment, then added, "He's wearing his dog tags."

There was a pause, then Sheriff Pecos Smith's words came low and slow. "I don't know who he is. Face in shadows, but none of us in the office can ID him. Deep gash across his chest from the amount of blood. Looks like jeans and a T-shirt. No tattoos showing. He'd been spread out on the dock north of town. I recognized the place from the two tire swings that have been there since we were kids."

Tucson could tell Pecos was nervous. His first crime as a new sheriff and it's a murder. Why couldn't it be a lost cat or even a drunk driver? "Breathe, brother, and tell me the facts."

"One of the deputies walked out on the dock. Kids sometimes go out there to smoke pot so he was looking for any evidence. He found several little snapshots of a body spread out on the town's most popular dock. Just pictures, no body. He brought the shots in and dumped them on my desk. A few were ruined by rain."

"Have you roped off the dock? You need to get out there before someone stumbles over the crime scene."

"Didn't have to. I passed there on my way in to work ten minutes ago. Nobody there. Someone would have reported a body if it was still there or even if they saw blood. So it must have been cleaned up. The kids won't be happy when we rope it off with crime tape. This was the first week it might be warm enough to swim."

"Anything else?"

"No."

Pecos took a deep breath. "I called Sheriff LeRoy. He said he gave me the keys to the sheriff's station at the party so anything dropped on my desk is my problem. He swears there was nothing on the desk when he left." Pecos let out a bark of a laugh. "Old guy said this was my problem, but I'll bet my first month's pay he's driving toward me right now. The pictures showed up on my first day, but I have a feeling the guy was murdered on LeRoy's watch."

"I'm on my way too. The Army CID may want to be involved in this." Tucson ended the call and whispered to himself that the pictures could be some kind of message to his little brother. A warning? A threat? A joke?

For a moment he didn't seem able to move. Jam was still against him. Tucson didn't want to let her go, and he couldn't pull her closer.

He finally pressed a kiss on her forehead. "I don't know when or where, but this isn't over between us, Jam."

She pulled his face down and kissed him hard, then whispered, "Come back to me. I agree, this isn't over."

He planted another solid, fast kiss as he lowered her to the floor, and ran down the stairs without looking back.

Chapter 8

Tucson

Sergeant Tucson Smith climbed into his rental car and headed to the center of Honey Creek.

"This town is just too cute to have a body lying around," he said aloud. Even the lamp poles looked like Mary Poppins should be dancing around them.

He shook his head as he morphed into the expert he was. He'd been on several missions for the army's Criminal Investigation Division. Sometimes going into hostile territory to retrieve fallen soldiers. Tucson knew what to look for.

With less than one hour before he had to start back to Fort Hood, he doubted he could help Pecos much. Seven hours before he had to report in to fly out with his team for parts unknown. Maybe, just maybe, he'd see something that might help them solve the body-on-the-dock case.

He'd wanted to spend his last hour in town making a memory with Jam to carry with him. Pictures of a murdered soldier were the last things he wanted to see. As an investigator he'd seen enough horror.

He'd never cared about collecting tender moments, like he'd had last night when he'd held her as she slept. But there was something different about Jam. She seemed so vulnerable, and he wanted to be the one to protect her.

For once he wanted to remember when he closed his eyes, and that memory was Jam.

Tucson could still feel Jam against him. Holding on tight. Melting into him. He had no idea what drew him to her, but the pull was strong. Who knows, maybe she was the one who'd save him. Lately, he'd felt more like a machine than a man. A soldier, nothing more.

And yet, this woman didn't belong near his world. Just a stranger. Barely real.

Dead bodies were real. Crime and murder were real. She didn't need him. His brother did, though. The army did. But not Jam. He tried to tell himself she was just a vision he saw once among the cottonwoods by the bank of a river. Tall. Slender. Beautiful. She'd smelled of cinnamon and was as starved of a lover's touch as he was.

He wasn't a man that women were drawn to. Too tough, he guessed. A childhood without love, a career where he usually worked alone or was gone on a mission he didn't want to talk about. He was a man who had nothing to offer a woman like Jam.

But those sky-blue eyes seemed to see deep inside him. This wasn't about sex or a port in a storm. She wanted a real bond that might develop into love if time allowed, and for some reason, she'd picked him. But there was no time.

Tucson pushed the feel of Jam to the back of his mind. His brother's call was a reminder that there was no time in his life for anything but work.

Chapter 9

Tucson

Pecos was waiting outside the sheriff's station as Tucson pulled up. Little brother looked like a man now. Tall, strong, and in his uniform, he seemed totally grown. Tucson no longer saw the kid he'd protected from the day Pecos was born.

Their parents weren't cruel, just neglectful. When he came home on leave, even from the first, he always went to the farm, not to visit his parents, but to check on Pecos. Tucson would help his little brother with the endless chores, and then they'd talk.

The two other brothers were nearer his age. They'd talked about their escape plans for years. But Pecos was so much younger and Tucson had worried what would happen when the three older brothers left home.

Pecos survived his raising thanks to the old sheriff and a few others in town. Now he was a husband to a beautiful, bright woman. A father of two and the youngest sheriff in the state.

Old Sheriff LeRoy Hayes had helped Tucson find his way a dozen years ago. He'd called in a favor from a friend in the army. Even today his commander would threaten to call the sheriff if Tucson even thought about stepping out of line. The old sheriff and the commander at the fort had been brothers-in-arms and no one understands that bond unless they've lived it.

As Tucson stepped from the rental car, Pecos was already talking. "Thank goodness you're still here. I didn't know who else to call."

Tucson moved seamlessly into the role he'd played for years in the army. "Rope off the perimeters around your office, including any door that could lead from your office. Don't touch any doorknob or light switch. I hope when you looked at the photos you didn't handle them."

Pecos frowned. "Give me some credit."

"You want my help or not, Sheriff? Fill me in." He fought down a smile as he called his kid brother "Sheriff."

Pecos nodded once. "Why rope off my office?"

"You'll want to know who sees the photos. Most people are curious, but the killer might want to get close to check his work." Tucson smiled. "Now, fill me in on everything."

Pecos reported facts in rapid fire. "The dispatcher was the only one here after the trooper brought the photos in, for maybe ten minutes. She would have seen the front door open. Only the deputies have keys to the back door and it locks automatically.

"The deputy on duty here left to pick up dinner. He went out the front door and crossed the street. The front door couldn't have been out of his sight for more than a few minutes. The photos had not been handled by anyone but the man who found them."

Tucson was moving toward the sheriff's office with Pecos at his side still talking. "I unlocked the office, saw the mess, and stepped back out."

Pecos lowered his voice. "I don't know who to trust. A

few of the deputies wanted the sheriff's job. They might be mad and playing a prank. That's why I had to call you. It could be a joke to make me look incompetent. If I call in backup on my first day and it's a prank, I'll never live it down. If it's not, I've got to get this right."

Both men moved inside the office, their hands behind their backs. Pecos quoted police procedure that Tucson knew by heart.

The brothers studied the photos.

Finally, Tucson whispered, "We'll probably not find any fingerprints or clues as to who trashed the photos. Most bad guys make a dozen mistakes." Tucson grinned. "All we have to find is one.

"The big question here isn't who took the shots. It's why. If this is real, why do they want you to know about this crime?" Tucson looked up at his brother. "I don't believe for a moment it's coincidence that these appeared on your desk on your first day in office."

The brothers were quiet as they went through standard procedures. Fingerprints were everywhere in the office, but none on the photos. The rain may have washed them away. Not one deputy had dropped by headquarters to watch. All were out on duty. So the snapshots might be real. The dispatcher said she was busy knitting and hadn't stopped to even go to the bathroom. No one in the holding cells, no janitors worked on weekends.

Finally, with magnifying glasses in their hands, the two men began to examine each small photo. They looked to have been taken moments after the crime happened.

First one: Body on dock. Spread eagle. Face turned slightly away from camera. Shadows.

Next: Left leg, appeared to be broken. No blood.

Next: Chest with dog tags around the neck but not readable.

Last picture: More blood. Obviously running down the sides of the chest and onto the dock.

"I feel like I'm watching a murder happen," Pecos whispered. "It makes no sense. Rainy. Cloudy, but daylight. Still, people driving by would've seen men there. And surely someone noticed a body. How could anyone miss the body?"

Tucson looked at the third photo. "Probably not broad daylight but it's hard to tell. I'm guessing just after dawn. Either the photographer was very careful, or the dead guy is setting up shots. The leg looks broken, but it might just be the angle of the shot.

"The killer could have placed the body while it was still dark. Then took the shots. I'll bet the weeds at the back of the dock blocked the view of the body from anyone driving by. Besides, there would be little traffic on a weekend morning."

The shift changed and deputies came in, one by one, studying the photos. None had any theories and all seemed to be taking it seriously.

As two deputies on duty examined the photos, Tucson watched the men. Neither tried to hide a smile. Both seemed willing to help.

At about ten the old sheriff, LeRoy Hayes, called in. As if he was still in charge, he informed Tucson that he'd called Commander Thompson and asked if Tucson could be assigned to the case since the victim was obviously in the service.

Tucson would have loved to have been in hearing distance of that conversation but somehow LeRoy had gotten his way. Tucson was assigned to Honey Creek until the case was solved or two weeks passed.

Pecos was too polite to tell the old sheriff to butt out, but Tucson made it plain that he'd be taking orders from the present sheriff.

Leroy grumbled but winked at Tucson to let him know Tucson was right.

As the brothers walked out, Pecos asked where Tucson was planning to spend the night. Both knew it wouldn't be at the Smith farm.

Tucson lied and said he had it worked out.

Pecos seemed too tired to ask another question. "See you at eight tomorrow. No sense working until it's daylight. I've already had the dock marked off. My deputy said he shined his lights over the entire dock and didn't see a thing."

No surprise. This crime, if it was a crime, was as strange as they come. All the pieces didn't fit and why would someone take photos, then remove the body and leave behind the evidence?

"See you here at eight, Sheriff." Tucson had so many questions he needed to write them down.

As he walked out into the cool night, the whole town seemed to be asleep. Honey Creek, he thought. The town he'd grown up in. The place he would have never returned to if it hadn't been for his brothers. Tucson was the oldest. His brothers were his responsibility. They always would be.

Tucson drove around the courthouse square. This town he'd always hated was now his home for a few weeks. He'd work the case all day, but at night he could only think of one place he wanted to be.

With Jam.

He told himself he'd just drop by and make sure she was fine tonight. Maybe they'd talk about what was happening. He'd said he'd be back. Who knows, she might be waiting up.

He drove the few blocks and then parked at the back of the café. One kitchen light was on and the back door was unlocked. Logic told him that meant he was expected.

Silently he climbed the back stairs and opened the second door on the left.

The moon offered just enough light for him to see her curled up atop the covers. She still wore her work clothes and shoes.

He tugged off her shoes and spread a blanket over her. Her midnight hair glowed in the moonlight. Too beautiful to be real, he thought as he lowered beside her.

He'd meant to simply watch over her for a few minutes, but when he finally closed his eyes, sleep overtook him.

His soul was home, he thought.

Chapter 10

Melody

When Melody's parents picked her up a little after five, she felt she was stepping out of a dream. She'd spent the whole day alone with Michael. They'd driven around the valley. They talked and laughed without having to whisper. They kissed a dozen times, and still she'd wished he'd kissed her one more time.

It was not surprising that her parents didn't notice her windblown hair and her slightly swollen lips. They were too busy talking about the great success of the workshop and all the things they wanted to add next time.

When they arrived home after an hour of talking, her mother seemed to remember Melody in the back seat. "I know it was a long day for you, Melody. Maybe next time you can stay with Grandmother A."

"I didn't mind."

"I hoped you walked around. Did you go over and get a Coke?"

"I walked around."

"Good," her mother said as if checking off a list. "You didn't talk to any of the college boys, did you?"

"No. I didn't." Melody climbed out of the car before her mother could start on the lecture about never dating.

As she ran for the house, she heard her mother call out, "Supper will be ready in thirty."

Melody dropped her books and reached for her phone.

**6:37: THANKS FOR THE LESSON. I LEARNED A
GREAT DEAL TODAY. HOME.**

She stared at the screen. No answer. Michael must be at the mess hall. He didn't talk much about what he did, but she thought he liked it. He called the fort home.

As she heard her mom calling her name, Melody put away the phone.

Mom called again. Sharp. Loud. Angry.

Melody rushed to the kitchen wondering what had happened with dinner.

As she rushed in Melody saw no food cooking. Her mother was standing in the center of the room with what looked like a death grip on her phone.

Her father was at the back door looking as puzzled as Melody.

No one said a word for a few moments, then her mother took in a deep breath and said, "Professor Clark just called to tell me that she saw you getting out of a car in front of the library. She wanted to congratulate us on finally allowing you to date. She had the nerve to say, 'It's about time.'"

Her father's voice came low. "Is this true, Melody? Don't you dare lie."

"I won't," Melody said in almost a whisper. How could she deny Michael after she'd just had the best day of her life. "But I will not answer questions."

Both her parents shot questions in rapid fire. "Who was

he?" "How did you meet him?" "How long had this been going on?"

She stood facing the firing squad alone. Not saying a word. All her meek life she'd never disobeyed. She'd been grounded once for not eating her dinner, and a few times for not making the grades they wanted her to.

The lectures began.

Melody didn't move, but in her mind she could almost hear Michael reading a book about the Blitz in London during WWII. At one point the couple made a pact to meet up at Big Ben at midnight if they ever got separated.

He'd told her they should name a place. Somewhere public, but not too public. A place they both knew.

"The dock in Honey Creek. No one would look for us there. The dock at midnight."

The dock at midnight. She almost said it aloud as her parents were dueling orders.

"I'll have your phone. You're obviously not big enough to follow rules." Her mother held out her hand.

Melody walked to her room. Pulled out her phone and hit Michael's number. One ring. She hung up. Again. Again. Three calls, one ring. Their code: "Trouble."

Then, feeling her whole body shaking, she deleted Michael's number.

The Avendales sat down to supper. No one ate much. When Melody stood and headed to her room, her mother's last words were, "We'll talk about this tomorrow."

At dawn Melody was dressed for church. Her father drove her to early morning choir practice without saying a word until he stopped. "See you in an hour."

"Am I allowed to go to youth meeting tonight?"

"I'll drive you." He hesitated. "How about you walk over to Grandmother A's place? It's only a block from the church. I think we all need some time before we talk. I'll okay it with Mom."

Melody waved goodbye and walked inside. Five minutes later she walked out the side door of the Sunday school rooms, crossed the parking lot with families moving like ants around the cars.

Two miles later she was at the Greyhound bus station. She bought a ticket to Waco without anyone looking her in the eyes.

She wasn't going to Waco, but halfway between home and Waco was Honey Creek.

By the time the church bells began to ring, she was boarding the bus. She knew her parents didn't make church this morning. They were home discussing her.

She'd wait on the dock tonight and every night until Michael came. The dock was her Big Ben. He might not come for a few nights or a few weeks, but he would come. He would eventually remember what he'd said yesterday when he'd told her how to hide and survive until he could get to her.

Chapter 11

Mr. Winston's Idea

After the luncheon Saturday, Mr. Winston walked Miss Lambert to her lavender-colored door above the pharmacy. When she asked if he'd like coffee, he decided to go wild and say yes.

"I think I'd like that, Lilly. There's a nip in the air." Having known her for years, her first name was new on his tongue.

She pulled the key away from the lock and looked over her shoulder. In the twilight he had no idea if she was smiling or frowning. She moved aside for him to push the door open and they both stepped in.

Her apartment wasn't new to him. He'd come to a Friends of the Library meeting many times with others. But tonight, he was her lone guest. He swore even the air felt different.

"I hope it's not too late for coffee. I could come back some other time if you prefer." Winston feared he'd stepped too far, too fast.

"No, no. It . . . it is fine."

"Good, there is something I'd like to ask you." He followed her into a spotless kitchen. All was in order, just as he knew it would be.

"Oh, a question, of course." Lilly finally smiled. "Ask away while I put on the coffee. You wouldn't believe the questions I get asked just because I worked in a pharmacy. I think everyone thought I sat around reading the back of the bottles all day."

She didn't look at him, but her voice had given up the panic mode. He simply stood watching her. He would not sit down until offered a seat. That wouldn't be polite.

When she finally turned his direction with a coffee cup in each hand, she said, "Please sit down. I have some real English biscuits I buy every Christmas for my holiday treat. I'd like to offer you some."

He took two without telling her that just because the tin had London Bridge on the container did not mean the cookies came from England.

After they both ate their cookies and half the coffee was gone, she smiled. "Now ask your question, Mr. Winston. You know if I don't have the answer, I'll be digging through the internet to find it."

He straightened. "Perhaps you should call me Charles. I've thought of asking this question for a long time, but I wanted to wait until we had a moment alone." He cleared his throat. "With neither of us ever being married, I don't want to frighten you, so I'd like to start with asking if you'd like to be engaged to me."

Lilly's eyes widened. He couldn't tell if she was shocked or having a stroke. "Oh dear. Lilly, I didn't mean to upset you. I just thought it might be nice since we are friends to take our relationship one step further.

"At lunch when we were talking about wish goals, I thought about you. I'd like to have the town think of us as a couple." He didn't add that saying they were engaged sounded much better than what people whispered now.

"They never married, you know." Folks would whisper, "Always alone."

He tried to keep his voice calm. "If we were engaged, we could spend more time together. I do enjoy your company, and I believe you enjoy mine. Of course, if you prefer . . ."

"Yes," she interrupted. "Yes, to being engaged to you. Though I think I know you well, Charles, this would certainly be an adventure. Think of all the interesting conversations we'd have since we don't have any grandchildren to talk about." Both fought down a giggle.

"No old spouses to complain about. No in-laws to report on. Imagine the topics we'd have time to cover." Winston patted her arm.

Lilly covered her laugh, then straightened. "We must talk about the rules of this engagement. I need to know exactly what you think it would entail. I agree to the engagement but not marriage. We are both too old for that nonsense."

Winston let out a long breath and slowly finished his coffee. "I agree."

Lilly smiled as silence filled the room. It seemed they were both deep in thought.

Finally, Winston took charge. "I think you are wise about setting rules. Having never been engaged, I may need a bit of help, my lady. I thought we might walk around the square on warm evenings."

"Oh yes, and we could stop in for an ice cream now and then." Her eyes finally met his. "Maybe watch a movie together."

"I'd like that, Lilly."

They sat staring at one another for a moment. "I was

asked once before," she whispered as if turning loose of a secret.

"Why did you say no?"

"I didn't love him, and he never showed any hint of loving me. He did like my cooking. Maybe he was confused." She looked at Winston as she set down the first rule. "Charles, do you have any problem saying that you love me? Preferably before we eat any meal I've cooked. I would like to hear it said now and then. That seems a part of an engagement."

"I agree and I promise to always be kind to you, dear lady."

Lilly smiled. "I'd like that, but you have always been kind to me."

He pulled a box from his coat pocket. "I've been carrying this around hoping for a chance to speak privately with you. Will you wear my mother's engagement ring? It was the only valuable I carried from Ireland and many a time I feared I'd have to sell it. Now I'm glad I didn't."

She didn't move.

Winston opened the box and slid the small band of woven gold on her slender finger. "If you change your mind about the engagement, all you have to do is tell me. I'd like you to keep the ring. I'll never give it to another in this lifetime."

They sat in silence for a while.

Finally, she asked, "Will you sit next to me in church tomorrow?"

"Of course. Will you kiss me good night?"

"I will as long as we are not in public. Will you take my arm when we walk?"

"I will."

He grinned thinking this was going splendidly. "We're doing something wild, aren't we. I'm a bit afraid, Lilly.

We'll be talked about. If you've no objection, I'd like to take you to dinner one night a week. Maybe Thursday, if you have no plans."

"That would be grand, and I'd like you to come to my house for a simple supper on Tuesdays. We could talk and maybe watch the news together."

Winston felt as if his heart was beating again after being dormant for years. He'd known Lilly since he'd first moved to Honey Creek, and she'd always been pleasant company. She was gentle and kind, a lady to the core. They always had interesting conversations. The possibility of having someone to share time with made the future seem brighter.

"It is getting late, dear. I must go. I'm guessing after we sit together in church, there will be questions." He kissed her on the cheek as he stood.

He made it three steps then remembered their bargain. "I love you, Lilly. I think I always have." She was staring down at the ring on her left hand. "Is there something else you'd like Lilly? I think this is the time to be frank with each other."

"Yes." Tears sat in her pale blue eyes. "One more thing. When you come Tuesday night, every Tuesday night if convenient, will you sleep with me? I've never . . ."

She didn't finish. She seemed to have trouble breathing.

Winston froze. He'd lived a very proper life, he'd thought, but there had been women. A few one-night stands in his twenties. A cook he'd been involved with for a few months in his thirties, but no deep feelings ever developed. A woman he'd grown up with in Ireland. He'd made love to her the night before he'd left home at eighteen and once when he'd gone back to Ireland. In between times, she'd married and divorced three times. She never kept the man, but she kept the land. He never even thought of offering marriage to her; after all, he had no land.

"Are you sure you'd want me to?" he asked his Lilly. "Someone might see me leaving come Wednesday morning."

"Yes. I'm sure. Will you?"

Winston straightened like a soldier accepting a dangerous assignment. "I will. And, Lilly, nothing will happen that you don't want to happen."

He made it to the door and was one step outside when he thought he heard Miss Lilly Lambert whisper, "I want it all."

As he walked home, lightning could have hit him, buffaloes could have stampeded over him, an alien ship could have beamed him up, and he wouldn't have noticed.

The shy, proper lady wanted it all, and he wasn't sure what that involved or if he was up to the task.

Twelve hours later, in church, holding her hand, Winston still hadn't figured it out. He didn't think this was one task he could ask divine guidance for.

But, thanks to problems at the sheriff's office, very few people noticed they'd sat side by side and Lilly had taken his arm as they'd left.

Winston patted her hand resting on his arm. He loved feeling the ring on her finger.

They talked of the weather and the sheriff's first case that needed solving as he walked her to her door. Then, he stepped inside so she could kiss him on the cheek.

As she did, he whispered, "I love you."

Then blushing for the first time in years, he walked away wishing it was Tuesday.

Chapter 12

Jam

Sunday

Tiny slivers of light sliced through the lace curtains on the French doors in her little room above the café. The second door on the second floor opened to a bedroom that had become her hideout when she was too tired to go home.

Jam listened as the huge old house whined and creaked. The refrigerator below beeped because it had somehow cracked open during the night. What sounded like squirrels scampered across the roof. The wind howled, tree branches and vines fought to get in, and shutters rattled. The floors creaked so loud sometimes she swore someone was walking upstairs on the small third floor.

She knew the sounds of the night in this old house, yet Jam would swear she wasn't alone.

Just a few of a dozen more things that needed fixing, she thought to herself. *Never enough time.*

Folks say you have to love an old house if you buy one because it's always needing a makeover. She did love this old captain's house that she'd changed into a café. But she also loved her little farmhouse and her grandparents' home that had sat empty for fifty years. The last farm, the last house on Sunflower Lane. She'd always thought it was waiting to become something grand.

The café was her business, but Sunflower Lane was in her blood.

Someday when she'd learned enough, she'd remodel the big old house on Sunflower Lane and make a place where people could come to learn, or rest, or even heal.

She didn't want to just feed people, she wanted to help people. There was a peace on her rocky land scattered with wildflowers. A peace she wanted to share with others.

Funny, she thought, she owned three houses and none felt like home. She simply floated between them like Goldilocks trying to find the one that felt just right.

She'd planned to go to her farm tonight. After all, Sunday was her only sleep-in morning. But Jam had hoped Tucson might come back if only to say goodbye. They didn't really know each other and a few kisses didn't make a relationship but she could hope.

Finally giving up, she fell asleep waiting and cuddled up with dreams.

Jam smiled as she heard the kitchen staff coming in to prep for the Sunday buffet. She'd told her staff she wouldn't be in, so she'd have to sneak down the front stairs unseen before they set up the buffet, or sleep until two when the café closed.

She rolled over, thinking sleeping was the best idea.

With no warning, she slammed into a huge boulder in her bed.

It took her a blink to figure out what it was atop the bedspread, then she just stared.

Sergeant Tucson Smith. Sound asleep. In her bed. She didn't know whether to scream or laugh. They were both fully dressed except for shoes, so nothing had happened between them, but this big hulk of a man seemed to have developed a habit of crawling into bed with her.

Apparently, she was sleeping with the world's largest GI Joe doll.

Patting his whiskered cheek, she whispered, "But, ain't he cute?"

Jam poked him three times before he opened one eye and growled.

She decided to laugh. "Sergeant Smith, you cannot sleep here. Aren't you supposed to be back at your fort?"

He scrubbed his face with one hand. "How'd you get in my bed?"

"It's my bed."

Looking around he said, "It is your bed. Would you believe I teleported up here?"

"Not a chance." Laughter flavored her words.

"I was so tired last night I just headed to the nearest bed. You'd said you were going to your farm earlier, and now I wake up and find you in my borrowed bed."

"It's my bed." She poked his chest. When he looked wounded, she laughed. "Why are you still in town? Maybe you're not. Maybe you're my morning dream."

He grabbed her hand and pulled her to him. After kissing her, he whispered against her ear, "I'm real, Jam. I'm no dream."

She put her hands on the sides of his face. Kissed him just like he'd kissed her. "You're real. But why are you still here?"

"I got posted to my little brother's new case thanks to that old sheriff. I'm now officially on assignment in Honey Creek." Tucson smiled. "It's going to be a tough assignment." He fisted his hand and lightly tapped her chin. "A secret agent keeps pulling me to her bed."

"Before I kick you out, you've got to tell me what happened last night. It must be big if they called in the army."

"Not the whole army. Just me, and I'm not talking until you feed me. I don't have the energy. I worked half the night, then spent a few hours watching you sleep. When I finally dozed off, you decided to cuddle."

"I'm not a cuddler," Jam insisted. "Every boyfriend since the second grade has told me that."

Tucson opened his hand and brushed her hair that seemed to be flying in every direction. "Every boyfriend since the second grade is right. I swear, under these covers is a land mine of sharp body parts. An elbow in my eye woke me once. Knee to my privates a couple of times. A shoulder knocked me in the chin and a breast slammed into my face when you rolled over and stretched. Oh, wait, that wasn't so bad."

She rolled to face him nose to nose, her head propped on a pillow. "I'm not interested in your injuries; I want to know what happened at the sheriff's office."

He leaned closer, almost touching her. "I can't tell you details. It's classified. Apparently, the former sheriff and my commander are old buddies. LeRoy pulled in a favor and got me assigned here for two weeks. All I can tell you is that there may be an active-duty soldier involved and I'm investigating."

"Are you investigating me?"

"I wouldn't mind. There is something about you that makes me want to get closer. When I saw you in the moonlight two nights ago, I swear you were the most beautiful vision I'd ever dreamed up. Then, as we talked and shared a meal, I just wanted to hold you, but you were sleepwalking tired and half drunk, so I settled for watching you sleep."

She studied him. "That is weird that old LeRoy pulled you in on a mystery, but right now you want to tell me why you crawled in my bed again? You've got some strange habits, Tucson Smith."

"I know. New habits. I never had them before I saw you crying in the cottonwoods. Everyone knows this place is haunted. Maybe you're the resident witch. Maybe I'm bewitched?"

"The house has ghosts, not witches. Get your town history straight. What made you think you were welcome? I could have shot you."

He winked. "You left the door open. You knew I'd keep my promise to come back. That's why you didn't go to the farm last night. You were waiting for me." He slowly smiled. "All you have to do is yell and your staff will head up here with butcher knives. I'm guessing they'd murder me first and then ask questions."

"Well, I remember locking the door, so you must have broken in." She touched the stubble on his jaw. "You afraid I'll scream?"

"No. Something tells me, Jam, that you are as attracted to me as I am to you. I've never felt a pull so strong. I don't want to rush this, whatever it might be, but I don't want to miss knowing you."

Jam brushed his brown hair. *Not long enough*, she thought, *but soft to the touch*. "What time do you have to be back at the sheriff's office?"

He checked his watch. "I'm meeting Pecos in a half hour and I need to check out a few things before I report in. Any chance we could have a date tonight before I sleep with you again?"

"I don't think I know you that well. I don't go out with every man who flops up on my shore."

"Honey, you've seen me naked and we've slept together

twice." He glowered. "And for some reason you're not afraid of me."

"Should I be?"

"No. Never."

She slowly closed the distance between them and kissed him tenderly. "If you ever hurt me, I'll have the ghosts up on the third floor murder you."

He laughed as he pushed her curtain of hair away from her face and kissed her cheek. "I've been looking in bars for the right woman for years. Who knew perfection was hiding out by the river? We've got a date tonight. I want to take you out. Any objection?"

"No objection. Just be on time. Dark-thirty sounds good."

"I'll be on time, or I'll call."

As he rolled off the bed and picked up his boots, she asked, "Anything else?"

"Yeah, wear something beside that uniform, Jam."

"Like what?"

"Anything else." He reached the door. "Or nothing at all."

Jam rolled onto his pillow and hid her face. She wasn't sure she was laughing or crying. It had been years since she'd flirted with even a smile. This man who came out of the river made no sense. For some crazy reason he was attracted to her. Didn't he see that she was too thin, too tall? She hadn't worn makeup since she'd turned thirty. She was the kind of girl who went out on friend dates with the crowd and didn't get kissed good night. She didn't know how to talk sexy.

She'd thought about marrying a coworker when she was twenty-two. They'd both been interning to be chefs in Dallas. The work hours were insane, and when they did have sex it was awkward. Jam thought of how Paul just faded away more than broke up with her. She couldn't remember the month he disappeared. No goodbye, no fights.

She thought the last words he said to her were, "I'll be working late."

She hadn't cried when she noticed all his things were gone from her apartment. A few months later, after her parents' deaths, she moved back home to Honey Creek. She'd settled into the house she'd grown up in and used the little inheritance from her parents to buy the café.

With all the work to do, the seasons flowed like weeks. She'd decided she always got the generic kind of love. Dates with friends. Never missing anyone when they walked away.

Only Tucson was different, and the wonder was he seemed as new to passion as she was.

"It can't last," she whispered into the pillow. But while it did, she'd enjoy every minute.

Chapter 13

McCoy's Refuge

McCoy woke slowly, taking in the room as if it were more a lingering nightmare than his life. Nothing on the walls, not even paint in some spots. Hard bed, one blanket, one pillow, a piece of leather tacked up as a window cover.

He vaguely remembered falling on the bed and the room going dark and then light again a few times. Half a dozen empty water bottles were on the box of a nightstand.

He had no idea how long he slept or what day it was. That seemed to be a habit since the hospital. Then the room had been bright and white. Now the walls were mud brown and the light was cave level.

Trolls wouldn't live in this place.

Thinking of trolls, there was one standing in the doorway, and he wasn't smiling. Grandpa Sadler Mason, his absent relative for twenty-nine years, might be the world's tallest troll, but he definitely was one. His silver hair was six months late to the barber, his hands were black from working on engines, and McCoy wouldn't be surprised if he growled at any moment.

When his steel gray eyes finally focused on his grandson, Sadler shouted, "You going to sleep all day again, boy?"

"I'm not a boy. I'll be thirty next fall. Not that you'd know." McCoy had to ask, "Did you even know I existed?"

"I did. Your dad wrote me a few times. He sent a picture of you once. On the back he wrote your name and age. Four, I think it was. Said your mom ran off and left you with him to raise."

"Did you write back?"

The old man shook his head. "Didn't have nothing to say."

"Were you interested in me? Are you now?"

"Sure." Sadler stood frozen for a while as if trying to think of something to say. Finally, he asked, "What do you do for a living, boy?"

"I'm a contractor. Mostly I build businesses and small strip malls. Lost my job when I wrecked my car and had to spend three weeks in the hospital." McCoy stared straight at his grandfather. "What do you do, old man?"

"I'm not old. I'm worn out. There's a difference. I work on farm equipment mostly, and I care for a few old donkeys more as a hobby than for money. You know anything about donkeys?"

"Nope." They might be talking, but McCoy didn't feel like he was getting any closer to the old guy. From Sadler's greasy overalls there was no doubt he was a mechanic. His hands were scarred and layered in grime.

McCoy might as well settle things between them. "I'm not asking for a handout. I could work around here for my keep. Your farm equipment might be in good shape, but your house and barn need work. I could make repairs for you."

When Grandpa didn't comment, McCoy added, "That bathroom floor is about rotted out and could use tiling. No bigger than it is, the job wouldn't cost much. I noticed when I came in that the porch is sagging. Might blow down in a strong wind. Near as I can see, every sink in the place is dripping and all the windows need caulking."

"I can do all that, boy, but I don't have time." Grandpa might not be smiling, but he'd stopped frowning.

McCoy nodded once. "If you don't mind me staying, I'll do it. All you'll have to do is buy the materials. I may have to start off slow, but in a few days, I'll be at full speed."

McCoy didn't feel like bargaining. His normally chaotic life had gone into overdrive, and he needed a place to stop and rest. "Yes or no, old man. I can call Leo and have him come get me if the answer is no."

The old guy smiled for the first time. "You ain't got nowhere else to go or you wouldn't have come here."

"True, but I've been down before."

Sadler scratched his head, and McCoy could have sworn he saw fleas flying out.

"Stay if you like. Fix what you want to, but I'll feed you for as long as it takes you to heal. You're kin. I'll help you while you're down."

"Thanks." McCoy was shocked. No welcome. No hug. Not one kind word for his only grandson, but somewhere under those dirty overalls was a beating heart.

His grandfather turned to leave. "I got food on the table. Usually have stew or chili."

McCoy raised one eyebrow. "You made stew?"

"No. I'll open it. When I go into town to get supplies, I'll stop by the grocery store and pick us up a dozen more cans. Supper is always stew, chili or takeout. Saves time trying to figure what to cook at night."

The world's tallest troll was gone when McCoy looked up, so he yelled at the empty room, "Mind telling me what day it is?" He fought the urge to slug himself for asking the same question the nurses had always asked. Now his grandfather would think he had brain damage.

"It's Sunday," Grandpa answered from the back of the house. "I came in to see if you were dead. Since you're not, we might as well eat."

"Can you cook anything besides stew and chili?"

"No. Two choices seems enough. After every breakfast, put your cereal bowl with leftover milk in the fridge to use again."

McCoy hobbled to the kitchen and was relieved when he saw two McDonald's bags. The old man had a sense of humor; he got McCoy the kids' meal.

They sat down in the two rolling chairs and ate without saying a word. It didn't take long for McCoy to figure out why Sadler used office chairs in the kitchen. If the old guy needed something, he just rolled a few feet and he could reach every inch of the little kitchen.

When he finished McCoy said, "Thanks for the meal." Then he lifted his broken leg off the floor and took his glass to the sink and his bag to the trash without getting up.

Sadler nodded.

Since neither seemed to want to talk, McCoy limped back to what was now his bedroom and decided to take a nap before he went to bed. He'd meant to dream of being back in Georgia with Breanna, but he could no longer remember her face.

How could he have forgotten her so fast? He'd put an engagement ring on her finger, but he'd never really imagined being married to her. She'd been tall. All his girlfriends were at least five foot eight and blonde. Most were happy to quit their jobs and move around with him. He made good money, and they didn't mind helping him spend it on weekends. But in the end, they all grew bored and left. They had discovered that after a twelve-hour day of hard work, he didn't much feel like partying.

As he closed his eyes, he thought he'd probably end up

living alone, just like his grandpa. If he lined up three photos of the Mason men, anyone would swear they were looking at the same aging man.

Sadler woke him an hour later to give him a book to read just in case he couldn't sleep. McCoy guessed if he stayed three months, he'd read the whole collection.

Long after dark McCoy heard the old man open the front door. From his window he watched his grandpa walk around as if on guard. Surely Sadler didn't think people would come onto his land at night. And, if it was true, McCoy might be stepping into more trouble than he'd bargained for.

An hour later Sadler came in. He must have gone to his bedroom across the hall because the house was silent.

McCoy decided to take a shower. He'd had enough sponge baths to last him a lifetime.

Maybe he'd hated them because he'd always had a problem with people touching him. He wasn't strange or anything. He loved touching a woman he cared about, but most of the time he didn't know how to act when someone hugged him.

Maybe he was just the product of being an only child raised by a father who'd neither spanked him nor hugged him, or even so much as held his hand.

McCoy never stayed long enough in a town to develop real friends, so his discomfort with being touched hadn't really been a problem.

He worked with his hands, molding wood and tile and brick to be useful, sometimes beautiful, but he'd never learned to be at ease around people.

Breanna hadn't been gone a month, and all he remembered of her was her soft hair. Hell, he might as well give up relationships and just buy a wig to pat on now and then.

"Something is seriously wrong with me," McCoy

mumbled as he moved through the silent rooms of his grandfather's house. "I have the bonding skills of a rattle-snake."

He stubbed his toe on his good foot and cussed the rest of the way to the bathroom.

The room was clean. He tied a trash bag around his foot and leg with tape and took his first shower in almost a month. He stood under the water until it turned cold, then he stepped out on a sagging hardwood floor and dried off.

He'd found his first project. The flooring was so rotten McCoy was surprised his foot hadn't broken through.

With Sadler in bed, McCoy began to explore the place wearing only underwear. The cabinets were mostly full of soup cans, but the cabinet doors were barely hanging on. The refrigerator rattled like a Model T and held milk and beer. A gun case was built into the wall behind the front door. It held only rifles, all loaded, which told McCoy the old man was worried about something. The case was locked, but the key lay on the top of the case for anyone six feet tall to see.

His plan to be helpful might just work if his grandpa could afford to feed him. He knew when he left, this place would be in much better shape. In a few days, he'd probably be hobbling around without crutches. He might not be able to repair the roof, but he could fix the floor on his knees.

When he stepped out onto the porch, the night was cool and the land was painted in shadows. The air smelled fresh, and the evening was calm. Silence wasn't something he was used to. He'd worked on noisy construction sites and slept in cheap hotels the past ten years.

Tonight, this world seemed new to him and it smelled of flowers.

McCoy didn't even hear the car pull off the county road and onto the dirt trail until headlights flashed. The little

Volkswagen moved toward him as if two beams of light were floating over the air.

He barely heard the engine until it cut off three feet from the steps. A woman with short curling chestnut hair jumped out and started delivering boxes to the porch.

When she raised her head, she didn't seem surprised to see a six-foot-three man frozen on the porch in only his white underwear. She looked him up and down and went back to work.

Finally, it dawned on him that he should have gone back inside, but it was too late now. She was already standing between him and the door. Without another look at him, she reached inside and flicked on the porchlight. Then she started counting boxes.

"You must be Sadler's grandson." She smiled as she studied him, bruises and all. "I heard you were staying here."

"I would claim no kin to him, but even I can see he's the wrinkled copy of me." He thought of crossing his arms over his chest to look less naked, but then the crutch would fall and so would he.

"I don't much care who you are, except you are the only company I've ever seen at this place. I'm just dropping off medicine."

"Is the old man sick?"

"No."

He moved closer. She'd already seen him so what did it matter how near he was? "You a doc?"

"Yeah. A vet. The meds are for the old donkeys. He's got a small herd on land big enough to graze a hundred more."

"How many does he have?"

"A few dozen, but they're half-wild. He buys them at the auctions when no one else bids. He turns them out in the back pasture this time of year. Sadler can give them the shots they need, but he may need a little help rounding them up. Can you handle the work, Grandson?"

"It's McCoy, McCoy Mason."

The little lady finally smiled. "I'm Doc Blanton. Baylor Blanton."

McCoy tried conversation. "You named after a pill?"

"No," she snapped. "I'm named after a college. You might have heard of it."

McCoy thought of telling her he wasn't from Texas, but if he appeared any dumber, she'd probably deworm him along with the donkeys.

He figured changing the subject might help. "How'd you get past the gate? Pop doesn't welcome visitors."

"I know the combination to the lock."

"What is it?"

She raised an eyebrow. "I'm guessing Sadler will tell you when he wants you to know."

"Want to tell me why the old man buys animals no one else wants, Doc?"

The vet shrugged. "Maybe he doesn't want them to be slaughtered."

McCoy almost laughed. "Yeah, I can tell he's got a big heart."

She started down the porch steps. "A heart is a hard thing to see." She was almost to her car when she added, "He took you in, didn't he?"

McCoy had no answer to that. He'd have liked to keep talking to her.

She frowned at him. "Might want to stay off that leg until it is checked out. Use the Mule if you wander around the place."

"Where's the Mule?" One more stray to keep up with, he thought.

She pointed at an ATV parked in a shed next to a barn.

This McCoy knew something about. ATVs were used around construction sites. "Looks like a Coleman Outfitter with a wide dump bed."

The vet smiled. "You may have to drive with your foot hanging out, but it will get you around. Mason may never paint his house, but his engines run. Every farmer and rancher in the valley has him tune up equipment."

"I can handle the ATV." He'd rebuild the entire engine before he'd even consider climbing on a horse or a donkey.

She finally grinned. "I bet you can, McCoy. Drive out and check the herd a few times a day. I can't prove it, but the donkey found dead last week may not have died of old age. I saw signs of poisoning. Sadler hates coming to town, so if he talks you into that chore, drop by my office. It'll save me a trip out next week. If you come, I'll buy you a cup of coffee and check your leg."

"Thanks, but I think I'll see a real doctor."

"I am a real doctor. The MD who runs the clinic in Honey Creek is on vacation for two weeks. If anyone gets sick, they'll have to drive fifty miles. You'll get really tired of driving the Mule that distance with your leg hanging out. Besides, you're a big enough animal for me to handle." She looked down at his bare feet. "I'll order you a size twelve boot when you're ready for that cast to come off."

"Twelve and a half."

"All right." She opened her car door. "Cute knees."

When she grinned, she looked more girl than woman.

If he stayed a week, McCoy had a feeling he'd be taking her up on that coffee. But right now, he'd sworn off women. He had no doubt Dr. Baylor Blanton would be worth taking the time to get to know.

"Night, cowboy," she said showing little interest.

The vet vanished before he could think of an answer. He

watched her little car drive away. "I'm not a cowboy," he said to no one.

Then, he swore. He hated smart women, and the doc was way out of his league. Breanna had never made him think. She'd laughed at his jokes even when he'd forgotten the punchline.

But smart women were always ahead of him. They were usually telling him what he was thinking even when he hadn't known he was thinking at all.

Chapter 14

Mr. Winston and His Lady

Mr. Winston sat in his garden thinking of his day. It seemed his world had changed. First, no one ever sat on either side of him at church, though everyone greeted him. The widows all sat together, but he'd never seen even a half row of widowers.

Families often took up a whole pew. But he remained alone.

Until today, when Lilly Lambert sat by his side.

As always, he'd been early to church. The organist was warming up. The deacons were getting all in order. The ladies who arranged the flowers were making a final check. And Miss Lilly, his Miss Lilly, was organizing the choir's music.

He watched her. Slender, graceful, shy. He'd kissed her on the cheek last night.

No one noticed, but he never took his eyes off her. When she walked toward him, she flashed a quick smile. Like they'd agreed they would, she sat beside him, almost touching.

He gently took her hand in his and turned it over so he

could see his mother's ring. "I see you haven't changed your mind."

"I have not. And you?"

"I feel the same. Will you join me in the parlor afterwards? There is a senior lunch."

"I will. I brought a pound cake."

"I'll be sure to get a slice." He thought of how calmly they whispered, but he swore he felt more alive than he had in years. He even thought of kissing her cheek right in church, but of course, he didn't.

As the widows took their seats on the two front pews a few stared, but none spoke. The church was filling up and the organ was playing.

Charles didn't hear a word of the sermon. He thought about the days to come. His life was full of friends and projects and committees he served on, and now he had Lilly. He wanted to hear about everything in her life. It would be grand to just talk about their days. Maybe they should make it a rule to call each other every evening.

They could call at nine just to say good night. He'd take her out to dinner on Thursday. She'd cook for him on Tuesday and on Sunday, who knows what they'd think of to do after church. A drive through the valley might be nice. A walk after lunch. Maybe a movie now and then.

She'd whispered that she wanted it all. That was probably what she meant.

She'd said she wanted him to stay the night on Tuesdays. He wasn't sure she knew what that meant to most people. Sleeping together? Making love?

They mixed with the others at lunch and when she held his arm as they walked to her apartment, he thought about what she might want.

When he reached her door, he waited. She was talking

about how good the children's choir was this morning and he was thinking midnight thoughts.

As she unlocked the door, he asked, "May I come in to kiss you goodbye?"

"Of course, but only for a moment."

He sensed she was blushing as he closed the door, leaned near, and kissed her cheek. "I love you, Lilly."

"Thank you for remembering." Then, she kissed him lightly on the lips.

For a while they just smiled at each other. Then he opened the door and took one step. "Until Tuesday."

"Until Tuesday." She was smiling as he turned away.

Now, as the sun set on his perfect day, he remembered every moment. He took in a deep breath of the smell of almost spring. For the first time in a long while, he couldn't wait to see what might happen next.

Chapter 15

McCoy's Pop

Monday

After sleeping most of the first few days at his "not so friendly" grandpa's house, McCoy slept most of the nights as well. He'd planned to stay awake long enough to think about the cute vet who made midnight calls, but sleep won out.

Sunday had been a waste of time. Mostly he followed Sadler around and listened to the old man talk about people who were dead or people in town that McCoy would probably never meet.

They drove out to the pasture and Sadler showed McCoy where the donkey was found dead. McCoy felt like he was on the world's worst sightseeing tour.

He did spend time thinking about how he'd fix the bathroom floor. By Monday he had a good start on his first project. He'd asked if the old man needed a shower for a few days.

All Sadler said was, "Not till Wednesday."

McCoy's leg hurt like hell, but he worked. Sadler dropped by now and then to watch. The good news was

McCoy found everything he needed: lumber, nails, saws. The house might be a mess but the barns were stocked and organized.

After almost a month without working with his hands, he'd forgotten how great it felt.

When McCoy noticed Grandpa watching, he said, "I'm almost ready for the vinyl. What color do you want in the bathroom?"

"I don't care. Make a list of any supplies you'll need and I'll drive you in. Put whatever you pick out on my account. While you shop, I'll go down to McDonald's and get us supper. I figure I should support our new business in town."

"You do know it's a chain, Pop?" McCoy was tired of calling Sadler "Grandpa," and Sadler didn't seem right. He decided to call him Pop. The few times his dad had talked about Sadler, he'd referred to him as Pop.

Midafternoon they headed to Honey Creek. Pop was grumbling about the idea of McDonald's as a chain. He said he'd been to both the other towns in the valley and hadn't seen one, so the chain couldn't be doing too well.

When Pop turned on the paved county road, McCoy took a long breath and relaxed. Since Sadler didn't seem to want to talk except to himself, McCoy went to sleep.

Twenty minutes later, when he got out of the truck, McCoy figured he probably looked as bad as he felt. He'd been wearing the same clothes since he got out of the hospital. The couple who ran the town's only hardware store, Jack and Joanie Johnson, babied him. If they could have talked him into it, they would have put him in a buggy and pushed him down every aisle. The hardware store had everything including dog food, plants, fixtures, pipes, and several shelves of clothes marked as Work Clothes for Farm and Ranch.

McCoy collected supplies for his next three projects and tossed in a couple of shirts, half a dozen T-shirts, underwear, jeans, and a pair of tennis shoes. He only needed one right shoe. Maybe he could bring the left one back for a half refund.

When he got near the checkout, he picked up four bags of cookies and a whole box of Butterfingers.

As Jack rang up the basket, McCoy said, "Hope I'm not going over Pop's limit."

Jack grinned. "There is no limit on Sadler Mason's account. Never has been that I know of."

While Jack loaded all the supplies into the back of Sadler's pickup, McCoy climbed in and said, "I bought some clothes. I'll pay you back."

Pop didn't even glance his way. He simply said, "We'll settle up when you leave. The way you work, even with a bum leg, I'm thinking I may owe you."

McCoy smiled. He'd almost gotten a compliment out of the old man.

"Where did you learn to work like that, son?"

"My dad taught me."

"And I taught him. He never did like to paint though."

"True. By the time I was ten, he made me do all the painting."

A comfortable silence settled between them.

Once home, they unloaded and ate their hamburgers, and McCoy was ready for bed. He pulled out one of the bags of cookies. "I bought you some cookies."

"I don't eat cookies," Pop said. "Never did."

McCoy put the bag on the table between the couch and Sadler's chair.

As he leaned back, he noticed a gold key mortared high up between the fireplace rocks. "You want to tell me why you put a key in the fireplace?"

McCoy half expected Pop not to answer, but he leaned forward and began speaking. "Years ago, I used to carry that key around. It was special to me. My grandfather gave it to me. One day when I was riding on the tractor, it must have fallen out when I was checking the fences. It was almost dark when I noticed rain moving in, so I turned toward home. Lightning flashed, and I saw the key in the dirt. I got off the tractor to get it just as lightning flashed and hit the very seat I'd been sitting on. I would have been fried if I'd still been atop the tractor."

Pop leaned back and smiled. "It's my good luck key, so I built it into the house so this place will never burn."

"Great story, Pop," McCoy managed to say as he fell asleep.

Chapter 16

Sergeant Tucson Smith

Dressed in civilian clothes, Tucson Smith met his brother at the dock where the pictures of the body had been photographed. Tiny little pictures like someone had used a child's camera.

Tucson stepped into his familiar role. Investigation. Paid attention to every detail. Measured everything, including the sun's angle. Searched for anything that was out of place. The army had trained him well.

As he worked, a hunch nagged at his brain. The angle of the shots. The light. The blood trails on the chest that looked the width of fingers. The blood must have come straight out of the victim's heart. A knife. A bullet.

No weapon photographed or found.

Tucson didn't say anything to Pecos yet, but the crime scene seemed to look more and more like a setup. The quality was poor, water spotted.

When they returned to the office, Pecos seemed to have a list of problems to solve. Tucson poured himself his third cup of coffee and sat alone in a back office to think. Why would someone kill a soldier? Or why would he fake his own death? Why did whoever took the pictures clean up the crime scene and toss the pictures to the wind?

After two refills of strong coffee, Tucson grew frustrated and stood and stared out a barred window.

But he wasn't seeing the alley. Tucson could not get the sight of Jam asleep next to him out of his mind.

No, he thought. It wasn't the sleeping he loved. It was the fact that she slept so peacefully beside him.

A lamb sleeping with a lion. From the moment he saw her crying in the cottonwoods by the river, he knew he'd never hurt her. They lived very different lives, but somehow they belonged together if only in the midnight shadows.

He knew he was already bracing himself for the goodbye, but he'd carry her in his memory forever.

He'd always thought of himself as a bear of a man, and Jam was definitely a gentle woman. But somehow, they were drawn to each other. He calmed when near her, and she must have also. Was that enough to build a relationship on?

Probably not.

An hour later when he walked in the tall grass beside the dock looking for clues, he mentally moved through his life. Because Tucson was the oldest, his father was always impatient for him to grow up. From the time his little brothers could walk, he was in charge of them. If they got hurt or broke something or didn't do their jobs around the farm, Tucson was blamed and punished.

At eighteen, when he'd joined the army, boot camp was easy compared to home. He beefed up and became hard as a rock mentally and physically. He decided he wanted to be the best soldier, then the best MP, and finally the best criminal investigator in the army. He'd been all over the world, sent in to solve crimes or retrieve the bodies, and now he was back in his hometown.

All his brothers had severed ties with their parents, but

not with each other. They'd married and had children that Tucson sent gifts to every Christmas. They talked on the phone, not of the past, but of the future.

Only Tucson kept up with their parents in a way. He checked their electric bill each month. If they were still paying the bill, they were still living on the farm. The first few years in the army he sent them his change of address every time he was reassigned. They never wrote.

At first Tucson came home on leave to check on his brothers.

Tucson smiled to himself. Once, while home, he'd threatened his dad that if he didn't make sure Pecos stayed in school Tucson would return and they'd have a talk. The words were the same words he'd used to beat his oldest son.

Surprisingly, Tucson had seen anger and fear in his old man that night.

As soon as Pecos left home after graduation, Tucson hadn't contacted his parents again. His brothers were his family now. The only family he'd probably ever have.

"Tucson!" his little brother called from the shoreline twenty feet away. "I think I found something."

"Freeze," Tucson answered as he moved slowly toward the water's edge. This area was not traveled. Too rocky for the swimmers. Too muddy to launch a boat.

Pecos stood still, like a huge marker at a crime scene, and Tucson moved toward him, taking pictures of bare footprints along the shore heading toward the water. At one point the victim with dog tags must have fallen back on the grass or been tossed. Fresh blood flashed in the sunlight. Only a few drops, but enough for a sample.

Tucson leaned closer, his camera clicking, then he bagged the blood. He had no proof the footprints or the blood belonged to the soldier. Kids ran the water's edge and jumped off the dock as a rite of passage into spring.

"You see it?" Pecos whispered.

"Yeah, blood."

"The footprints could have just been a swimmer, or maybe our dead guy isn't dead, but why go in the water this way? It's rocky and there's stickers. If he's going toward the water, why not just jump off the dock, and if he's bleeding, why go in at all?" Pecos's brain was running on the same track as Tucson's.

Pecos answered his own question. "Because from here no one would see him. Tree branches block the view of the dock and water. Bare feet running away unseen, then slipping in the water. What do you think?"

"The photos were taken well after dawn and apparently our victim got up and walked into the water. I saw no shoe prints so our soldier might have been alone."

"He couldn't be. Someone had to take the pictures." Pecos shook his head. "Maybe the victim was being carried?"

"Probably not. Again, no shoe prints. The killer wouldn't take off his shoes to carry the dead guy to the river. He could have tossed him from the dock. Or, swimmers could have gotten here early and he'd had to hide on this side of the dock."

"We are back to why was he barefooted," Pecos thought aloud. "In the cool of dawn, whoever took the pictures would be dressed, and the only one barefoot would be the dead guy."

Tucson tossed another idea in. "What if the dead guy wasn't dead? After the pictures were taken, he climbed off the dock and ran for the water?"

"He looked pretty dead to me. Cut from Adam's apple to belly button."

Tucson scrubbed his head as if he could wake his brain up. "What I don't understand is why would someone take pictures and then get rid of the body. Why not just leave the dead guy?"

The young sheriff looked worried. "I'm starting to believe there was only one person on the dock. The victim, the photographer, the killer . . . all one person. I just can't figure out how he did it."

Tucson shrugged. "Maybe the question is why, not who."

By noon the brothers were back at the sheriff's office examining the photos that were now poster size. By four they were interviewing every kid who swam that day. None had stayed long. The first outing of the year was cold once the swimmers were wet.

They learned little. One kid, about fifteen, said he thought he saw a black pickup at the site when he arrived. None saw blood or anything out of order.

At seven, Tucson stepped outside and called Jam.

When she picked up, she didn't give him time to say a word. "You're not coming, right?"

"Right."

The line went dead.

Tucson dropped his phone in his pocket and walked back inside. At midnight he decided to crash in the empty holding cell, but his thoughts were with Jam in her little bedroom. Second door on the second floor.

He told himself to forget her. She was just a woman he'd found crying in the cottonwoods. She wasn't real. She wasn't his. The last thing he wanted in this life was to worry about a girlfriend.

About one a.m. he cussed so loud the dispatcher two rooms away probably heard him. He called himself every kind of fool. What kind of man watches a woman sleep? Or climbs in her bed . . . twice? How could missing Jam feel like a physical pain inside him?

When he finally fell asleep, he dreamed of her by his side. It was like the world had shifted and she was now somehow a part of him.

Chapter 17

The Café

Tuesday

Jam woke up with a headache that followed her around all day. She hadn't slept well, and the third time she yelled at one of her staff, they mutinied. With the kindness of a caregiver, her cook told her to take a walk or the staff would.

Nodding, Jam picked up a dozen of her fresh muffins and ten minutes later she was serving them to everyone in the sheriff's office.

She'd reacted to Tucson's call too fast last night. She might not get to apologize, but at least she could smile at him.

As she moved around the sheriff's office, even the drunk with one arm chained to a chair thanked her for the treat.

With two muffins left in the basket, she tapped on the sheriff's door. She could see through the glass that the new sheriff and his brother were poring over papers on the desk. She noticed that Tucson was back in uniform this morning.

Pecos opened the door, still talking to Tucson. He stopped in mid-sentence when he saw she was staring at his brother as if he was a wild animal in the office.

Tucson didn't move. He didn't even blink. Neither did she. She didn't know whether to yell at him for standing her up or apologize for hanging up on him.

Clueless, Pecos stepped in between them. "Jam, I'd like you to meet my brother. He's just in town for a few days to help me out with a case." He pointed at Tucson as if she might have missed two hundred pounds of muscle. "Tucson, this is a friend of mine. Looks like she brought us muffins. She owns the Honey Creek Café where we had the party Sunday." Pecos paused, becoming aware that no one was listening.

They didn't say a word to each other. Pecos looked back and forth between them as if he was watching invisible tennis. "I'll get us some fresh coffee. Have a seat, Jam. My brother will eventually figure out how to talk."

Jam took one step into the office and Pecos darted out with two half-full coffee cups.

Tucson's voice was low. "I don't want to talk to you. I wanted to see you."

"Me too."

"But you hung up on me."

"I'd been thinking about you all day, Tucson. Of course I hung up. You just blew me off."

She took a step toward him and set the basket on the only corner of the desk that wasn't covered.

He didn't smile or apologize. His eyes had a hunger in them that frightened her a bit.

"I don't want to talk here, Jam."

Anger flared. "Fine. No date. No conversation. It was nice knowing you, Sergeant."

As she turned to leave, Pecos rushed through the door. Coffee flew, spilling across her white uniform.

Jam squealed more from surprise than pain as hot coffee splattered across her midriff.

Tucson moved so fast he was pulling her back before she thought to move.

He swung her around and shoved her out of the office. Three feet later, he opened the women's restroom door. "Get that jacket off. I'll find the first aid kit."

Pecos just stood in the hallway's entrance, turning his head sideways as if trying to figure out was going on.

"First aid kit?" Tucson snapped.

The sheriff pointed to the counter. "Should I get the firemen next door?"

"No. Let me have a look first." Tucson picked up the kit and disappeared into the women's restroom.

Jam had her chef's coat halfway off and was starting to feel the burn just below her ribs to her waist.

"What are you doing in here?" There was barely room for two, and he seemed to be breathing in all the oxygen. All her anger and hurt focused on him.

"I'm helping." He set the first aid box down and started wetting paper towels.

Without hesitating he opened her top and lay the towels across her middle.

Gulping in a scream, Jam closed her eyes, and tried not to faint.

He turned her around, resting her back against his chest as he kept replacing cold paper towels against her red skin.

She didn't cry out. She just welcomed every cold compress. Slowly she calmed and started to breathe.

"Is she all right?" Pecos yelled through the door.

"The burn's not blistering," Tucson said as he brushed

his chin against her hair. "Just first-degree burns in a few places."

"Jam, what can I do to help? I'm so sorry," Pecos yelled.

"It was my fault as much as yours." She fought to keep her voice level. "Your brother is applying cream now."

Pecos sounded confused. "You sure you're all right in there with my brother?"

"Yes. I'm fine." She patted Tucson's hand as it moved slowly across her bare skin. "The bull is being gentle."

"Relax, Jam." Tucson winked at her. "This will cool the burn down."

As he wrapped the scalded skin just below her bra, he whispered, "Take your bra off. You'll be more comfortable."

"Not a chance," she said, as she watched his reflection in the mirror in front of her.

He slipped the open coat off her shoulders and let it drop, then unbuttoned his tan shirt and helped her into his uniform. The short sleeves hung past her elbows.

She turned to face him. "Thanks," she whispered. She placed her hand on his chest. "I'm sorry I hung up on you. I just felt . . ."

He kissed her forehead. "I know. When I said I didn't want to talk to you, I meant I wanted to hold you. Fall asleep next to you. I didn't know how to say the words." He kissed her lips lightly. "I swear, Jessica Ann Mackenzie, I've never felt this way. For the first time I'm starting to understand addiction and for me, it seems to be you."

She heard what sounded like a crowd asking questions from the other side of the door. One offered to drive her home, another thought they should drive her to the clinic.

"Later," she whispered against Tucson's ear as she pulled away. "This is not the time or place." She pressed her hand against his heart.

When she opened the door, their moment together was

gone. But when she glanced back there was no longer anger in his eyes.

With half the sheriff's office staff following, Tucson walked her to a cruiser. Pecos had arranged for one of the deputies to drive her home and another to follow in her car.

When Tucson leaned in to put her seat belt on so the shoulder strap wouldn't touch her bandages, he whispered, "Later."

She stared into his chocolate eyes now full of concern. "I'm all right," she said softly as she fought to keep the pain out of her voice. "I'm a chef. We all get burned now and then."

There was no time to talk, but he'd said a great deal with his actions. For the first time in her life, it seemed someone cared about her.

Chapter 18

McCoy's Hell

The first light of dawn woke McCoy. Four days out of the hospital and he seemed to be getting worse. He'd have to get better to have the strength to die. He thought of taking the pain pills. That would ease the pain in his leg, but then his brain would slow like muddy water was sloshing around between his ears.

He felt like he'd slept a season away. His body was stiff from sleeping on Pop's old couch and he was starving.

McCoy reached for the cookie bag he'd opened when he relaxed on the couch, but it was empty. Who knew ginger snaps evaporated overnight?

Not bothering with the crutch, he hopped to the bathroom. Either his left leg was healing or he'd grown used to the pain.

Pop was sitting at the tiny kitchen table reading when McCoy limped back to the couch.

"You ever think of waking me up and telling me to go to bed?"

"Nope." Pop pulled his cereal bowl out of the refrigerator.

McCoy leaned back on the couch and closed his eyes so his body could wake up one limb at a time. The room was cool and silent. Well, soundless except for Pop's crunching.

Giving up on trying to sleep, he reached for a crutch. When he hobbled over to the table, the old guy didn't offer to help him get his bowl or the cereal box. He just watched while McCoy pushed his way around the kitchen in the office chair.

Finally, Pop asked, "You wake up on the wrong side of the couch?"

McCoy stared as his grandpa laughed at his own joke.

After finishing his first bowl, McCoy poured milk over his second helping and said, "I'm taking out the toilet and shower today to lay the tile. You got a problem with that?"

"No. If you'll let me know when you're ready, I'll help you lift them out. I don't want you falling and breaking the other leg. Then it'd take forever to get the job done." Pop went back to reading. Three pages later he added, "We'll move them to the back porch. I'm expecting company."

McCoy studied the old guy. He lived in a shack with engine parts as yard art, and he was worried about curb appeal? Damn if Pop wasn't growing on him.

They worked together until dark and that night McCoy took a shower in a bathroom with a solid floor. Pop didn't say a word about McCoy's work, but when he limped down the hallway, McCoy saw Pop at the doorway of the bathroom with a hint of satisfaction on his weathered face.

That night McCoy stood at his bedroom window and watched Pop walk his land with a rifle resting on his arm.

All seemed peaceful, but the old man was on guard. His head was up, not searching on the ground, but maybe waiting for someone to come at him.

McCoy decided he'd take the ATV and drive the fence line tomorrow. Maybe set a few string traps. They wouldn't stop anyone, but when he checked them, he'd know if someone was trespassing.

Chapter 19

Mr. Winston's Waterloo

Mr. Winston wanted to pick Lilly a small bouquet from his garden, but it was too early in the year. He thought of cooking something to take to her, but he wasn't sure that would be right. After all, she'd invited him to dinner. Candy seemed a bit over the top.

So, as he waited for Lilly to answer her door, his hat and a grocery bag in his hands, he tried to remember to breathe. This was Tuesday. She'd invited him to dinner and asked him to spend the night. He wasn't entirely sure what that entailed, but he was ready for whatever she asked of him.

When she finally opened the door, she looked as nervous as he felt. He couldn't be sure, but he thought she had on a new blouse and skirt.

"You look lovely tonight, Lilly," he said thinking that she truly was.

Her "thank you" was so low he wasn't sure he heard her.

He set the paper bag on the corner of the couch and followed her to the kitchen.

"Something smells delicious." His second compliment.

"I wasn't sure what you liked, so I cooked a chicken and mushroom soup with cornbread."

"That's grand." He stood four feet away from her. "May I help?"

"No, everything is ready."

They began their first private meal together. He pulled out her chair. She dipped the soup. He complimented the cook after his second bite, which he'd read was always proper. They talked of foods they liked and each listed dishes they hated. His list was short, but hers was a bit longer.

He insisted on helping her clean up, then they sat in the living area and watched the news. During the commercials, they each commented on what was happening in the world and the upcoming weather.

Then, both were silent for a while. He started conversations that she didn't pick up. She asked about his day and he couldn't think of much to report. They even said the same things twice just to have conversation. Finally, he stood and said he'd be heading home.

At the door he turned to kiss her good night and noticed a tear on her cheek. "What's wrong, dear?"

"Nothing. I just thought you might stay. But it's all right. We don't know each other well enough."

"Do you want me to stay?" Winston had not noticed one hint that she was interested in anything but conversation.

"Not if you would be uncomfortable." Another tear dropped off her cheek. "We have time to think about things, or maybe this is a fool's game we're playing. I just thought . . ."

Winston took one step toward the door and picked up the paper bag he'd carried in. "I brought my pajamas and my toothbrush. If I spend the night, I'd like to hold you. I think that would be a good start."

She smiled. "You came ready to stay with me? Has anything changed your mind?"

"No, dear. I just need to know I'll be welcomed."

She pushed her tear away. "I've never been held all night long. I think I might like to be."

He frowned. "I forgot to pack my slippers. I'll try to remember them next time."

"All right." She didn't move. Apparently, the conversation had gone too far in talking about night clothes.

Winston decided he'd be standing in the living room, holding his bag for the entire night if he didn't act. After all, he'd had a bit of practice in this kind of thing and he guessed she had none.

He offered his arm and they walked toward her bedroom. "If you'd like to change in the bathroom, I'll change here by the bed. Then, while I brush my teeth, you might like to get under the covers so you won't be cold."

Lilly nodded and disappeared in the bathroom.

She appeared ten minutes later in a modest gown and a robe to match. He kissed her on the lips lightly and said he'd be back. When he returned, he saw her robe on a chair and Lilly was under the covers. Winston slid in beside her and opened his arms.

She hesitated, then rolled against him.

He circled his arms around her and whispered, "I think we will begin a beautiful journey tonight. I'm no expert, but I know making love is not about just sex. It's a nearness. A warmth that grows. Someone told me once that it's a matching of heartbeats."

Lilly brushed his jaw as she looked up. "I'd like that. What do we do first?"

"We hold each other. Touch each other if we like. We get so comfortable that your warmth becomes part of me, and my hand moving over your body will always be a caress."

There was nothing else to say. As they learned each other, a closeness grew and Winston knew loving Lilly would always be a joy in his heart.

He felt like he'd waited almost a lifetime to find her. They might not have much time left of life, so the nights they were together were going to be all the sweeter.

She fell asleep first, then he took a deep breath and joined her. His last thought was a prayer for one more night of such peace.

He awoke long after sunrise, and she was still in his arms. He slipped from her bed and dressed in the bathroom. When he came back, the bed was empty.

Winston found her in the kitchen making coffee. She was wearing her robe. Her hair was out of place and she wore no makeup. For a moment he saw the girl inside her. Beautiful. Shy. Kind. He realized then that he wasn't loving her in her twilight years; he was loving all the ages she'd lived through. The memories, the dreams, even the scars left by life.

What an adventure to learn all of her.

"I have one thing to say to you, Lilly," he said frowning.

"What, Charles?" He saw worry in her light blue eyes.

"One night a week is not enough, dear."

She laughed. "I agree. Maybe we could come back here after we eat out on Thursday. We could have coffee and dessert before we retire."

He nodded once. "And then I'd like to sleep beside you." Before she answered, he added, "And since we're spending Sunday together, I think Sunday night you might stay over at my house."

"I think I'd like that very much. I might even buy a new gown and robe to leave at your place."

"I'll clean out a drawer for you."

She handed him his coffee and said, "I do believe, Mr. Winston, we've gone wild."

"I believe we have."

Chapter 20

Sergeant Tucson Smith

Wednesday

For the third night in a row, Tucson worked with his brother until after midnight. Tucson was calling in favors from military police all over the country. The picture of the soldier's body spread out on the dock didn't match any soldier who had gone AWOL in the last month.

The dog tags looked relatively new. There were no scars visible on the body. Estimated height five foot nine, weight 170 pounds. Hair so short it could have been light brown or blond. Age estimated as between nineteen and twenty-five. No tattoos. No rings or piercings.

Tucson rubbed his eyes and swore. "The guy isn't giving us anything. Not even a wart or a scraped knee. He either ran away as soon as he was sworn in or he's been finished with boot camp long enough to heal from the bangs and bruises of training." The tags were obviously a clue, but all other information was blurry.

Pecos reached for his jacket. "You're talking like the guy is still alive. He looks pretty dead to me and he'll still be dead tomorrow."

"Maybe he faked the whole scene. I'll need more than a picture as proof." Tucson was still staring at the pictures of the body on the dock. "Just a theory. No sign of a struggle. No sign he was dragged."

"How do you explain the bloody cut running down his chest?"

"Ketchup or hot sauce? He wouldn't be the first soldier to fake his own death. Or maybe he used bagged blood or even paint. If he staged the shots, he might have cut his foot when he ran to the river and we were lucky to find a few drops of his blood. Real blood."

Pecos shoved his big brother toward the door. "It's time we call it a night. Dead or alive, he'll still be our puzzle come morning."

As they walked out of the sheriff's office, Pecos added, "Kerrie said you're welcome to come home with me. Our couch is comfortable and the babies will only wake you up a few times a night."

"Tell Kerrie thanks, but I think I'll check on Jam and then get a hotel. I'm so tired tonight that if the second coming happens, I'll miss it. I'm too exhausted to walk into heaven."

Pecos didn't bother to ask questions. He just waved as they both climbed into their cars.

Tucson smiled as he headed toward Jam. He knew he wouldn't be welcome to sleep on the unused half of her bed tonight, but he had to make sure she was resting easy. The coffee burn may have cooled, but the wound might wake her if she rolled over on the tender skin.

The back door of the café wasn't locked, and she'd left a light on near the staircase. He helped himself to a glass of milk and one of Jam's famous muffins, then headed up the stairs. The second room on the second floor was quickly becoming his favorite place.

Silently, he opened her door and to his surprise Jam was sitting up in bed reading a book. A pillow rested over her middle.

"You awake?"

"My staff made me take the day off. I slept all afternoon and then decided I'd stay awake until you came."

"You knew I'd come, but I'm not staying." Tucson sat a few feet away. "You mind if I take a look at the burn?"

"No, but you have to share that muffin."

He gave her half.

When the snack was gone, she asked, "How'd you know what to do? Just something you learned in the army?"

Jam didn't move as he unbuttoned her pajama shirt from the bottom up. "I had three little brothers. By the fourth grade I'd read the first aid book from the Boy Scouts a dozen times."

She laughed as he gently pushed her top open all the way to the bottom of her breasts.

Her skin was spotted with red marks. One was as big as the palm of his hand. No ugly blisters. There would be no scars.

"How bad does it hurt?"

"I'm fine, Tucson, but I could use more cream. The supplies are in the bathroom."

He collected the salve and gauze and went to work. Jam watched his big hand moving over her middle. Almost a caress.

"I can do this myself, you know."

"I know, but I like helping." He grinned. "Correction, I like touching you." His fingers brushed over the bottom of her breasts that barely showed.

"You can't stay tonight. My staff will be in early to check on me."

"I know. Much as I'd like to watch over you, if I reached for you in my sleep, I might hurt you."

A thud came from above, and they both looked up. Tucson felt his body go on full alert.

"Just the ghosts. Don't worry, Sergeant, I'll protect you."

Something rolling across the floor rattled overhead. "Are you sure someone's not in the attic?"

"Trust me, I've climbed the stairs a dozen times over the years after hearing something. Nothing. Maybe the wind blew a window open or the old heater rattled. Rotted boxes tumble off rotted shelves. Nails pull free and pictures fall. Birds fly into the vents. A brick falls off the decaying chimney. I've seen it all, but not once have I found a ghost."

When he didn't relax, she added, "There are four small bedrooms upstairs. Folks claim the captain's four daughters lived up there. When they died, they all decided to haunt the third floor because their father could not climb the stairs thanks to old wounds. The legend goes that they'd laugh as he aged, knowing how he hated to be alone and crippled.

"People claimed the girls would stomp and dance, knowing he couldn't get to them. Some say he went mad cussing his daughters before he died. My staff all claim they've heard his daughters. A few say they've seen shadows moving in the dark dining rooms. But I never have."

"Stop," Tucson demanded as he buttoned up her pajamas. "You are creeping me out."

"Don't tell me my big strong soldier is afraid of ghosts?"

"Of course not." He kept looking at the ceiling as if laughter might drift down. "I just don't want to leave you alone if there is danger."

Jam had a strange look on her face. Like she was considering options. Slowly, she said, "There might be danger tonight. My grandmother believed death rides on moonless nights. Would you hold my hand until I fall asleep?"

"Of course." He leaned against the headboard and offered his hand.

She settled into the covers. In truth, she didn't look very afraid, but Tucson liked the idea of holding any part of the lady beside him.

Tucson studied her for a few minutes. "You're smiling, Jam, and you don't seem to be in any pain." Tucson kissed her cheek. "But I think I'll stay here with you a bit longer. Just until you fall asleep. Just until I know you're safe."

She didn't turn loose of his hand as she closed her eyes and relaxed. He laced her fingers in his and did the same. As he drifted off, he thought of how they fit together. No woman had ever felt so right.

At dawn he was still beside her when the crew below arrived. Half awake, Tucson nodded at one of the staff as she poked her head in Jam's room. Then the girl placed her finger to her lips and silently backed out.

Tucson decided somehow it was his calling in life to sleep with Jam. Not be her lover. That didn't seem in the cards. He was her guardian angel. His job was to watch over this kind, creative woman.

He didn't know if he was in heaven or hell. All he did know was he was right where he was meant to be.

Chapter 21

The Café

Thursday

If her staff thought it strange that Jam had a sleepover with the sheriff's brother, no one said a word.

Just before the front door was opened, Jam pulled on a T-shirt and went downstairs to tell everyone what to do while she planned to take the day off.

She caught him watching her from the second-floor shadows. When she neared, Tucson whispered, "You're a general to the troop, honey. They all love you."

Pulling him back to her room, she answered, "They are all like family to me."

Before he could say more, she handed him a newspaper and a little picnic basket filled with breakfast breads and bottled milk.

When he raised an eyebrow, Jam added, "The girl who didn't see you in my bed this morning handed this to me."

They both cuddled back into the covers and ate their snack while Tucson read the paper to her.

Pecos showed up at the café's back door about nine with

a bag from the cleaners. She came down as soon as she heard his voice.

Jam smiled at the new sheriff everyone loved and pointed at the stairs. "Second floor. Second room. I think your brother is in the shower."

He nodded and headed up.

Turning to her crew, Jam asked, "Which one of you called the sheriff?"

To her surprise all of them raised their hands and started talking at once. The grill cook thought Tucson was lost. Two of the waitresses said they assumed he was drunk. The dishwasher claimed he just invaded, and the sweet hostess said she thought he was a medic who was probably just hungry.

None of her staff seemed to think that the good-looking soldier might have just come over to sleep with the boss.

Jam didn't know whether to feel insulted or blessed with such clean-minded employees.

She collected two coffees and headed upstairs.

At the slightly open bedroom door she paused. Tucson was pulling on his trousers. The hair on his chest was still damp. She'd seen his body before. In the shadows by the river and again in her kitchen, but she'd never seen him with sunlight bouncing off his freshly washed body.

He was fantastic.

Pecos's words finally registered. "What are you doing in Jam's bedroom, brother? My wife's mother is a cousin to the Mackenzies. I don't know how you pick up women around the fort, but Jam is not a one-night stand. Did you even use protection?"

"Are you giving me the birds and bees talk, little brother?" Tucson sounded more confused than angry.

"No," Pecos snapped. "It's just that Jam is my friend

and almost kin. I'm warning you that you'd better not hurt her."

Tucson laughed. "Pecos, you do know we're both in our thirties, and I'm not going to lie to her or you, brother. I'm crazy about her. She's beautiful, talented, kind . . ." Tucson paused then added, "And way too smart to get involved with a soldier. In truth I think she sees me as more of a guardian angel than a lover."

Pecos didn't back down. "The staff says you just wander in whenever you want to."

Jam had heard enough. No one in town thought of her as "someone to date," "someone to introduce to their sons or brothers" or even "someone to have an affair with."

No one but Tucson.

She set the coffee down on the hall table and walked into the bedroom. She didn't even glance at Pecos as she moved toward Tucson.

When she was two inches away from him, she spread her hands over the warmth of his chest, raised to her tip-toes, and kissed him. Not a friend kiss or a thank-you kiss but a full-out passionate kiss.

He didn't react for a moment. Then, like a man learning to breathe, he kissed her back. His arm circled her and pulled her closer.

This was a kiss like she'd wanted that first night by the river. A kind of kiss he'd always give her.

His hands were gentle at her waist as if he feared he might hold her too tight.

When she broke the kiss, she pulled away a few inches and stared into his warm brown eyes. Slowly she smiled as she saw the promise of more.

Jam turned toward the sheriff, her hand still on Tucson's chest. "Morning, Pecos. I didn't notice you were there."

"Goodbye, Sheriff," Tucson said still staring at Jam. "I'll meet you at the office in an hour."

Pecos raised his hands and mumbled something about taking his birds and the bees talk somewhere else.

"Close the door on your way out." Tucson lowered his head for another kiss. His hands moved over her hips as the door closed.

When they finally came up for air, Jam pulled away as he tugged her T-shirt off. "Now, we have to be careful." She began her rules. "You can't touch my front from below my bra to my panties. And you can't lie on me. And . . ."

"Jam, we'll figure it out." He lifted her and took two steps to the bed. "Why'd you kiss me like that?"

"I was tired of waiting, and I figured if I kissed you in front of the sheriff and your family, you'd know I was serious."

Two hours later, in the middle of the lunch rush, Sergeant Tucson Smith walked through the kitchen and out the back door. He didn't say a word to the people who had called the law on him.

He simply smiled. He'd thank them later.

Chapter 22

McCoy's Fairy

Thursday

A little after dawn, McCoy decided to caulk the windows and doors of Pop's old house. Pop, of course, showed no interest and disappeared. Half an hour later a tiny face materialized in the corner of the porch window. Huge green eyes, ginger-colored ponytails over each ear, and freckles sprinkled across her cheeks and nose.

McCoy set down his tools and limped outside. He didn't know much about children, but this one didn't look old enough to go to school. "Can I help you with something, kid?"

"I live just down the way. I cut through Mr. Mason's land to get home," she said with her tiny fists on her chubby waist. "You a robber, mister?"

"No, kid, I'm Mason's grandson." McCoy couldn't help but wonder how young women were when they learned that look that says, *I'm not sure what you're doing, but it must be something wrong.*

The kid never broke eye contact. "How did he get you?

Mom says he's not married and doesn't have any children. I think you have to have a grown-up kid to get a grandson. And"—she looked at his cast—"you're broken. He should send you back."

McCoy had trouble coming up with an answer to that. "Just lucky, I guess," he said. "He let me stay."

She shook her head. "You don't look lucky. You look busted, mister. What's wrong with your leg? Does it hurt? Will it fall off if you take that cast off?"

"I was in a wreck. Now and then it hurts. No, my leg will not fall off. Now my question: Are you a little Shaylee?" He fought the urge to pat her on the head. She was so cute.

"What is a Shaylee? I never heard that word." She tick-tocked her head, making her ponytails fly.

McCoy wished he could lean down to her level. "It's a fairy princess from over the hill. I read about them in a book on Ireland."

She studied him for a moment as if he was her first encounter with an alien.

"I'm Sarah-Jane Mackenzie's oldest." She took a bow and then danced around him. "Mackenzies and their kin are all that live on Sunflower Lane. It's a rule."

"Sadler's not a Mackenzie." McCoy had never heard the name.

"He married a Mackenzie. My momma keeps a chart."

McCoy didn't argue. In a town this size he wouldn't be surprised if half the people were related.

"You need a puppy," she finally said when she'd twirled until she was dizzy. "I'll let you have your pick."

"Nope," McCoy answered as he saw an old gardener's wagon at the side of the porch with a half-dozen pups wiggling around inside.

"I got to give them away." She was tearing up. "My

momma says we can't have more dogs than kids. It's a rule around these parts."

"Not my problem." He needed to get away before she started crying. He hated it when women cried. Even this pint-sized one.

When one tear fell, McCoy broke. "I've never had a dog. Wouldn't know how to take care of one." She just stared at him so he had to think fast. "I got to go to the vet in town today. I'll ask her if she can help you."

"I'll go with you. My wagon will fit in the back of the pickup." The fairy girl was on the move.

"Don't you have to ask your mother first?" McCoy studied her. He knew nothing about kids, except he used to be one.

"My mom works until five then she has to pick up my little sisters. She says I'm free-range from the time I get off the bus until she gets home. I got one rule: Stay out of trouble and check in with Mr. Mason if I need anything."

McCoy heard the barn door swing open.

"Hi, Sunshine," Pop yelled as he walked toward the house. "What do you need?"

"I need a ride, Mr. Mason. I got important business with the vet." She danced off the porch and ran to him.

McCoy was surprised when she took his hand and tried to pull him along faster.

"You got to take your broken grandson to the vet, and I'm riding along."

Before McCoy could object, the pups were loaded up and the fairy girl was waiting in the cab.

Pop and McCoy climbed in with the girl between them. Pop whispered, "When the fairies come we always lock the gun case behind the door."

"I'll remember," McCoy answered. That feeling that

Pop was waiting for trouble settled over him, but now wasn't the time to ask.

The little fairy told him she was five and her real name was Olivia, but he could call her Sunshine. Mr. Mason was her best friend. She had two sisters who looked like her.

All the way to town, she never stopped talking or wiggling.

McCoy just nodded now and then, and Pop coughed down a laugh when Sunshine told them trips to town come with stopping for snacks.

As they reached Honey Creek, she finally turned her attention to McCoy. "Don't you think it's a little strange that your doctor is a vet? My teacher says vets take care of dumb animals who can't take care of themselves."

Pop laughed, but McCoy just said, "That's me."

When they got to the Blanton Veterinarian Clinic, it was a much bigger operation than he'd thought it would be. A clinic, two barns, and pens about a half mile from town. The MD on vacation had asked the vet to take some X-rays but McCoy felt a bit strange limping inside a tiny waiting room. All the people holding dogs and cats just stared at him.

Pop and the fairy didn't even bother holding the door open for him, they just headed for the corrals to see the newborn colts.

McCoy limped to the desk.

A middle-aged woman dressed in orange, from her sweater to her sweat pants, was at the desk. While she hummed in time with her gum chewing, she took his information.

She asked him his address twice like it was a trick question, and he'd have one the second time around. "Second farm on Sunflower Lane."

Orange Lady frowned. "Shouldn't be too hard to find since there's only three farms out that way."

When he mentioned he was Sadler's grandson, she smiled and told him he was expected. Then she slipped on orange sandals and took him to a small room for an X-ray.

"Martha will take off your cast and take your pics. The vet told us you were coming. When Dr. Hudson gets back, he'll probably want you to check in with him as well. He'll need these X-rays to see how you are healing."

"The vet and the town's medical doctor swap patients?" McCoy found that hard to believe.

"In emergencies. Dr. Blanton doesn't mind, but Dr. Hudson hates it. He claims her patients have fleas."

"How long has Baylor been a vet?"

"Your vet, Dr. Blanton, took over the practice from her dad a few years ago," the orange lady said as she walked out and called back, "Stay put or we'll put a leash on you, cowboy."

"I'm not a cowboy," McCoy said to no one as he tossed his Stetson on a chair.

Ten minutes later, Martha, an Amazon warrior of a woman in a lab coat, took X-rays, fitted him for the boot, and showed him to an office, not an examining room. Her conversation seemed to be limited to dog commands. Roll over. Lift your leg. Sit up.

She pointed to a chair and said, "Stay," then walked off.

He relaxed, thinking at least he wouldn't be on an examining table whose last patient was a cat.

In defiance, McCoy stood at the window watching the fairy nicknamed Sunshine try to give away a pup to everyone who walked by outside. People stopped and seemed to listen to her sales pitch, but no one walked away with a dog.

When the woman he'd seen a few nights ago delivering medicine to Pop's porch rushed in, she announced, "I'm not treating you, Mr. Mason. I only ordered you a boot and took X-rays for Dr. Hudson. How does the new boot feel?"

"Great," he answered, obviously lying. "Any chance you'll buy me that coffee you promised? I've been drinking Pop's mud for days."

She looked like she was in a hurry, but she nodded. In daylight she was certainly easy on the eyes. He wouldn't mind spending a few minutes in her company. Baylor was one of those rare women who would look like a girl until she was into her forties. Probably in her sixties no one would guess her age. Her small frame could almost let her pass for a boy in her jeans and flannel shirt.

Dr. Baylor Blanton wasn't tall or blonde. Not his type. Her short curls were more chestnut color, little to no makeup, and she didn't come to his shoulder. She wasn't slim, no model look, he decided. More healthy looking with her sunburned nose and full lips that really didn't need any lipstick.

He decided she could have been eighteen or thirty-five.

McCoy knew he sounded brain-dead, but he usually talked to women who giggled and patted on him for no reason at all. Most of the time he didn't care if they could string a sentence together.

But today he really needed to talk to someone besides Pop and the fairy girl.

Baylor smiled as if she had read his mind. "Fair enough, but if I have a cup of coffee with you, you'll have to carry boxes back to Sadler's place. It'll save me a trip tonight."

He sat down while she stepped out of her office. A

minute later she was back and handing him a paper cup. It smelled great. As she leaned against her desk, they toasted, both smiled.

Only, the strange thing was, after weeks without talking to a woman, he found he couldn't think of anything to say. She was smart, and his brain had been scrambled. She had a job, money, a car. He was homeless. She was probably lowering her IQ just standing in the same room with him.

He felt like the dented can of spinach on the grocer's shelf. No one was ever going to pick him.

When he looked up, the vet was studying him, probably thinking the same thing.

If they'd been pretty much anywhere else, he might have smiled, maybe even flirted a little, but this didn't seem the time or place.

After a few minutes of silence, McCoy broke. "Say what you want to say, Doc. Ask me any question or give me a lecture. Just stop staring at me like you're trying to guess what species I am."

She laughed. "Okay, I do need to talk to you. I'm glad you're in town, McCoy Mason. Sadler may need you more than you think. There is a big outfit coming in that wants to develop mini-ranches. Homes just big enough to have a barn out back. They plan to sell them to all the folks working from home." She laughed. "The best of both worlds, they say. Country living in a community with tennis courts."

She took a drink and added, "Only the farmers who don't want to sell are being pushed, maybe even threatened. I'm glad Sadler has you. He doesn't have to stand alone."

"Glad I'm of some use." McCoy wondered why Pop

hadn't mentioned his problem. "I'll stand with Pop, but I doubt anyone will push that old man around."

When he looked up, she was still staring at him. Without a word, they seemed to agree to help.

Baylor bumped his good leg with her knee. "You've got an easygoing way about you. I think we could be friends if you decide to hang around. I'm always running double time, and I have a feeling you're a calm kind of guy."

She'd delivered her entire speech without taking a breath. He'd need to speed up his hearing to keep up with her. Was she flirting with him? Probably not, she'd used the "friend" word.

He thought about saying that they could be a lot more than just friends, but he had nothing to offer her. Plus, she was more a woman he'd be friends with, nothing more. Oh, she was cute, but her clothes looked just like his and he'd guess she had no idea how to flirt. She was one of those women who had all the right parts in all the right places, but she didn't know how to be a woman.

McCoy swallowed down cuss words with his coffee. The doc wasn't a car he could examine piece by piece. He needed to stop thinking about women in parts. If she had any idea what was on his mind, she'd probably slap him. Or slug him. Or put him to sleep, not in a good way. And he deserved it. What kind of idiot only remembers his fiancée's hair?

He'd give friendship a try. "I'd like it if we became friends, Baylor. Your life seems to be your job, and I admire that. I'm pretty much that way when I'm working. From the day we break ground on a construction site until they cut the ribbon open for business, that's all I think about."

"I understand." She leaned back against her desk and

relaxed for probably the first time all morning. "Maybe we could talk sometime."

A talk, he thought. *Not a drink or a meal. Just a talk. Definitely just the friend category.*

For a few minutes they simply drank their coffee, then he told her about the fairy girl who'd shown up this morning with a wagonload of pups.

They watched the kid through the window and laughed when she finally found a home for one. She cried and hugged the pup so hard the dog barked.

"I'll make a few calls and post a note on the adoption board. We'll find them all homes."

Baylor sounded so caring he thought of asking if she'd put a note for him on the board. Something like, "Broken down guy, not a cowboy, in need of direction."

McCoy watched her, wondering what kind of man would be lucky enough to win her heart. Probably a heart surgeon or some guy in the Peace Corps. McCoy pulled back into the present and glanced at the fairy girl and her pups. "Find a home for all but one. Pop could use a dog. I'll put in a dog door before I leave."

"Will that be soon?"

"No. Since I have no direction right now, here is as good a place as anywhere." He kept staring out the window at the pups and felt a kinship to them.

McCoy finally turned back to Baylor. "Thanks for getting me the boot. It'll make working around the farm much easier. While I'm here, I want you to know if you need anything, just call. I don't know much about animals, but I'm good with my hands. I can figure out how to fix just about anything."

"Thanks. It might be nice to have a friend to call."

He stood slowly. There was that "friend" word again. "What do I owe you?"

The lady was all professional now. The moment they'd had, if they'd had one, was gone. "No charge. Your grand-father doesn't charge me for keeping my trucks running."

"Like I said, if you ever need that favor, just call."

She finally met his gaze. "You sound like your grand-father." As she opened her office door, she added, "Take care of him."

He walked away thinking she hadn't even offered to shake hands.

That night as he watched Pop walk the land, again with a rifle resting in his arm, McCoy knew something was up. Maybe Baylor's words were warning him. The doc might have only heard rumors, but something was not right. Trouble seemed in the wind.

When they'd stopped at the bakery on the town square, everyone in the place seemed to know Pop. McCoy and the fairy girl just sat and ate donuts, listening to a mailman tell Pop all the news. A body was found on a dock just outside of town. The army had sent an investigator because the dead guy had on dog tags.

Finally, the mailman remembered his route and Pop moved to the counter to order one of every kind of donut. McCoy whispered to the little girl, "You all right, kid? I'm not sure you needed to hear all that talk."

With chocolate on both sides of her mouth, she whis-pered back, "I got a question."

"Shoot, kid. I'll do my best to answer."

She looked very serious. "What does 'nude' mean?"

"It's like naked."

"Oh, what is the difference?" She propped her chin on her palm and waited for wisdom.

McCoy gave it his best try. "Nude is when the doctor tells you to take your clothes off. Naked is when you wake up on a barroom floor and can't remember where you left your clothes. That usually happens to me after one too many beers."

She went back to eating, and McCoy decided he'd given the fairy girl too much information. Her mother would probably be over later to club him. Then he'd have to explain the difference between clubbing someone and hitting a fool.

At the rate this was going, the whole town might vote to have Dr. Baylor put him to sleep.

Chapter 23

Mr. Winston and His Shy Lady

The air was a bit chilly as Winston and Miss Lilly walked back from the Honey Creek Café on Thursday night. The owner, Jam Mackenzie, had made a special corner for them, away from the chill of the opening door and out of sight of most guests. She had even put a candle in the center making their table for two romantic.

Lilly talked about her day, and he mentioned a movie he'd watched. If anyone could have heard them, they'd have thought the two senior citizens were having a bland conversation, but to Winston and Lilly, they were having a grand time. Under the table he patted her knee now and then, and she smiled every time.

She took his arm as he walked her back to her apartment. Neither talked as they strolled, but Winston couldn't stop grinning. One shy woman had changed his life.

When they stepped inside her apartment, she asked if he'd like a dessert, and he answered, "I'd like to hold you, dear."

Lilly nodded, and they moved to her bedroom. The routine had been set. She changed clothes in the bathroom while he changed in the bedroom.

She slipped into bed while he brushed his teeth.

And then, he climbed in beside her and held her. They didn't talk much. They simply enjoyed the nearness of the other.

Growing bold, she moved her fingers between the buttons of his pajama top and then giggled as if they were teenagers.

"You're hairy, Charles. You have fur."

"That I do. Are you furry too?"

"No." She blushed, laughing softly.

"Lilly, would you mind if I check for myself?"

"All right." She moved her fingers to unbutton the first button of her gown.

He stopped her. "Please, allow me, dear."

All talking stopped for a while, but when they both drifted to sleep, her hand rested on his heart and his fingers caressed her breast even as they slept. Both wanted to travel slowly into this new journey, not run. Each moment was a joy to treasure.

At dawn they both laughed about what they'd done, and their kisses came easy during breakfast.

They were falling in love for the first time.

Chapter 24

Sergeant Tucson Smith

Friday

Rain pounded on the roof of the sheriff's office all afternoon. Tucson spent most of his time talking on the phone while examining reports of AWOL cases. He'd been an investigator for most of his career in the army. He'd done so many recovery missions they haunted his dreams. But this body . . . this body didn't look right. Blood on the chest, but not dripping onto the dock. His body was pale or ash gray in the morning light. If his body had been dumped on the wood, Tucson expected a bit more of a rag doll look or a stiff appearance, as if rigor mortis had set in.

For the most part, he liked working in the field, even war zones, but he endured the paperwork. Crime scenes told a story so much clearer than photos, and this crime scene had been cleared.

He'd felt tied to a desk all morning. The master sergeant at headquarters was sending him faxes, open files, and now and then, wild guesses. Most of the sheriff's staff believed they were looking for a recent deserter. And the killer or victim, if he staged the scene, wanted the army to think that he was dead. Why else would there be photos and no body?

The dock didn't make sense. It was too clean, too staged, too public. The bare footprint in the mud was another thing that made everyone question if the corpse didn't get up and walk off. The killer would have had shoes. The victim was the only one barefooted.

If someone wanted to kill a soldier, or anybody really did, they might take pictures for trophies, but why scatter them in a public place? The killer had to wait until light, stage the scene, kill the soldier, then get rid of all traces before anyone noticed. Why do it in full daylight twenty feet away from a well-traveled road and why have dog tags if anyone seeing the photos couldn't see them?

Another theory: The whole "dead body" scene was staged, photographed, and cleaned up. If the dead guy in the pictures was helping, it would go twice as fast.

But why pretend? Soldiers didn't have to die to get out. They could quit.

Obviously, the dog tags were left on so whoever saw the photos would be able to ID the soldier. But a drop of blood hid the name and numbers. Just *O-Positive* was readable on the tag. The most common blood type.

Another fact: Tucson had no guarantee the footprint was the dead guy.

If someone wanted to leave proof of a soldier's death, why not show the tags clearly? The photographer hadn't checked the photos? They were in a hurry?

Questions. No answers. Was the guy active duty? Suicide or murder? Real or a prank?

Tucson had been surprised how many soldiers walk away from their post. Maybe this guy faked his death so he wouldn't be hunted, but in truth, the army didn't send out search parties.

Most of the soldiers reported missing were only out for a night. Maybe a weekend with a girlfriend or too drunk to come back or simply having car trouble. Then there were the emergencies at home.

Maybe some were just tired of army life. Tucson had learned most went back to Uncle Sam on their own.

He was surprised that only about one percent were charged and served time. They lost any rank and sometimes pay.

But in this case, somebody wanted the new sheriff to know the soldier on the dock Saturday was in the army. Soldier O-Positive.

Tucson stood up and stretched. He needed a break. "I'm going for a walk," he said to no one in particular. He grabbed Pecos's still-wet slicker and left.

The rain didn't bother him. Tucson felt like he'd marched a thousand miles in bad weather.

For a while he didn't think of anything. He just moved with the wind. He'd clear his mind and go back fresh.

As he passed the Honey Creek Café, midnight memories filled his mind. He'd made love to Jam so slowly it was a sweet kind of torture. They might barely know each other, but to him she was like coming home. The first woman he'd ever met who would be hard to leave.

Holding her and knowing it was only for a few days was heaven fenced by heart attack. But if she wanted to make love again tonight, he'd sacrifice himself.

As he left town, he headed toward the dock where the pictures of the soldier had been taken. Half a mile later, he was standing on the side of the road staring at crime scene tape flying in the wind.

If there were any clues the deputies hadn't found, they'd be gone now. Trees by the river were sweeping low, brushing over the boards that the body had been spread out on.

"Tell me your secrets," he whispered to the night. "What happened here?"

A prank or a crime?

Memories of running off the dock and splashing in the water as a kid came back to him. He used to love summers when they'd sneak away for a few hours of fun. His dad was strict on chores, but most of the time he paid little attention to his sons. Often, he was gone, and they'd work together on the list he left, then take off.

As soon as Pecos could walk, he was following along. Tucson and his two middle brothers would take turns carrying Pecos on their shoulders. The fourth son might have been ignored by his parents, but he was loved by his three big brothers.

In the rain, Tucson saw his childhood clearly for the first time. It hadn't been all bad. His dad was a cold, hard man, but the brothers had each other. They'd had swimming on hot days and fishing at night. They'd had mud fights and flashlight wars and sleeping on the flat roof of the kitchen. When one had been sent to bed without his supper, the others would run reconnaissance.

Tucson stopped in the middle of the road. Since the day he'd left, he'd only remembered the bad times. A mother who never seemed to care. A father who was always angry or absent. The hard work that never seemed to be done.

His childhood had colored his life in black and gray. But no more.

That stops now, he decided. He'd choose to remember staring at the stars from the roof and walking a mile upstream so he could float down. The stars were so close he thought he might touch one and the river rocked him as he drifted.

He'd remember laughing hard when they talked Pecos

into trying to ride a turkey and a hundred other times the Smith boys had laughed at themselves.

Tucson grinned as more memories flooded in. The time they tried to dig to China. A hideout they'd built in the trees. Hiding comics in the attic.

In long strides he turned and headed back to town realizing people didn't always change when something huge happened in their life. Sometimes revelations struck in the silent rain as well.

The storm raged and night shadowed him as he passed the dock once more. He slowed, letting his mind move back into the problem at hand.

A blink of light flashed from the river's edge.

Tucson stilled and watched.

Another flicker of white came from the overgrown side of the dock. Tucson vanished into the shadows and stood perfectly still.

Someone was out near the water, moving cautiously over the wet bank. The black outline was medium height, willowy in the wind. A dark hoodie covered his head and hung low on his body. The stranger was moving slowly along the edge of the river as the beam of light swung back and forth on the rocky ground.

Tucson moved closer. He wished he'd brought a flashlight or a cell phone or even a gun.

No one would be searching in a storm unless they'd lost something very important.

Ten feet away, he saw thin fingers trying to hold the light steady. Five feet away he saw red polish on the nails. He was following a woman.

He trailed as she walked toward the café's lights far down the river. She never looked up or she might have seen him. Her concentration was on the flashlight's beam. She was looking for something that was worth facing the storm to find.

Tucson could see the back of the café in the distance and guessed she'd have to turn back soon or risk being seen.

Lightning flashed and thunder raged like music to the drama being played out. The wind snapped a branch above her. The girl glanced up for a moment and slipped on the wet bank. The raging water swallowed her in an instant.

He reached for her, but she was gone. He only had a moment to react and he didn't hesitate. He took two steps and dove into the water.

The storm howled and the river splashed, but he focused on a panicked cry that seemed to be echoing all around him.

Tucson pushed his head out of the taunting waves long enough to find his bearings.

He thought he saw a blink from the flashlight then all went dark.

He swam toward the light and dove deep into the mocking water.

Stretching his arms wide, once, twice. The third time he touched something. One more sweep and he had her hoodie, then her shoulders, and finally her waist. With one arm around her, he climbed the waves and headed to the shore.

The current had carried them closer to the café. When he pulled her on the bank, she was limp. Dead weight. Tucson swung her over his shoulder and marched toward the café's light.

When he pounded on the locked door, he saw Jam rushing to answer.

"Don't tell me you've been swimming in the river with your clothes . . ."

Jam froze as she took in the thin body folded over his shoulder.

"Call 911." Tucson pushed his way in and lowered the girl to the floor.

The dishwasher, who had been sweeping up, dropped his broom and hit three numbers on his cell then handed the phone to Tucson.

Jam didn't ask any questions. She just started pulling clothes off the girl.

"What is your emergency?" The dispatcher's voice seemed to whisper in the silent kitchen.

"I've got a possible drowning victim. Kitchen of Honey Creek Café. Send an ambulance and fire truck."

"On their way." The dispatcher barked a few orders then said almost calmly, "Your name?"

"Sergeant Smith. If my brother is there, send him out. If he's not, call him."

"Will do," the dispatcher said, then yelled for the sheriff.

Tucson could hear more yelling on the other end, but he handed the phone back to the dishwasher. "Thanks. You mind waiting outside to direct them in?"

"Don't mind at all." The man who usually moved at sloth speed took off at a run.

For a moment the kitchen was silent. Jam had rolled the girl to her side. Water dripped from the stranger's mouth. When she coughed up a gush of river water, Tucson and Jam both let out a sigh.

She tossed him a few towels then she rolled one beneath the girl's head.

"Where did you find her?" Jam whispered.

"In the river. I saw her fall in."

"And you went in after her?"

He nodded. She was going down, making no effort to swim.

Both knew he'd risked his life. The river gives back only bodies in a storm. Many fishermen had learned that the hard way.

Chapter 25

The Café

Jam leaned against the hallway wall beside the second bedroom on the second floor. Her part-time hideout was now a recovery room. The girl who'd almost drowned in the river was sleeping. She seemed such a fragile creature, all bones and auburn hair. She hadn't talked much other than to thank Tucson and give the bare facts to the sheriff.

She was walking along the bank of the river. A branch broke and frightened her. She slid into the river and the water seemed to pull her down.

Folks seemed to be hopping out of the river on a regular basis these days, Jam was thinking. First Tucson and now this girl who had no identification or car parked anywhere nearby. She refused to go to the hospital and swore she was eighteen, so there wasn't much Pecos could do except tell her not to walk by the water's edge in the dark on a rainy night.

He decided to let her rest a bit. Then he'd drive her home.

Jam didn't know what to do with the girl either. She said she'd taken a bus into town to meet her boyfriend. But he didn't show up. She refused to give any information about him, not even his name.

The sheriff got nothing except her first name was Mel.

Pecos couldn't arrest her. Apparently, it wasn't a crime to remain silent.

The girl asked if she could clean up. Jam showed her upstairs and offered her a jogging suit to change into.

When Jam returned to check on her, the girl was curled up in the middle of the bed, sound asleep. She looked so fragile, so young, so lost.

The second problem was still in Jam's kitchen. Tucson Smith. He was looking like a mud man again. He'd waited around until the EMTs said the girl was fine. They wanted to drive her to the nearest hospital, but she'd have none of that. So the sergeant stayed after the firemen left. Since he'd found her, she seemed to be his problem.

While Jam was upstairs with their surprise guest, Tucson stripped down and yelled that he'd wash off outside with the garden hose.

When she started down, she could hear the Smith brothers arguing.

Pecos did not think it was funny and threatened to jail his brother for indecent exposure. Even if it was dark, Tucson could not stand outside on the café lawn and strip.

Since everyone, including the dishwasher, had gone home, the sheriff finally just handed his brother a few towels and blocked the door until Tucson was dry enough not to mess up the newly mopped kitchen floor.

"You know, brother, I don't think you're housebroken," Pecos yelled. "If you'd find a wife, she might train you. Kerrie's got me clamping little hooks on my dirty socks so they'll come out of the dryer together. I didn't even know socks had to match till I got married."

Tucson growled. "I don't ever see myself doing that. Some men don't like to be caged."

Pecos laughed. "Yeah, you will. I love the cage. Of course, we have two little ones waking up the whole house every few hours. I figure once both babies start talking, I won't say another word until they leave for college. Another thing I've learned. Girls, no matter their age, talk more than boys do."

Jam sat down in the shadows of the stairs and listened to the brothers. She loved hearing Tucson relaxed, and everyone in town knew Pecos was crazy about his wife.

"How many kids you going to have?" Tucson asked.

"As many as Kerrie wants, I guess. She plans to finish school this year and maybe start law school. So, we might slow down the baby factory for a while." Pecos laughed. "When she takes the bar, we'll be law and order."

Tucson pulled on his trousers and a T-shirt. "You're happy, little brother, aren't you?"

"That I am. I've got lots to learn about the law and lots to learn about being a parent, but I feel like I'm playing in the World Series of life. One hundred percent in the game."

Jam smiled. The young sheriff had figured life out. There was a kindness in Pecos that everyone could see and a kind of handsome that only Kerrie saw. But, for Pecos, that was enough.

She joined them and offered milk and chocolate pie. Pecos said he had to get home. On his way out he yelled, "Call me in the morning when our mermaid wakes up. I'm not sure what crime she's committed, but I have a feeling she needs our help. One of the deputies drove the road by the river. Not one parked car, so maybe she did catch a ride into town. And maybe whoever was coming to meet her didn't show up. It seems to me she's too young to be on her own and too old to be bossed around."

Pecos waved as he left.

Tucson moved Pecos's abandoned slice of pie onto his plate. "Any big town would just let her go on her way. She's not a kid."

"I'll let her do that, if that's what she wants, but she'll know we're here to help her if she needs it."

"Small towns," Tucson added.

Jam bumped against the sergeant. "Where am I going to sleep tonight? All the other bedrooms on the second floor are used for storage and one of us has to stand guard."

"Where am I going to sleep if you don't have a bed? I was hoping to bunk in with you again," he laughed. "How about the four bedrooms on the third floor? I'm willing to share a room with you. After all, I survived last night."

"The attic bedrooms? The captain's daughters' rooms? I am not sleeping with ghosts. I would rather sleep in the old tent I loan fishermen who're caught in the rain. Besides, we can't leave the girl alone."

"Go check on her and put on something warm. We'll take turns sleeping." Tucson had finished his glass of milk and started working on his brother's pie.

Jam didn't argue with his command. It had been a long day, and keeping watch on her guest was about to make the night longer. She climbed the stairs and checked on their mermaid, then took a shower before putting on fluffy pj's and thick socks.

When she returned, Tucson surprised her by having set up a little tent on the landing. It took up all the space and smelled a bit like fish. He'd turned the opening toward the upstairs so as she walked down, she stepped into the tent.

He'd spread out two sleeping bags. One to use as a mattress and another as a blanket. If he left his feet hanging out, they fit very nicely inside.

She crawled in. "Nothing is going to happen between us tonight. You do know that, don't you?"

"Of course. We're on guard." He settled in. "But I'll be dreaming about the wild night in a tent that we could have had. You have any problem with that?"

"Yes, I do. Now I won't be able to sleep, thinking about what you might be dreaming about." She lay on her back, their shoulders touching. "What if your thoughts are X-rated?"

"You can bet on that, Jam."

They were silent for a while, listening to the rain and each lost in their own thoughts. Finally Jam said, "We don't go together, Sergeant. You live out of a duffel bag and travel the world. Me, I've never been anywhere much. I like having roots. I'm not that interesting. I've never even shot a gun, and you've probably been shot by one. If you ever did spend time with me, we'd run out of anything to talk about. I get excited over trying new recipes. I'm . . ."

Snoring came from the other side of the tiny tent.

"Tucson, are you listening? I don't think I'd even be fun in bed. I don't even know what the 'wild things' are. If we became lovers, you'd have to explain things. Not that sex is all I want us to do. That is if you want us to be anything like friends or lovers. We don't make sense. You're hours away, so once you go back to the fort it will be hard to even get together, and I never take a day off.

"Tucson?"

She rolled to her side and faced him.

In the dim light she made out his face. He was sound asleep.

"Never mind." She tapped his shoulder with her fist.

He didn't move or wake, but when she did it again, he opened his arm and she moved against his side.

They fit, she thought as she drifted into sleep. Maybe talking was overrated.

Chapter 26

McCoy's Worries

When Pop drove McCoy back from town on Friday, the fairy girl said she had to go home, but she left the last pup with Pop. He complained that he and dogs didn't get along, but the puppy followed the old guy around, lapping up every bit of donut dropped, and slept with his head on Pop's boot.

McCoy wanted nothing more than to sleep. His leg hurt from being moved every which way and his head hurt from thinking. But he had work to do. He finished the caulking and worked on leveling the porch.

To keep the pain out of his mind, he started thinking about the vet. Baylor Blanton was pretty, but obviously she wasn't interested in finding a man. Baggy jeans, no makeup, hair with no style but curly. If she was looking, she needed to put a bit of bait on the hook.

Come to think of it, he liked seeing the real woman first, before she got all dolled up. Then there'd be no surprises when she changed back into her usual self, or when she rolled over in the morning.

It was terrible when a guy took his dream girl home and the next morning woke up with a nightmare. Men made things easy since they looked pretty much the same. What you saw was what you got. Take it or leave it.

And, apparently, no one wanted him. Not one person had ever said "I love you" to him and meant it, including his parents or his newly departed fiancée.

The only nice thing Breanna Bell did before she rode back to Georgia in the moving van was return the ring. When it came time to leave this place, he planned to pawn the diamond and hit the road. For right now, it was stashed away in a pocket of his work clothes. He'd never propose to a woman again.

When he headed to bed, he decided he wouldn't mind taking Baylor out for a night. She was nice to talk to. They could be friends. He didn't have any girl friends, but he could work on being a friend.

Closing his eyes, he decided "friends" might be all he could handle.

Hell, he didn't even have a home, or enough money to date, or any clothes to wear. Double hell, he realized, if they went out, she'd have to open the door for him.

McCoy decided to work harder and forget both the pain and the vet. His logic was downright depressing. His dreams were nightmares and his prospects were lousy.

At dusk Pop woke him to tell him supper was ready.

Half a can of soup and three donuts later, McCoy was ready to go to bed again. He grabbed one of Pop's Western books, said good night, and disappeared in his room.

He'd barely gotten settled in when he heard the house phone. A few minutes later, Pop poked his head into McCoy's room. "You know anything about elevators, boy?"

"A little. I've helped install a few. I ride them now and then. Does that count?"

"Well, our mayor called and says the one at the courthouse is broke, and she tried to get someone to repair it, but no one will come out this late. She's got two court reporters who claim they will not come in tomorrow if it's not fixed. She must be pretty desperate if she called me. Everyone knows I only work on farm equipment."

"I could take a look at it first thing in the morning." McCoy picked his book back up.

Pop didn't move.

"Anything else?"

"Yeah, get dressed. I'll drive you to town. There ain't no tomorrow in this job."

"But . . ."

"Now!" Pop yelled. "She wants the elevator fixed now. This is an emergency, son. You can charge double. If you fix it, of course. Mayor said a fireman will let you in and show you where everything is. She claims, unless there is a fire, the men will be on call if you need something moved or lifted. They are just across the street and probably have nothing to do except keep an eye on you."

The idea that he might earn money got McCoy moving. Within ten minutes they were on their way to town. At the courthouse, Pop helped him carry in a mechanic's toolbox and then said he'd be over at the pool hall.

"You're not going to stay around and give me a hand?"

Pop smiled. "I'll check on you at midnight when the hall closes. If you haven't figured it out by then, I'll take a look at it."

McCoy was glad no one was around because he spent the first hour cussing the elevator. But, part of what he loved about being a contractor was figuring out the puzzle of making things work. And this was a challenge.

The firemen checked on him every hour. They brought coffee the first time and spaghetti the second time. McCoy took time off to eat and thanked them for not bringing canned soup.

The volunteers were near his age and a few offered suggestions. When McCoy said he wished he had a few cables and some oil, one of the guys said he'd go over to the hardware store and get any supplies needed. He was the Johnsons' nephew and had a key.

As the hours passed, McCoy slowly figured it out. Once the elevator was working, he rode it up and down half a dozen times just for fun.

By the time Pop came back at midnight, McCoy was sitting outside the firehouse waiting for him. As they drove home, McCoy went over every detail about what didn't work and what finally did.

To his surprise, Pop paid attention.

When he fell back in bed, McCoy couldn't remember ever being so tired. His leg hurt and his hands had several cuts, but he felt great.

He was so exhausted he didn't have the energy even to dream.

Chapter 27

Mr. Winston and His Ladies

Saturday

This rainy-day Saturday was not their normal luncheon day, but Geraldine Mackenzie had left a message on Mr. Winston's house phone.

Lunch today. Eleven o'clock. By the river.

He was a man of routine, and this sudden change left him flustered. He had talked to Lilly last night, and she hadn't mentioned a lunch, so she didn't know about it either. Saturdays were always his day to dust his big old house and wash the sheets. After all, Lilly would be staying over Sunday night.

They'd agreed not to see one another on Fridays, Saturdays except for the once-a-month lunch by the river, or on Mondays and Wednesdays. That way on Tuesdays, Thursdays, and Sundays they'd have things to talk about.

Winston grinned. He loved being engaged.

He might have liked to talk about why Geraldine called their group together, but there was no time. His whole Saturday routine was off because of the unplanned lunch.

The thought crossed his mind that maybe the ladies

hadn't invited Lilly. Maybe they were planning a surprise birthday party for her. No, that couldn't be right. Her birthday wasn't for four months.

He'd just have to go to see what was so important to call a lunch.

At exactly eleven o'clock, he walked up to the café. The storm had ended last night but clouds still filled the sky. Not a good day for an outside table, but he hadn't planned this.

Winston relaxed. The table was set for four. His Lilly would be coming.

If it was no one's birthday, he hoped it wasn't another of Nancy's schemes to borrow the church minibus for a senior citizen trip to the casino in Oklahoma. She swore they'd sing hymns all the way there and back, but the preacher didn't go for the idea.

The last time she'd tried to rally the troops to go, the preacher gave three sermons about how the devil's ways were road markers on the way to sin.

This morning the two Mackenzie widows were waiting for him with big smiles, which usually meant trouble. Winston often thought there were too many Mackenzies in this town. A third of the population was either named Mackenzie or kinned to one. He swore Honey Creek had a three-party system. Democrats, Republicans, and Mackenzies.

Winston coughed to hide a laugh. He couldn't wait to tell Lilly his thought.

He remained standing, knowing Lilly would be arriving at their table in four minutes. He could set his clock by her being always five minutes late.

While he waited, the widows gossiped about how a young woman fell in the river last night. Oh, she was all right, but she couldn't be much on brains to walk close to the river during a storm.

Winston never quite understood why when kids spend all summer jumping in the river, no one says a word. But let one "poor soul" fall in by accident and there's always fear of death, or attempted suicide, or insanity. After the reason for falling in was determined, the people of Honey Creek would begin a game of naming every person who'd ever died in the river.

Winston almost laughed, thinking it was like a dozen drunks trying to name all seven dwarfs.

Nancy interrupted his thoughts by saying, "It is probably attempted suicide. She was lucky Pecos's brother saw her fall in. I heard it was raining hard and she was wandering by the dock where that dead body was photographed. If it was dead. My cousin says it was probably a joke. Betty, our dispatcher, said he didn't look dead to her. She saw the photos, poor thing, but it's part of her job."

"Betty saw a naked body?" Geraldine looked shocked. "I didn't know that."

"He wasn't naked. Our chatty mailman just added that fact to make the story more interesting."

Nancy frowned. "Oh, of course Betty saw the pictures. A dispatcher is just like a deputy. They know the facts. She described the scene in detail at the church women's lunch."

Winston had to change the subject. "I think the girl was probably looking for her young lover. A devil of a wind blew her in as the raging river pulled her down."

Both ladies ignored him. "And what was the sergeant doing out near the river in a storm? I heard one of the waitresses at the café say he'd already jumped in the river this week. Maybe he doesn't have the sense God gave a duck. Our mailman mentioned Tucson Smith has been in combat."

Nancy always had an answer for any question. After all,

she'd taught fourth grade. It was required. "Oh, Geraldine, of course he's been in combat. He's in the army so all he thinks about is fighting and dying. Those soldiers always do strange things. Probably just part of his training. Did you look at him? He could probably walk through a brick wall without a scratch."

"I never heard of river walking being part of combat training."

Winston turned his back to the ladies so they wouldn't see him roll his eyes. He'd lived among these Texans half his life and still didn't understand their thinking. Last winter, two fishermen flipped their boat, and the sheriff insisted they go to suicide prevention classes for weeks. Both gave up fishing for golf.

Winston remembered a saying he'd heard once. *Logic rides a drunk horse in West Texas.*

When Lilly arrived, she gave a quick smile at Winston and let him pull out her chair.

He couldn't resist brushing her shoulder before he stepped away. Greetings were exchanged as Jam brought out small salads.

"This is a treat to see you, ladies and Mr. Winston. A surprise," Jam said.

"We've something to discuss, dear," Nancy announced. "Please see we are not disturbed until our meals are delivered."

"Of course." Jam took the request as if it were a sworn oath.

When they were alone, Nancy looked from Lilly to Mr. Winston and started without delay. "It has come to our attention that you two are going out alone. Now, sitting in church might be all right, but going out alone, well, that means something."

In her low voice, Lilly asked, "What does it mean, Nancy?"

All four were silent for a minute then Geraldine whispered, "People will think you are a couple, dear. You're together. You are dating and no telling what else."

Winston straightened. "We're not dating. We're engaged. We plan to continue going out together."

Both widows looked so shocked he almost felt sorry for them. "Remember last week when we talked about wish goals? Well, Lilly and I have never been engaged, so we thought it might be fun. We are not thinking of marriage. We just think it would be nice to be engaged."

"What if we all just decided to have fun? Do whatever we want to do? Go wild? I'd like to run and jump off the dock, but you don't see me doing that." Nancy huffed.

Geraldine's mind was sliding down the rabbit hole with her sister-in-law. "I'd like to go to the horse races and wear a big hat with flowers on top." She giggled. "I'd bet twenty dollars on the prettiest horse and yell for him to win."

Nancy giggled. "I'd like to play spin the bottle. I never got to play it when I was young. I love games."

Winston sat back and watched the three respectable women let their imaginations fly. They were suddenly Honey Creek's episode of *Girls Gone Wild*.

Even his sweet Lilly said she'd like to play poker with real money and ride on the back of a motorbike.

Lilly laughed and mentioned their hairdresser, Cindy, said she'd like to eat a whole blueberry pie, and Ona, the town's only master gardener, said she'd like to arrive at the garden show one year wearing nothing but sunflowers.

Nancy loved the idea of an illegal poker game. "We'd invite anyone who knows the game and tell them to all take different ways to the secret place."

Geraldine fantasized about having a sit-in on the town

square about changing the reindeer lamp ornaments to chipmunks.

Even Winston laughed at that idea and promised to make a sign if they marched.

When Lilly winked at him as Jam brought the lunch, Winston almost dropped his glass of tea. It wasn't just a wink. It was a wicked wink.

He barely managed to keep up with the rest of the conversation at lunch. He was too busy thinking about what he might do. He wasn't interested in going crazy. He just wanted to be with Lilly.

Maybe next Tuesday night, when she cooked dinner for him, he might go to bed without his pajama top on. She seemed to like his chest. She'd called it fur.

They ate lunch and talked, and the laughter never stopped.

As always, he and Lilly walked the widows home and then turned toward Lilly's place.

"I think we've started something, Lilly."

"I'm afraid so, but isn't it fun?"

When he walked her to her door, he kissed her right outside for anyone passing the pharmacy to see.

Scandalous!

Chapter 28

Melody's Escape

After sleeping different places for almost a week, Melody welcomed the bed. Among the pillows and soft covers she felt like she was being cuddled in an angel's arms.

She had posted a note on the refrigerator to her parents when she left home. She'd lied and said that she planned to stay with Grandmother A for a few days. That might give her a day or two head start but she had no doubt they knew she was gone by now.

If she'd had a phone she might have called just to let them know she was all right, but without telling them where she was. They'd be angry and demand to know more, but she'd grown up over the past week, and she would hold her ground. She would never be their little girl again.

She'd also never tell them how hard her journey had been. The loneliness. The cold. The fear.

Michael was working his way to her. She'd wait as long as she could.

She had no idea how this would end. But she knew one fact. She'd do it again and again as long as there was a chance she could be with Michael.

Melody pulled the pillow against her back and pretended he was sleeping beside her.

Chapter 29

Sergeant Tucson Smith

After sleeping in a tent, Tucson had woken alone to the banging of a fully operating kitchen. Mixers were grinding. People were yelling in some kind of code and running and stomping around like Irish Riverdancers. Gone was the woman he'd slept with along with his X-rated dreams.

His day went downhill from there. He'd slept in his clothes again, and Jam barely took the time to wave at him when he poked his head out of the tent.

So, after checking on the mermaid, his plan was to drive over to the cleaners, wait until they opened, then change into his only other clothes in a closet the cleaners called a dressing room. He was bouncing from uniform to suit every other day, and the cleaners were getting rich.

Yesterday, Tucson finally called Fort Hood and asked a friend to pack at least three uniforms and some running sweats and overnight them. They should be coming in tomorrow. Overnight in the hill country always took two days, sometimes three.

Since he was on loan from the fort, he should be in uniform at work, but in off-hours he didn't like to stand out in town, so he might as well buy more clothes for dates.

Dates, he laughed. He hadn't even used that word in years. But, while he was in town he planned to take Jam out every night. He wanted her in his arms dancing, in his bed and sitting across from him at breakfast. Their time might be short but he wanted memories to keep. He craved her close and needed her to know that someone cherished her if only for a few weeks a year when he could make it back to Honey Creek.

Maybe, for a woman who said she had nothing but work, a few vacations to meet him would be enough to fill that little tickle for adventure inside her. They could talk on the phone, text one another, and meet anywhere in the world if they wanted to be alone. Or, if she needed to stay here, he'd come to her and step into her busy, chaotic life.

But he had to fit in her world and western style was all that he could find in town besides T-shirts. He'd dress like a Texan when they went out. Tonight on their first real date, all Tucson wanted to be was a man taking his girl out.

When he walked into the sheriff's office a half hour later, Pecos smiled. "I thought you might sleep in, brother."

"No. Would you believe the kitchen is in full swing by dawn? I slept on the landing last night. Thought I'd better watch over our mermaid." He took the chair in front of Pecos's desk and stared at his brother.

Pecos waited and finally broke the silence. "What's on your mind?"

"When I saw the girl walking the edge of the river, she was looking for something. Not watching where she was going or trying to follow a path. For her to do that in a rainstorm tells me whatever she was trying to find must be very important."

"So, you don't think she was attempting suicide?"

"No. But I think her being there has something to do

with those pictures of the dead soldier. O-Positive-dead-guy and our mermaid have something in common. Star-crossed lovers maybe? Friends? Relatives?"

Pecos leaned forward and asked, "You didn't happen to see her carrying a purse? All she had in her coat pocket was a couple of twenties."

"No. It was dark and raining. I made out a flashlight and then saw her drop a backpack as she fell in the water."

Pecos nodded. "When the firemen were checking her, I noticed the backpack. One of the guys must have seen it on the bank. I unzipped it and only saw a few rag dolls inside. Which might mean she's younger than we thought."

Tucson didn't argue. "I'm guessing you checked missing persons?"

The sheriff nodded. "I came back here and searched while you were cuddling up the Jam."

"Fat chance." Tucson wasn't ready to talk about him and Jam being a couple, so he stayed on point. "I would have guessed the girl as seventeen or eighteen, but she might be sixteen or younger if she's carrying dolls. Who knows? She wouldn't answer any questions last night."

"I've checked on the missing persons website twice this morning hoping someone put her in the site. No one fits. If she ran away, nobody seems in any hurry to find her. I'll widen the search to statewide."

"Looks like you're doing all you can, little brother."

Pecos shook his head. "First week on the job and I've already got an unsolved death case and probably a runaway. I'm working fifteen hours a day and solving nothing."

"Go home to your family, Pecos," Tucson said, suddenly wishing that he had a family to disappear to. "It's Saturday. I'll hang around here and go over everything one more time. Then, I'll go back to the dock and look around.

Maybe she stashed the purse somewhere but not likely. If we do find an ID, we'll have one problem solved."

"You won't find anything. The storm will have washed anything away." Pecos stood and pulled on his jacket. "Maybe something will come up. We can't hold the woman, but try to talk to her. She knows something about the guy. I feel it. Since you saved her life, she might talk to you."

"I'll try but I'm not good at this kind of thing. I can't play the warm and fuzzy type people want to talk to."

After Pecos left the station, Tucson spread out the notes and the few grainy photos of the body on the desk one more time. The more he studied the shots the more he thought it was staged. The crime scene was too clean. The body looked as if it was placed there, not killed on the dock.

Then, he saw it. The one clue he'd been waiting for. The dead guy's hand moved slightly from one shot to the other. It looked the same, but when he compared the finger to the groove in the dock, the pose was different. Little finger half an inch away from the groove in one shot and touching the line in another. Right hand with fingers together in one shot, spread out in the other.

He took a long breath. They were dealing with a trick someone was playing, not the death of a soldier. The only reason he couldn't read the tags was because the pretend dead guy had made a mistake. He'd accidentally splashed a bit of fake blood on the tags. The only reason he'd wanted to wear tags had to be to show his name so he could be logged as presumed dead.

Now there were two questions: Who was the guy? And why did he want to be presumed dead?

The urge to call Pecos was strong, but his brother needed

a break. Tucson decided to relax. Nothing was going on. He'd tell the sheriff in a few hours when Pecos called in.

To Tucson's surprise, he liked the atmosphere in the small office. Deputies circling through, checking in, checking out. They treated Tucson as one of the team. He tried to be friendly to the locals, but he didn't have Pecos's winning ways. Most locals who came in to report something lost or to pay tickets ignored the big soldier in the room.

Tucson had always been tall for his age. He'd always been the kid too big to hug. He remembered the time when the fourth-grade teacher hugged everyone but him. He told himself it was because he was the only kid who could look her straight in the eyes, but in truth, he'd just never been cuddly.

So, he became muscular, hard inside and out. But this was his hometown. Maybe he should try to smile at people.

Finally, one man waiting in the line to pay a ticket said, "Look, there's Jam's soldier. I saw him on her porch the other day."

Suddenly all eyes were on Tucson.

A lady said she saw him with Pecos on the dock. She claimed the big soldier was helping out his brother. Wasn't that sweet.

Another told the crowd that Jam called her soldier "Sergeant."

All at once people started talking to him. One lady even asked how Jam was doing. The bone-thin mailman said Jam was sweet. "You better treat her right, Sergeant, or you'll be answering to me."

A farmer in the back laughed. "Yeah, you and a dozen of her cousins."

When the mailman held up a fist that he'd obviously never used in a fight, everyone in the room laughed.

Tucson smiled. Somehow being "Jam's soldier" made him not so frightening to the locals. A Mackenzie had claimed him, so he was trusted.

About noon a cowboy limped in using a crutch more as a weapon on strangers coming too close than to help him walk. He tripped one of the deputies leaving and somehow got tangled up in an extension cord before he made it to the sheriff's office and Tucson.

"Can I help you, cowboy?" Tucson tried to sound friendly.

"I'm not a cowboy," the man said.

Tucson didn't bother to smile. "You could have fooled me."

"I need to talk to the sheriff. I may have some information."

"He's off today." Tucson leaned around the not-cowboy wearing Wranglers, a pearl snapped shirt, and a Stetson. The office was suddenly empty.

"Where is everyone, Betty?" Tucson yelled like he was the self-appointed loudspeaker.

The dispatcher down the hall yelled back, "They went to lunch. Everyone knows they all leave between twelve and one so if we've got a citizen in the office, he either can't read the note on the door about 'gone for lunch' or he is new to town."

Tucson yelled back, "Any chance you could help this outsider, Betty?"

"Not unless it's an emergency, and he'll have to call it in. I'm not allowed to leave unless I have to pee."

The not-cowboy started laughing, and Tucson considered slugging him.

Tucson leaned halfway across the desk. "You are a stranger in town, right?"

The tall man in western clothes leaned in. "And so are you."

Tucson decided if he knocked the man out, problem solved. No one was around to notice. No more questions. By the time the not-cowboy woke up, one of the deputies might be back.

But hitting a guy wobbling on one crutch didn't seem right. "Have a seat, cowboy. I'll do my best to help you."

"Name is McCoy Mason and Betty's right. I'm not from around here. I'm just recovering from a car accident at my granddad's place out on Sunflower Lane."

"I've heard of that lane so I'm thinking I should talk to you."

Mason folded into his chair like tall, slender men do, and Tucson dropped in the sheriff's office chair as if testing the weight capacity.

"Nice to meet you. I'm Sergeant Smith on loan from Fort Hood." Tucson was quickly reaching the end of his small-talk skills. "How can I be of service?"

"I know who you are," McCoy said. "I heard all about you from the mailman when I was at the bakery."

Tucson rubbed his forehead. "I'm not surprised. This town doesn't need phones. I think the gossip transmitters in their brains are somehow connected."

"I wouldn't know about that, Sergeant. I'm just visiting."

"Like I said, how can I help you, Mr. Mason? I've heard all the gossip so you can skip that."

"Well, it's just a hunch, not even a clue, but when I hopped off the bus a week ago, a nice guy named Leo picked me up and drove me to my grandfather's farm. At the time I'd just gotten out of the hospital and was barely awake, but I remember Leo saying no one ever gets off the bus on the late run. He has a shop next door to the stop and he told me the bus never even slows down."

Tucson tapped his pencil. "Is this going anywhere, cowboy?"

McCoy met his stare. "Two nights ago I drove by the bus station. The bus stopped and a girl jumped off and ran into the night. I didn't see much, but I remember she had a plaid backpack."

Tucson started taking notes. "This could be helpful. How about we go through everything one more time? Any detail could be helpful. If I can trace the bus route, we might figure out what town she is from.

"I'll print out the route."

McCoy Mason seemed willing to help. "I'm guessing she's not from the valley. It bothers me that she ran from the bus. Like she didn't want anyone to see her get off."

A half pot of coffee and an hour later, Tucson was convinced the girl he'd seen by the river and McCoy's traveler were the same. Everything matched with McCoy's story, even the backpack. Same dark reddish hair, same willowy build, almost a woman but not quite.

"Thanks, McCoy. Can I buy you lunch across the street? They serve breakfast all day."

McCoy guessed. "Nobody to eat lunch with, right, Sergeant?"

"Right."

"Then I'll take you up on the offer. All my grandfather serves is cereal."

Five minutes later McCoy ordered the "everything but the kitchen sink" breakfast, and Tucson did the same. As they ate, Tucson shared a few details, well-known clues. To his surprise, McCoy began to put the pieces together.

He'd told Tucson the facts and the guy started asking questions.

This not-cowboy had a sharp mind, Tucson thought.

McCoy held up his fork. "Let's consider the 'death scene' was staged. Kids just playing around. If the girl from the river is involved and the photos are of a young man, we might assume they knew each other.

"Maybe this girl was just taking pictures. Maybe they were on a date. Maybe they were in love. Maybe they decided to meet again at the dock, but for some reason he didn't show up. Why else would she be coming to Honey Creek? Why would she hang out on a dock after dark?"

McCoy shook his head. "What if she noticed the pictures were missing and thought she might have left them on the dock."

"But why wouldn't she come back with the soldier or at least come back to look for the photos in daylight?" Tucson answered his own question. "Because he's a soldier and couldn't get away."

McCoy nodded. "Maybe. Or maybe he is dead."

Tucson added, "And why was she carrying dolls? That bothers me, cowboy."

McCoy ignored the nickname. The waitress had called him that twice. "Forget the dolls, Sergeant. Why Honey Creek? The town's cute, but it's not a destination on any tourist map."

More questions than answers began to fly between the two men. Why the dog tags? What would they use for blood if the photo was staged? Why the public place?

McCoy was still eating his last biscuit when they headed out to the crime scene.

When they got in Tucson's rental car, he asked McCoy,

"Mind telling me why you dress like a cowboy if you're not a cowboy?"

"Long story. Abridged version: Moved to Houston for job. Girlfriend came along for fun. I had a car wreck on I-45. Spent three weeks in the hospital dying. Girlfriend left with all my stuff. I lived. Only had the new clothes I bought for a rodeo date I missed because of the wreck."

"Did the girlfriend ever come back?"

"Nope. She's still mad that I stood her up on our date. She said she really, really wanted to go to the Houston rodeo. So, I forgot her number. Fact is I kind of forgot everything but her hair. You think I've got brain damage?"

"No." Tucson pulled up at the dock. "I had a girlfriend once whose voice haunted me for months after we broke up. I don't remember anything else about her, but I'm afraid when I die her voice will still haunt me."

As they got out of the car, McCoy asked, "You think we're broken somehow? I've heard of men who write poems about their lost loves, and I'm not sure I could compose a sentence."

"Definitely broken." Tucson pulled out a notepad as they stepped on the dock. "Back to my problem. What do you think we're looking for?"

"I don't know, but we'll know it when we see it. Let's start along the trail. The bank is dry enough to walk on safely."

Tucson studied the trail, but McCoy kept looking up. Finally, the cowboy saw something out of place. A ribbon tied on a branch. A marker maybe or a memory symbol.

"Did the girl on the bus wear a ribbon in her hair?" Tucson asked.

"I don't remember, she might have. The back was knotted almost like a crazy bun."

Tucson frowned. "I don't remember any ribbon but she might have tied it to the branch to mark the spot she fell in."

"That makes no sense," McCoy reasoned. "Marking the spot where an accident happened."

"Maybe it wasn't an accident? Maybe she thought that was where our dead soldier went into the river."

"Great work, Sergeant. You've got a body that might not be dead and a near-drowning that might not have been an accident."

Tucson shook his head. "I'm brain-dead. The more I think about it, the more confused I get."

"That's my excuse. Find your own reason, Sergeant, for not putting all the pieces together."

They were almost to the Honey Creek Café when a spring shower stopped all progress for clues.

When the sergeant saw McCoy struggling to run, he looped his arm under McCoy's shoulder and they fell into step like two boys tied together in a three-legged race. Both were laughing as they reached the café.

Tucson left McCoy on Jam's porch and went back for his car.

When McCoy climbed in a few minutes later, Tucson said, "I got a call from the office. Betty says you got an old man and a fairy-sized girl waiting on you at the station."

"Yeah, they follow me around. I think they might have a bet on how long it'll be before I fall again."

When Tucson walked in a few minutes later, there was a fairy girl sitting in his office chair whirling around and around.

An old man, who had to be McCoy's kin, was standing in the doorway to the dispatcher's room. He appeared to be flirting with Betty.

"These two yours, McCoy?" Tucson asked.

"Yep. My grandfather and my guardian fairy."

Tucson laughed. "And I thought I had a strange family."

After he waved goodbye to the girl, Tucson walked back to Pecos's office and noticed the cell phone he'd left behind had a voicemail notification on it.

He tapped the play icon. Four words. "The mermaid has disappeared."

Chapter 30

Melody in Shadows

"Michael? Michael? Are you up here?" Melody Avendale didn't dare raise her voice. "Michael, please be here." She clutched her plaid backpack against her chest as if it would protect her. "Please be here."

The dusty boards on the third floor creaked as if angry that she'd woken them from a long sleep.

"Mike? It's me. I made it to Honey Creek like you told me to if I was in trouble, but I can't find you. Please say something. I'm scared. I called and gave you the signal. I know you'll come get me. I went to the dock first, but you weren't there. Then by luck a man saved me when I fell in the water. He brought me to just where I was heading. The Honey Creek Café. You were right—perfect hideout."

Something rattled at the far end of a hallway, but she saw no movement. Four doors lined the hall like guards. All open. All dark, as if daring her to come in. At the end of the corridor was one high window. It provided a ray of sunshine that illuminated the dust dancing in the light like schools of tiny fish swimming in a sunbeam.

Melody kept moving silently. She'd lost her shoes in

the river, but the lady at the café had given her socks. She progressed slowly, sliding along the floor as if ice skating.

"Michael, are you here? Oh, please be here. You told me where you used to hide and this is the last place I can remember to look."

She made her way down the passageway, looking into every bare room. No one answered her whispered call.

When she reached the end, she crumbled below the window and began to cry. She'd been everywhere Mike had talked about. All the places he'd hidden when he'd run away from home as a boy. She'd stayed two hours at each place, waiting for him.

The garage where the school district housed their four buses was her first hideout. She'd found the coffeepot on the workbench in the back, just like Mike said it would be. Never washed, just rinsed out. Peanut butter crackers in a tin so the mice wouldn't get to them.

A tiny farm on Sunflower Lane was her second stop. He'd said no one lived there anymore, but the house was stocked with canned goods. The lady who owned the cottage came there some mornings to plant a garden and some nights to cry.

Melody ate soup and peaches at the little house, then cleaned everything up. She liked that place. It had been a happy home once, she thought, but now it was sleeping away sorrow.

The next hideout she found was the fisherman's shack used only in summer. Melody didn't like that place. It smelled and had no food.

And now she was in the last place Michael had found when he was a kid. The third floor of a café. She'd tried to slip in earlier, but there'd been too many people around. Then, after she'd almost drowned, a man carried her right to the café. All she had to do to find Mike's hiding place was climb one flight of stairs.

But he wasn't waiting for her here either. It had been days since she'd called him and left the code. Something must have happened.

She'd wait. He'd find her. Surely he'd come today.

Melody could almost hear his low voice whispering to her as they sat side by side in the library. "If trouble ever comes, meet me in Honey Creek."

She tugged out the last piece of braided ribbon she'd worn in her hair when she'd last seen him. He said he loved the colors: shiny blue, waterfall silver, and midnight velvet. She tied the four-inch strands to the latch on the window. If he made it here, he'd see the ribbon. He'd know she was near.

Mike had told her that when the time came for them to disappear, he'd call three times and only let it ring once. Her clue to slip away as soon as she could. He promised he'd be waiting. But she'd had to leave home without her cell, since her mother had taken it.

"I'm going to find you, Michael." Her words carried on the still air but they brought her no comfort. He'd talked about disappearing and spending the rest of their lives together. In three months, she'd be eighteen and no one could stop her. He'd told her he'd been running all his life until he saw her.

Melody had left one strip of ribbon at each hiding place. He'd see it and know she was near, waiting for him.

Each hideout was exactly as Mike had described. Their plan had to work.

But the plan to be together hadn't gone as planned. She'd been the one to call three times and let it ring once each time. She'd barely had time to delete the calls before her mother took the phone.

When she reached Honey Creek, she couldn't find him and feared something was wrong. Maybe he hadn't heard the rings. Maybe he'd changed his plans. Or worse, what if his plan no longer included her? She was seventeen. He could get in trouble. Maybe arrested.

Maybe it was a good thing he wasn't here in Honey Creek. She was alone but at least he was safe. Her money was almost gone, though. She had nowhere to go and no way of knowing what should happen next.

But she knew how to hide. He'd told her what to do. If he'd survived as a little boy, she could stay invisible until he found her.

A tiny mouse slowly came toward her. Five feet away he stopped and studied her.

"Hello." She brushed her tears away. "I guess it's you and me against the world. You may not know this, but I'm a mouse too."

That had been her father's name for her when she'd been little. He was kind but the few times she'd tried to stand up to him, his stern stare sent her running. Her mother always let her father hand out the first round of lectures. Not one verbal attack, but several until they were sure she'd never question, or argue, or disobey again. He'd always end with, "We love you, Melody. You're our little blessing and we're going to look after you as long as we live."

Her parents were teachers who'd married late in life and had her in their forties. She had no doubt they stayed up late every night planning what they'd teach her come dawn. Now and then she thought she was more their project than their child.

Smiling at the mouse she whispered, "I ran away. My parents are probably going crazy, but I love Mike. If I lie and say I'm eighteen we can get married. Then, I'll call them and tell them. Mike says once we're married, they can't pull us apart."

She pulled a cookie from her pocket and tore a piece off. When she tossed it toward the mouse, he darted away, then slowly came back for the food.

She'd planned to walk all the way to the dock before it rained last night. She wanted to check to see if Mike had left a message. Then, when it was late, she'd sneak into the back of the café and hide on the third floor.

But the storm came early and she'd slipped on the wet grass along the river's edge. Then a big man with arms as thick as tree trunks pulled her out. No anger, no lectures, he just brought her to the café.

She sometimes thought of people as animals. Frightened mice. Free flying birds. Bulldogs always on guard. But the man who saved her from drowning was a Clydesdale.

She used the pack for a pillow and her sweater as a blanket as she curled up beneath the window. She felt safe here. The strong man was near and so was the kind lady.

She was cold and worried and alone, but she wouldn't give up.

"If it doesn't rain, I'll look for Mike when it gets darker," she told the mouse. "Months ago when he'd been planning our someday, he'd said he'd meet me at the dock at midnight. Only he didn't exactly tell me what day. I'll go there every night and hope. I thought he might be hiding in the trees somewhere along the river's path to here, but he wasn't."

She didn't bother to wipe her tears away as she told her problems to the mouse. "That's all I could do. Keep waiting for him. If I call my parents, they'll never again let me out of their sight. And if they knew I was going to Mike, Dad would probably have him arrested.

"But I believe Mike. He swore he loved me, and he

said we'd be together. All I have to do is keep believing.
He'll come.

"Moonbeam dreams," she whispered. "And sunrise
laughter. That's what he promised."

She'd wait until midnight then make her way to the
dock. Stay off the roads. Walk the river's edge again. Find
where she'd tied the ribbon.

If it was gone, she'd know he was looking for her. Then
she'd stay still and wait for him to find her.

Chapter 31

Sergeant Tucson Smith

From the time he walked into the Honey Creek Café, Tucson had to follow Jam around to get information. She was full into the Saturday lunch run and had no time to stop for a chat.

He thought of pulling her into a dark corner and kissing her hello, but finding a dark corner isn't easy in a packed café.

No one in the kitchen had seen the girl walk out this morning. She'd taken all her things and simply disappeared. No, she hadn't told Jam anything about where she came from or why she was by the water on a stormy night. In fact, she hadn't answered a single question.

When a third waitress bumped into him, Jam shooed Tucson away with one hand. "That's all I know. Get out of my kitchen, Sergeant."

Tucson knew there was a chance that this girl appearing by the dock might have nothing to do with the O-positive, dog-tagged body, but he had a feeling in his gut the two were somehow linked.

The guy looked young. Young enough to have a girlfriend who was still in high school. But if she came in on a bus and McCoy said he didn't see anyone pick her up, maybe she was surprising Mr. O-Positive.

Tucson went out on the shady porch of the café to think. If she was traveling into Honey Creek, she was not from here. So, maybe O-Positive was the one from this valley. If so, someone might recognize the kid. If he had dog tags, he might have enlisted near here. The closest recruiting office was on the Clifton College campus, about thirty miles away. It might be worth a visit to the office.

A recruiter also wasn't likely to faint at the sight of a dead body.

"If the recruiter remembers him, they'd have a name," Tucson said aloud.

"You want some lunch?" Jam interrupted. "Or are you too busy arguing with yourself?"

"No, no lunch. I just had breakfast with a friend."

"You have a friend?" She sounded surprised then added, "You have someone else who is willing to feed you?"

He laughed realizing she probably thought since she found him, he was now hers. And as hers, she should know all about him.

Tucson raised an eyebrow and tried to ignore her comment. He considered himself a man who'd never belong to any woman, but he wouldn't mind getting to know this one a bit better.

"How about we have a date tonight, Jam? We can try again. A real date. I'll show up. You'll wear a dress."

"What about your search?"

"Nothing is going on with the investigation. The girl probably has nothing to do with the guy on the dock. Maybe she's just a runaway. I bet she'll turn up when she gets hungry. I'm guessing she's probably from the valley and just wanted to give her folks a fright." He grinned. "How about I investigate you tonight?"

"Okay, you win, a date. I can do that. What do you have in mind?"

"You wear something besides your uniform. We go out for a drink. I hear they have a great singer at a place over in Someday Valley." When she looked confused, like she'd never heard of the concept of going out, he added, "We can talk, maybe hold hands. Eat food someone else cooked. Make out in the car on the way home, clothing optional."

"I think I might like this dating idea. A night out eating and drinking. No uniforms. No clothes later."

Tucson grinned. "You got the basics down."

He'd never been an eating out and flowers kind of guy, but Jam could turn him into one. The whole town was right about her. She wasn't a one-night stand kind of woman. He might not be the marrying kind, but for a while it would be nice to have someone care about him. Someone he could care about. Even the townsfolk calling him "Jam's soldier" was growing on him.

He thought of the woman an old man named Mr. Winston called his "lady." Tucson had seen them eating lunch by the water. He couldn't make out what they said, but he noticed Winston sometimes held her hand or brushed her arm gently. There was something special about belonging to another, even for a short time.

Maybe eventually, Jam would travel to where he was stationed. Or, when he had to leave Honey Creek, they'd meet up in Dallas for a weekend or fly somewhere neither had ever been. He'd never had a person to explore new places with. Someone to write to and call when he just needed to talk.

Jam could be all of that.

And, if she wanted more, like a house and kids, he'd let her go to follow her dream, but they'd always have memories to share. Maybe they'd still write love letters now and then. He kind of liked the idea of having someone to whisper "I love you" to if only for a while.

Tucson didn't want to think too far into the future. He knew they didn't have one. But for a few months, they'd have a "now and then." Maybe that would be enough.

On impulse, he put his hands on her waist and moved her into the shadows laced in morning glory vines. His body pressed against hers as he kissed her tenderly.

She smelled of honey and ginger and passion. Her hands remained at her sides, but her kiss was hungry. They'd spent the night in the tent as friends, and now the drought was over.

When he broke the kiss, he whispered against her ear, "No matter what happens tonight, I want you next to me."

"Sounds like an order," she whispered back.

"Call it anything you want. A request. A goal. A prayer. Just be with me tonight."

"I'll think about it." She brushed her fingers along his jaw. "Fact is, I'll be thinking about it all afternoon. Don't be late. Pick me up at exactly seven."

"Sounds like an order."

She moved so close her lips brushed his ear. "It is. I plan to make several demands tonight."

He pulled her closer. "I love a bossy woman."

"Good. Get used to it. I've been missing out on life for a while, and I plan to jump into the deep end with you, Sergeant."

He loved staring in her sky-blue eyes. She might be Sunday morning proper, but those eyes held midnight promises.

Pecos yelled from the other end of the porch, pulling Tucson away from heaven.

After dragging in a long breath of honeysuckle air,

Tucson took one step away from Jam before his brother reached them.

"Grab your coat. We've got trouble at the dock!" The sheriff was shaking his head as if plagues were rolling into his county on double-decker buses.

"The dock just down the road? The crime scene? That dock? What now? Another body?"

"Dozens!" Pecos shouted as he jumped off the porch without wasting time with the steps.

Tucson followed. "Don't joke about a crime scene. What do I need a coat for? It's eighty degrees."

They climbed in the cruiser as Pecos filled him in. "We got a gang of drunk girls jumping off the dock topless. I've got to get them reined in before word gets out or any kids see them."

Tucson grinned. "And to think it's not even spring break. How wild does Honey Creek get then?"

"It never gets wild around here. Nothing ever happens. They must have thought they could get away with it on my watch, and that is about to change."

As Pecos drove, Tucson asked, "Don't tell me you never went skinny-dipping in the river. It's a rite of passage in the valley."

His little brother smiled. "Just once, on the day of my high school graduation. Kerrie kidnapped me after the ceremony, and we came out here to swim without any suits. Best day of my life back then and best memory ever."

"What happened? Did old LeRoy catch you?"

"No. He didn't catch us, but I knew I'd marry her and love her forever." Pecos smiled. "Some mornings I slap myself when I realize I get to wake up beside her. She's only got one flaw. She thinks I'm perfect."

Tucson laughed. "Remember that day, Sheriff, when we see these kids skinny-dipping today. They may be breaking the law, but maybe they're thinking they are just having fun. Go easy on them."

When they pulled up to the dock, a dozen bikinis were draped over the line of police tape left from last week.

First warning: Tucson noticed several of the tops were huge. A few of the cup sizes looked like they could carry cantaloupes.

Second warning: Tucson heard screaming mixed in with the laughter.

Both men took off running, but the crime scene was worse than they could have ever imagined. The entire membership of the Honey Creek Bridge Club was splashing around in the river wearing only inflated tire tubes around their waists. Tucson prayed they had on bottoms. White hair, wrinkles, and sagging was all he saw.

War zones were less frightening.

Pecos tossed a rope, but the only one wanting to be rescued was the preacher who kept yelling, "I've got my eyes closed, Sheriff. I didn't see a thing. I've fallen in Sodom and Gomorrah. Sulfur and fire will fall on me any moment."

The preacher said he had his eyes shut, but he managed to catch the rope, Tucson noticed.

It took both of the Smith brothers to pull the preacher in. He was the only swimmer without a tube to hold on to and who was fully dressed. "Bless you, brothers. Bless you. I fell in and have nothing to do with this riot."

Tucson shouted over all the laughter, "Preacher, we're not going to arrest you. As far as I know, swimming with your clothes on isn't a crime. I've done it a few times myself lately. But, what are you doing out here with these ladies?" Tucson was careful not to say "old" ladies. There was no telling how they'd take that.

"You can open your eyes, Preacher." Pecos fought down

a smile. "Looking at swimmers, dressed or not, isn't illegal either."

"I didn't see a thing," the preacher testified again. "I heard this sinning was going to happen, and I came out to stop it. When I failed and slipped off the dock, I decided to baptize a few of these sinners before they drowned."

"How many did you bring into the flock?" Pecos said with almost a straight face.

"None. They all swore they'd already been washed in the blood. A few even bopped me on the head with floating branches for questioning their righteousness. There's so many Baptists mixed in with the Methodists I couldn't tell who kept hitting me, but I'd bet it was one of those Methodists. They're wilder, you know. Plus, of course, I kept my eyes closed so I couldn't point out the violent ones."

Tucson helped the preacher to his car and suggested he keep his eyes wide open while he drove home.

When Tucson got back to the scene of the crime, Pecos was trying to talk the women into calling off the party.

No luck. One announced that since they still had on bottoms it was half a crime and no one ever issued half a ticket.

After ten minutes of Pecos's threats, one of the ladies found a two-inch leech on her arm, and they all screamed and headed toward shore.

Sam Houston's raid on San Jacinto couldn't have been any louder.

"Turn around, Sheriff!" one of the Mackenzie widows yelled. "And you, the sheriff's big brother, turn around too."

One pointed at Tucson. "You were in my third-grade math class and minding me doesn't have an expiration date, so look the other way, Tucson Smith, if you know what's good for you."

One of the ladies said she wouldn't mind seeing him naked. Maybe they should demand he join them.

The giggles were getting wilder by the second.

The Smith brothers had seen enough and gladly turned their backs as the ladies waddled out of the river like ducks. Both men stood perfectly still, even though a few tire tubes rolled their way.

When they heard cars start, Tucson whispered, "You going to arrest them?"

"No. Like the preacher, I didn't see a thing. What about you?"

"I wish I could unsee the whole incident. I wouldn't be able to look one of those women in the face while I arrested her. At least two were my teachers. Can you believe that? I always thought they never left their classrooms, and now I learn they go out skinny-dipping after they retire."

Pecos laughed and slapped his brother on the back. "I'm not even writing this up." They headed back to the cruiser. "No one would believe it anyway."

"Well, I'm telling Jam all about it on our date tonight. Of course, I'll swear I didn't see a thing."

Chapter 32

McCoy's Windfall

McCoy spent the afternoon finishing up Pop's porch. Now, maybe it would stand for another hundred years.

After working so late last night on the mayor's elevator, he was surprised his leg seemed to hurt less today than it had. He was getting his strength back. His men used to claim that he could work as fast as three men on a job. He'd always taken pride in that.

When Pop left to deliver one of the city trucks with an engine he had rebuilt, McCoy worked faster, hoping to surprise the old guy with a painted porch when he got back.

This place, this land was starting to grow on him. He liked seeing nature in every direction. The little road fit its name. Sunflower Lane. Nature seemed to smile between the few houses scattered around. The huge trees huddled around a grand old house at the end of the road. The flowers budding between rocks on Pop's land. A cottage surrounded with sleepy gardens.

McCoy loved the way sunrise spread out and gave him a welcome every morning. He liked watching the weather roll in. He and Pop sometimes sat on the porch just to watch, not worrying about rain or wind ruining his workday.

McCoy grew used to the stillness of Pop's land. For the first time he knew what peace looked like. He wasn't just standing on the farm; he was becoming a part of it. The tranquility of the breeze. The scent of the earth. The vastness of the sky. All were seeping into his soul.

He was starting to see why Pop never left this valley. The house had a calmness about it, almost like it was listening.

Hell, McCoy even liked the old key in the fireplace mortar. It might be worthless, but somehow it was a part of this place, just like the rubble of the stage station, and the pole barn that housed hay, and the old windmill that had clinked out time for decades.

Funny how when you can see across land, you can see the past and the future as well. Something about watching nature change seasons must ground a man.

Once he healed and went back to work, McCoy had a feeling he'd miss this little farm. He'd have to come visit from time to time. Pop was family. Real family, even if the old man didn't seem especially happy to see him appear every morning.

As McCoy opened the can of yellow paint meant to brighten up the porch, he considered his next projects. Maybe painting the inside of the house. Maybe building on a room, not just a shed for the washer.

Pop had no dryer. Said he didn't need one as long as he had wind, but McCoy guessed that come winter, Pop might enjoy not having to wait until the pipes thawed to wash his dirty clothes.

The old man's routine was to wear clothes three days,

then wash everything together after he had a full load. That might explain why all his clothes had faded to dirt brown.

As McCoy began the painting, he thought he heard gunshots. Not close, but near enough to have been on Mason land.

But Pop's land was fenced with no hunting signs on every fence.

Another shot shattered the calm day. Definitely gunfire. Then several came in a row almost like firecrackers.

Panic sped up his heart and for a moment he couldn't decide what he should do. The trouble Pop had been guarding against may have found them.

McCoy knew little about guns. He'd gone hunting with men he'd worked with a few times, but he really didn't get the idea of killing deer for sport, and he didn't want to get close enough to a wild hog to shoot it.

He knew Pop didn't let hunters set foot on his property. If trouble had stepped onto Mason land, McCoy might have to make a stand.

Wait a minute, when did this farm become part of him? He was just recovering here, not guarding the place.

Before he could think about it, he noticed three little ginger-haired girls standing just off the porch. The first was Olivia, and the other two were each stair-stepped down a year or so in age.

Looking at the three, he had no doubt Leo had been right; there were fairies on Pop's land. Their sundresses were crisp and clean. All three had their hair braided down their backs.

"Morning, Sunshine," McCoy said.

She marched up on the porch and pointed at the two smaller clones of her. "These are my little sisters. They both belong to Sarah-Jane too, but they don't talk much.

They wanted to see Pop's broken grandson. I told them I have no idea where you came from, but they still have questions."

One of the new fairy girls was studying him and the other one was focused on sucking her thumb.

McCoy tried to keep his voice calm while more gunshots rent the air. "Hello, fairy girls. It's nice to meet you, but now is not a good time for a visit. Maybe you should go home and come back later." Their house was in sight of Pop's back door and in the opposite direction from where the shots came from. A path was well worn between the neighbors.

"We can't," Sunshine answered. "Mom told us to stay with Pop for an hour. She's entertaining Harvey. Probably a tea party."

McCoy raised an eyebrow. "Harvey doesn't have red hair, does he?" He tried to keep his voice calm as he tried to herd them toward home.

All three girls nodded, but not one of them moved an inch toward the path home or in the safety of the house.

He knew little about girls, but he'd seen commercials on TV. "I've got some cookies in the house. Would you ladies like to have a tea party all by yourselves?"

They all three nodded again.

Five minutes later, he put three cups, probably stolen from Denny's, and a plate of sugar cookies on the table. "When you finish, I'll get down Pop's dominos and let you build something. For some reason he's got three sets. I'm sure he won't mind if you mix them."

While the girls had tea that tasted just like Dr Pepper, McCoy decided to call his one friend, Sergeant Tucson Smith at the sheriff's office. He might know what to do.

Half a dozen words later, the sergeant said he was on his way.

McCoy heard three more rounds fired while he waited with the girls. He made sure they were well away from the windows.

As they played, McCoy checked the lock on the gun case. He made sure the girls were having fun and then said he was walking down to the gate to let a friend in. "Keep the pup in the house, girls. He needs you to play with him for a while."

Once again they all nodded, and the littlest one gave the puppy a cookie.

Before McCoy could limp to the gate a hundred yards down the road, Pop turned off the county road in another city truck that sounded like it had worse engine trouble than the last truck.

By the time he punched the gate's code, the sergeant drove alongside him, yelled a greeting, and then followed Pop in.

McCoy swore Pop was yelling questions before the truck's engine rattled to a stop. How many shots? Any very close together as if more than one shooter? Did McCoy hear anything else? Did the shots sound like they were coming from the road or the pasture?

McCoy had few answers, but that didn't stop Sergeant Tucson Smith from asking the same questions.

After a few minutes all three agreed McCoy would stay with the girls.

Tucson and Pop would drive the boundary of the farm looking for the source of the gunfire.

McCoy decided he was probably overreacting. It might be kids shooting rabbits or maybe someone on the neighboring farm doing some target practice.

Or, he thought as he walked back to the house, Olivia's mother might have had enough of entertaining Harvey and decided to kill the sperm donor.

As McCoy limped back to the house, he heard laughter. Ten feet closer he saw chaos and angel smiles.

The three little girls were sitting on the porch with yellow spots on their faces, arms, and legs. Even the puppy was covered in yellow paint.

Olivia laughed. "We've got chicken spots."

He saw the can of paint he'd opened just before they arrived. This was all his fault.

Pop and Tucson were back before McCoy could get the girls washed up. Yellow paint was pretty much on everything in the house. The floor. The walls. The furniture. The dog.

Tucson looked worried but didn't say a word about what they might have found when they'd driven all four sides of Pop's land. He just nodded once at McCoy as if to say they'd talk later.

The sergeant stayed outside making calls, but Pop picked up the littlest girl and headed toward the kitchen sink. He wiped a spot off her toe. He looked around and said, "You know, I like yellow. You might as well paint the whole room this color."

Then he leaned down to the other two girls' level and said, "How about I walk you three home? We'll stop along the way and pick flowers for your mom. When she was little, she'd come over here every spring and spread wildflower seeds. In another month I'll have so many folks from town coming out to see them, it'll look like a busy highway to my place."

Sunshine took Pop's free hand. "I need to talk to you about something. I'm old enough to count money now. I've been thinking that we should put a Kool-Aid stand at your gate. I would have asked your broken grandson if he wanted to help, but he thinks Dr Pepper is tea, so I'm not sure he could handle Kool-Aid."

"We'll talk about it on the way home." Pop used the wagon that had carried the puppies to haul the fairy girls home. The last little pup pounded along as if he was part of the parade.

As soon as the wagon was out of sight, McCoy turned to Tucson. "What happened?"

"We drove the perimeter. It looked like someone shot two of the donkeys your pop keeps over near a pile of rocks in the north quarter. The old man crawled through the fence and knelt by each one. I could see him patting their necks but I couldn't make out what he was saying."

The big sergeant was silent for a moment, then added, "I remember he had a small herd, even when I was a kid. Everyone knew he bought old donkeys and sometimes broken-down horses at the local auction. He thought they should live out their years in peace, running free. Some folks think it's a waste of grassland and money these days to keep them, but I don't understand why anyone would just shoot them. Sadler keeps that pasture locked. The shooters cut the fence to get close enough to the two donkeys. Both animals were shot a second time in the head." He hesitated. "We couldn't see the rest of the herd. They probably took off when they heard the shots. All I can figure is that when Sadler drove off his land this morning, they saw their chance. Probably didn't know you were here."

Tucson swore, then added, "From the footprints, I'd say there were at least two men, maybe a third who stayed at the fence line. This wasn't just someone shooting from a car for fun. This was planned out. We found a paper wrapped in barb wire. It was the latest offer for Sadler's land."

"You think they'll be back?" McCoy hated the idea of these strangers on the farm.

Tucson shrugged. "I'm not a cop, but I've got a few skills that might help." He looked out toward the clouds along the horizon. "This sure is a beautiful place. It makes me think of settling down. Strange how a man gets used to the noise of a town but when you're out in the open country it's like the silence has been missing from your life and you didn't know it."

"Not so quiet today," McCoy answered.

"These guys are probably hired to shake your grandfather up so he'll sell. They don't see the beauty of the land. They're working for someone who only sees the money to be made. I'm guessing they won't give up until your grandfather sells. They see him and the donkeys as just something in their way. The businessmen might never do anything illegal with their own hands, but they might hire someone to make their problem go away."

"Pop will fight," McCoy whispered. "And I'll be right by his side."

For a moment, McCoy was surprised by his own declaration. It came from some part of him that he didn't even know was there.

Tucson added, "Strange how a location calls to you. I've met people who have to be by the ocean or the mountain air. I've seen military men travel for twenty years and then one day it's like they find home. The developers don't know what this place means to Sadler."

"I've even heard some people say they love the noise of New York or the light in Paris." McCoy added, "But I never thought for me it would be rocky ground, wildflowers, and fairy girls running around."

Taking one long breath, Tucson came back to the problem at hand. "I called the vet. From the number of shots you heard, th1160

ere may be other animals wounded or dead. We need to search for them before dark. Sadler will be back by the time the vet gets here, and we can start searching. I'll stand guard at the road for now. Pecos is calling a few ranchers to come in on horseback to help. This place isn't that big, but it's rocky, uneven land. We should be able to cover it before nightfall. If the vet finds animals hurt, she'll do what she can."

Tucson frowned. "This doesn't make sense. The donkeys were tame enough to come up to the ATV when I went out to check on them a few times. I knew Pop has been harassed with developers wanting to buy his farm and told me he caught a few men on his land once last winter but I didn't think they'd go to this extent."

McCoy nodded. "Pop said, at first, they were from some museum, wanting to investigate what they thought might be a historical site. But he claimed they looked too rough to even know how to spell 'museum.'"

"I doubt these guys were curators." Tucson added, "I do remember when I was a kid there were tall tales about a treasure buried beneath the rubble on Mason's land. One of my English teachers made us read early newspaper accounts of several groups searching for the lost stagecoach gold. Mason played along and let the whole class come out to dig around the old site. If the middle school couldn't find gold, I'd bet it's not there but we had a great field trip. Finally, after Sadler's wife died, he stopped letting people dig."

"So, Sarge, you're saying it might be land developers or, on a long shot, museum nuts? But either way . . . why kill the donkeys?" His question seemed to echo between them, until McCoy decided to answer his own question. "Maybe . . . because Pop cares about the donkeys. Maybe they think that if they kill what he loves he'll lose interest in the farm."

As the morning passed, they were no closer to finding any answers. Tucson made a few calls to local museums, and they said they knew nothing of any digs going on in the area, but they'd check.

After the vet arrived, McCoy drove her to where a rancher found the small herd. One animal had been grazed across the back, and two donkeys had managed to run into the trees before they'd bled out and died.

When he saw Baylor cry after examining them, McCoy fought back the urge to give her a hug.

When the ranchers rode off to finish searching, McCoy let her know: "If you need a shoulder to cry on, I've got two open."

She managed a smile, her eyes still welling with tears. "I always cry when animals die."

"What about when snakes die?"

Baylor pushed her tears aside. "No, not snakes."

"Frogs? Wild hogs? Alligators?"

"No."

"Hamsters?"

"Maybe. Definitely cats, dogs, horses."

"Doc, you're a real softy," he said, satisfied that he'd given her a chance to recover.

An hour later it was getting dark and they'd found no more donkeys down. He took his time driving her back to Pop's house. Most of the Mason land had never been plowed. It was as natural as it had been a hundred years ago. Uneven, with the shadow of a road that stagecoaches had once rolled over. Nature's beauty was all he saw.

All his life he'd seen buildings, roads, bridges. Never just the land. Nature, the earth, had always simply been a blank canvas for what man created. He'd always seen buildings as improving the landscape, but now he wasn't so sure.

Baylor talked about what it must have been like long ago. She guessed that this small, rocky strip of land had been forgotten by the first settlers, not really good for farming or easy to fence, but somehow the wildflowers grew here. Masons must have liked it rocky.

McCoy told her what Pop had said about Sunshine's mother planting flowers here, and it turned out that her grandmother had done the same.

She agreed. "My assistant said she heard that Sadler Mason married Olivia's great-grandmother. She died the next spring, but she left Sadler with a son. Sadler scattered his wife's ashes across his land. That might explain why three generations of her kin living nearby dusted the place with flowers. They had no grave to take flowers to, so they brought seeds."

"I'd like to believe that." McCoy turned to face the wind. "You've just given me my first family story worth keeping. His wife was my grandmother, and she sleeps among the flowers."

"The fairy girls are your cousins." The vet laughed. "All I got in my family is drunks and vets, but you've got fairies."

McCoy wondered if his dad had ever heard the story. He'd told McCoy once that he'd grown up mostly traveling around, but Sadler had a place near Honey Creek where they'd stay some winters. McCoy's dad said he wasn't surprised when Pop retired there. He'd told McCoy that Sadler wouldn't sell the worthless spot of land no matter how bad times got.

They were almost back at the house and could see Pop sitting on his porch with a rifle across his lap. It had to have been over fifty years since Pop's wife died, but he'd never sell the land. His wife was there among the flowers and, in a way, he was still with her.

"Any chance you'd stay for supper, Doc?"

"What are you having?"

"Take-out. If you'll drive me into town."

"It's a deal." She picked up her bag and handed McCoy an envelope. "I almost forgot. The mayor gave this to the sheriff, who gave it to me when he heard I was coming out. She would have mailed it, but it would have taken three days."

"I'm not surprised. I've met the mailman." McCoy opened his mail. One page with a big *Thank You* written on it and a check for four hundred dollars.

Last year he'd made over a hundred thousand in pay and bonuses, but this one check made him feel rich. "I'm buying dinner."

When they stepped up to the porch, McCoy told Pop the dinner plan. Baylor patted Pop's hand and told him not to worry about the trespassers. The sheriff was making rounds past his place every hour.

"I'm not worried about the shooters," Pop grumbled. "I'm watching out for Harvey. I told him when I took the girls home that I'd shoot him if he set foot on the place next door again without a wedding ring in his pocket. He told me to mind my own business."

McCoy had to ask, "And what did you say, Pop?"

"I told him I'd be locked and loaded. This shotgun might not kill him, but it'll put holes in him from his red hair to his big toe." Pop laughed. "I'm hoping he tries me.

It'd be worth going to jail for a year or two, and you'd watch over the place while I'm gone. Harvey will either be married or dead by the end of the month."

McCoy started to remind Pop that he was leaving as soon as he was running full steam, but held back. Lately he wasn't so sure. His to-do list was getting longer, not shorter.

Maybe he should hang around and make sure his pop wasn't driven off his land. The old guy was tough, he'd fight, but he might not win the battle alone.

Chapter 33

Sergeant Tucson Smith

Saturday Night

The beer was cold. The guy singing had talent. The bar was almost a romantic place to be, with more couples sitting around than singles trading pick-up lines. But mostly, all Tucson could see was Jam.

His first date in ages.

Jam Mackenzie wore a blouse the color of her eyes that hugged her body and was low enough to tease his dreams. He had no doubt she knew exactly what she was doing to him. Well into their thirties, they weren't first-time lovers. Both had been on their own for years. She running a very successful café and he traveling the world in the army.

Both had dated seriously before, but somehow this was new. Maybe it was because they met in darkness and opened up to honesty from the first. She'd been his crying lady in the cottonwoods, and he'd been her soldier who came out of the river.

She'd been like a spirit, no more than a will-o'-the-wisp in the breeze that night, and she still didn't seem completely real. He'd always thought relationships simply grew, but with Jam he'd fallen for her at first sight.

He had no agenda tonight, no plan. He just wanted to be near her. In the months ahead, when he was flying for hours with nothing to see but midnight sky and oceans, he'd think of her. He sensed that she would always be a part of him. A memory he'd pull out now and then and smile. Maybe he'd even see her when he came back home for leave. They'd be more than friends, less than lovers.

Who knows, she might teach him what love meant.

If they'd met in the trees beside the river when they were in their teens, would they have been one another's first love? If their paths had crossed in their twenties, would their lives have blended or at least paralleled?

But now, in their thirties, both their lives seemed set in stone. She loved her small-town life. She was a success in her world surrounded by friends and family. He craved the adventure he lived. He traveled. His work was challenging, sometimes dangerous. He had no plan to stop.

They didn't fit together. Still, Tucson had never been drawn to a woman like he was to Jam.

In the low lights of the barroom tonight, she was playing with her wineglass and looking like she was trying to start a conversation.

He was happy just watching her, being close, knowing they were together.

"Any breaks in the cases piling up on the sheriff's desk?" she asked politely.

"Yes. Pecos finally got a lead on the girl who fell in the water. She might be from a town south of here. One of the deputies saw a report of a missing high school girl. Her parents didn't report her right away because they thought she was staying with her grandmother, which was always where she went when they'd had an argument.

"Pecos is questioning the parents tomorrow morning, but since the girl in the water disappeared on us, we don't have anything conclusive to tell the folks who might be her parents."

Jam frowned. "That's all you got to tell me, Sergeant?"

"Not much happening. Your turn. You hear everything in town while you're serving food."

Conversation didn't come any easier to her than it did to him. They were both straining for something to talk about.

Finally, she said, "I think I remember seeing you in school a few times. You were a few years younger than me, right?"

"One year behind you, but we ran in different circles. You were popular, into sports, even in the school play. I was in ROTC and skipped class every time I got the chance. I graduated a semester early so I could go in the army as soon as I turned eighteen." He brushed his hand over hers. "You were a Mackenzie. Everyone knew you. Your family is royalty in this valley."

He noticed how her blue eyes seemed to smile. She liked his touch.

"There were four of you Smith boys. I always thought you all looked alike." She laced her fingers in his. "You were the oldest. The ringleader."

Tucson laughed. "I felt like I raised my brothers. Maybe I did. I still worry about them. We all got our mother's dark hair and eyes. I don't remember her ever saying anything to me besides orders, so army life was home to me. I joined up first and my brothers followed. I started out as a marine but switched to the army. My brothers still kid me about it. We may not see each other often, but the last few years we've kept up with each other online."

She started slowly moving two fingers over his palm,

driving him crazy as she talked casually of his family. "I barely remember Pecos in school."

"He is several years younger. He went his own way. Only, like us, he left home as soon as he finished high school. The day after graduation he packed and walked out. As far as I know, my parents have never even checked on him, and he lives a few miles away from their farm." Tucson wanted to touch her all over as he held her hand. His body was still, but his mind was already making love to her.

For now, they'd talk. He'd watch how she moved, how often she leaned near and he'd test where she liked to be touched. They would have their date, talking of regular things, but he planned to move closer as the night aged. This woman drew him as no one ever had.

Tucson had played this game before. His light brushes would become bolder. Her voice would turn velvet. Only, now he didn't see it as playing. This time it was loving.

By the time they got back to the café, he'd be holding her against him. Whispering in a low voice. Looking into those laughing eyes. And by midnight they'd be making love in that little hideaway room on the second floor. Jam's long bare body would be beside him, warm and willing. He'd ask what she wanted and then give her far more.

His voice remained calm as he wished the midnight loving would come faster. First, they had to simply hold hands, laugh, get to know one another better. Small talk and big expectations to come. They'd make a memory neither would ever forget.

Tucson tried to keep the conversation going as he lightly moved his hand along her slender leg. "Sheriff LeRoy has his faults, but he helped Pecos get his start. Gave him a job as a dispatcher and that led to his interest in the law." Tucson laughed. "Of course, once he met Kerrie, she told him what to do. She was going to college and he had to go along with her."

Jam raised one eyebrow as his fingers trailed halfway up the inside of her thigh. "And you'll never let a woman own you, right, Sergeant?"

"Right." He'd be straight with her from the first. No promises he wouldn't keep. No matter how much he wanted her, when the time came, he'd walk away. "I remember you in school, Jam. You were Jessica then. I used to get you and your cousin Jennifer mixed up. Your hair was really long then, and when you rushed down the hall it would swing over your hips."

"You remember my hair?"

His grin was a bit wicked. "No, I remember your hips and a few other body parts. I was a teenage boy, what else can I say."

She blushed. "I don't remember ever speaking to you."

He brushed his hand over her leg, loving that she didn't shy away. "You said 'hi' to me once, but I didn't answer you."

"Why not?" She leaned closer.

"I was younger than you. You dated guys older than me. Jocks with cars and money to take you on a real date."

"A real date like this?" she asked as she leaned closer. "If I'd looked into your eyes, Tucson, I would have talked you into taking me out, even if you were younger."

He swore she was playing peek-a-boo with her breasts. Almost showing too much, not showing enough.

When he finally looked up, she winked at him, confirming his suspicions. She was thinking in the same direction he was. Without much thought about being in public, he closed the space between them and kissed her.

Their lips might be the only thing touching, but he maintained he could feel her with every cell in his body.

As he broke the kiss, he whispered, "A real date tonight.

A hundred times better than we could have imagined in high school."

"Way overdue." She stood and offered her hand. "A real date comes with a dance."

She moved into his arms. Close. Matching her steps with his. They knew dancing was simply the beginning of what was to come. He was near enough to smell her hair and begin to learn the feel of her breast brushing against him.

Tucson nestled his face against her throat loving the softness of her skin.

He hadn't recognized her at first a few nights ago but now he'd know her even blindfolded. The nice girl had matured into a beautiful woman. Not the kind of woman he would usually go for, he reminded himself, but maybe Jam was the kind of woman he needed in his life. Jam Mackenzie was smart, and funny, and sexy as hell, and she didn't even know it.

She wrapped her arms around his neck and whispered, "I'm starving."

Without turning loose of her hand, he headed out of the bar.

As the evening moved from dinner at a truck stop café thirty miles away, to driving a long circle around the small towns in the valley, they talked easy in low tones. He'd never remembered telling a woman so much about himself, his family, his work.

They stopped at Lookout Point to watch the night sky. He stood behind her, holding her against his chest.

They looked at the first stars as their bodies seemed to be blending. His body enveloped her with warmth.

"I feel safe in your arms," she whispered.

"You are," he answered. "The only thing I worry about is holding you too tightly."

Her laughter brushed against his ear. "If you do, I'll bite your ear."

Then the sweet girl in his arms gently bit his earlobe and the sergeant had to fight to keep his legs from buckling.

He kissed her playfully as they walked back to his car before he did something in public that should only be done in private.

On the drive back to her place, she told him her goal of someday owning an inn on land along a road called Sunflower Lane. The big old house had been built by her grandfather, but she planned to enlarge it by adding wings on both sides. There would be a dining room that would seat thirty and a parlor that would open up big enough to have a small wedding. Behind the house she'd build little bungalows hidden among gardens and trails where couples could walk and whisper of their future. It would be a sweet, calm place where all were safe.

She wanted it to be where young lovers would come to hide out and old lovers would come for Sunday dinner to remember. A calm haven. Meals would be served mostly to guests in rooms or on balconies, with the food prepared at the Honey Creek kitchen.

When Tucson pulled up to the café she was still talking. "But my goals may change. When I started at the café, I thought I'd just make the B&B upstairs, then I realized it needed to be more than a few rooms and I wanted something that was far more than just a place to spend the night. I didn't want just a place people stay while traveling, I want it to be the destination."

"You're a romantic, Jam, with big plans." He swept her hair aside and leaned over to kiss her neck.

"And you're not romantic?" she laughed as she climbed out of the car and he followed.

"Not at all. Not a romantic bone in my body." His hands brushed over her shoulder, then circled her waist. "Tell me more about your inn." He pushed the silk of her blouse back and kissed her shoulder as she unlocked the door. "I can't get enough of you, Jam. I want to hold you. Watch you sleep. Talk to you. Oh, one more thing. I want to make love to you."

She seemed to have trouble forming words for a moment. "The inn would be . . . a retreat . . . where people could come to relax . . . and unwind."

He loved that his touch was making her lose her train of thought. He pushed her bra strap out of his way.

"There . . . There." She took a breath and tried to continue. "There would be romantic walks and shady places to sit. Young couples could come to plan their futures and those who'd lost their partners would stay to heal."

He'd reached the swell of her breasts with his kisses. Every sense was coming alive in him and he knew the same was happening to her.

"I'd call it the Sunflower Inn . . . because the pasture has sunflowers lining the drive. And on Sundays lifetime lovers would return."

Her words were so soft he barely heard, but her body was warm and melting into him. All she'd have to do was step away, but she didn't.

"Tell me more," he whispered as he began unbuttoning her shirt.

"Sadler Mason's place is on the front side of the road."

Tucson stepped away just enough to see her face as his hand covered her breast.

She closed her eyes. "In spring all along Sunflower Lane's rolling land, it looks like a huge bouquet."

Tucson could almost see her dream, but he no longer wanted to talk. "Shush, darlin'. The time for talk is over."

Jam was lost in his dream now, as he distracted her by nibbling down her neck.

He couldn't lie to her. He was happy with his life, content, challenged, but she was like a piece missing that he'd never thought to want.

He straightened. "I'm about to get closer to you, Jam. Any objection?"

It made no sense. He didn't just want her. He needed her, and he'd never needed anyone.

She was becoming his "home." Not a place but a feeling. She was something he had never known to crave.

There was a whole world outside this valley, and he wanted to show it to her. They'd wake up in Paris and see the Eiffel Tower out their window as the sun rose, or walk the colorful streets of Tokyo, or float down the River Thames and hear Big Ben chime the hour. For the past dozen years, he'd explored alone. Now he wanted her with him.

Only she didn't want him. Oh, maybe to play with. To date. Maybe sleep with. But not to love. Her world was already full and he had the feeling she wasn't going to let him too close. Her roots were planted here and he had no roots. One night, or a few days may be all they'd have.

A memory, not a lifetime like some lovers get.

In a way, she was like him. Terrified. She was afraid to leave, and he was afraid to stay.

It was almost midnight when she unlocked the back door of the Honey Creek Café. They stood in the doorway and kissed like teenagers saying good night on the porch, then he lifted her in his arms and climbed the stairs without a word.

"Any objection if I sleep with you, Miss Mackenzie?"

"None at all. I was hoping our date might not end until breakfast."

They both kept their words light but the depth of feeling in her eyes might drown him. In the shadows of the bedroom he undressed her slowly as if the beauty was too pure to see all at once.

The time for conversation was over. Now all they wanted to do was hold on tight to one another for as long as this lasted. Reality would eventually pull them apart, but not tonight.

Tonight, they'd both pretend that dawn would never come.

They were young enough to believe in a dream for a while and old enough to know it would end as quickly as it began.

But for tonight, they wouldn't think about anything but being alive and almost loving someone.

Chapter 34

Melody Explores in Silence

As Melody Avendale watched the owner of the Honey Creek Café lock up the place at sunset and leave on her date, Melody began to make a plan. The owner of the café left with the big man who had pulled Melody out of the river last night.

A date, she decided. They wouldn't be back for hours.

Tucson and Jam had been laughing as they ran to the sergeant's car. They might be in their thirties, but Melody swore they were acting like teenagers.

For a while, Melody sat perfectly still, realizing she was totally alone. She could leave and look for Michael, but she'd have to be back before the owner returned.

Mike, her best friend, her one love, grew up in this town. He had explained that there had been two ways to get into the café when he was hiding out on weekends when his dad-of-the-month was drunk.

A few loose boards by the back laundry room that could be pulled open enough to slip in, and a window in the formal dining room used for parties. Mike said the latch had been broken for years and either no one but him noticed or no one bothered to fix it.

Mike had discovered the window as a kid. He'd stayed on the third floor for three days on his first visit. The owner must have inherited some money. She was cleaning this place up so she could open the café. Every day she tested recipes and then left them for the carpenters to have for lunch the next day. Mike would carefully slice off his supper once Jam Mackenzie left to go home at night.

He'd listen to her talk to people who dropped by her soon-to-be café.

Mike told Melody that he thought of the owner of the café as his almost-mother. She never knew he was there, but she was taking care of him better than anyone ever had.

When he was twelve and the café had been running for a few years, he sometimes stayed the night on the third floor, usually when his foster parents were on a rampage.

About then he discovered libraries. First the school libraries, then the public one on Main, and eventually the Clifton College Library where he met her every Saturday. As a kid, if he stayed lost in fiction, he stayed out of trouble. Between reading and sleeping on the third floor now and then, he made it through high school invisible to most.

Mike had told her about the time Jam had a date with a man she'd known in college. Mike had heard Jam telling a friend on the phone that the guy had just called out of the blue.

They'd almost caught Mike stealing supper when they came back to the café kitchen for dessert after their date.

He managed to hide in the corner of the landing. Halfway to safety on the third floor and halfway to the back door. Afraid to make a move, all he could do was watch them talking half a floor away.

Mike had only been twelve, but he recognized a jerk when he saw one. Jam's date mostly just bragged, and drank, and then bragged some more.

When she told her date it was time for him to go home, the guy said that it was too far to drive back to the city. He'd had too much beer to get behind the wheel. Then he laughed and said they were not finished with their date.

When she didn't see things his way, he slapped her hard and told her the night wasn't over yet, and called her ugly names.

Jam yelled for him to get out and the man started shoving her almost playfully. When she ran for the door, he hit her so hard she fell, sprawling across the floor.

He jerked her to her feet, grabbed her shoulders, and shoved her hard again and again toward the stairs. She fell against the stairs busting her lip and bruising her cheek. She began to scramble up the stairs to avoid his kicks.

She looked up as she got to the landing, her face bruised and bleeding. Her blue eyes stared straight at Mike as if she didn't believe he was real.

Michael nodded once. Letting her know he was on her side.

"Once she passed me," Mike had told Melody, "I stretched my body out as far as the shadows could cover me. When that jerk came storming up the stairs after her, I stuck my arm out and grabbed the cuff of his pants. Then I watched as his foot missed the next step and he went down, slamming against the wooden stairs so hard it echoed across the huge kitchen."

Mike continued in a whisper. "Jam's blood might be spotted on the steps, but several of the guy's teeth were also left behind. His face bounced like a basketball on each step as he skimmed down."

Mike smiled grimly as he told Melody the rest. "I slid back into my hiding place just as Jam appeared at the top of the stairs with a Colt that one of the Mackenzies must have brought back from the Civil War. After two missed shots, the jerk managed to get to his feet and run."

A few days later, Mike heard that some guy from Dallas was passing through town and had a wreck on the curve near the café. Broke one leg, shattered an elbow, and knocked most of his teeth out.

Mike had saved his almost-mother. Now that Melody knew Jam, she understood why Mike risked his life for her. Jam was kind.

In a way, the café was a part of their story now. She'd met Mike thirty miles away but she'd known from the first that he was one of the good guys in the world. No matter how hard it was, she'd wait for him. People say kids seventeen and nineteen can't love fully, but she knew that wasn't true. She loved Mike with all her heart.

He was kind also. His almost-mother must have taught him that.

Melody made her rounds of Mike's hiding places, then climbed back through the unlocked dining room window before Mike's almost-mother returned with the man everyone called the Sergeant.

As she passed through the kitchen, she collected her supper. No one would miss a glass of milk or an apple or muffins left over from breakfast. Jam always had snacks for the staff.

Climbing all the way to the third floor, Melody had eaten her only meal of the day. Then she began to explore her hideout before the sun's glow was gone. Last night it had been too dark. Now she wanted to learn the rooms so she could move about them when all turned dark.

At first glance she'd thought the rooms were empty, but there were signs that little girls had once lived in them.

Childhood drawings of castles inside an old wardrobe. Forgotten mirrors on the wall for people less than five feet tall. Pieces of furniture that were broken or too big to fit easily through the door were shoved into corners.

Melody, tired and frightened from being alone, sensed a sadness in the rooms. Vines had grown over the windows, so thick little light came in and a silent desolation lingered.

Mike once said that a few days after he'd saved the café owner, Jam had told everyone a stranger had broken into her place, and she had fallen while running up the stairs. That had explained her bruises and twisted ankle. She said that a ghost had tripped up the robber as he tried to follow her.

The sheriff wrote down the account as if it made sense. He bagged the teeth and took them to the traveler in a hospital. LeRoy must have figured that claiming a ghost saved her might not make Jam a good witness so he supposedly threatened the stranger while the guy sucked his meal through a straw.

Whatever ghosts that might exist on the third floor, Melody decided they must like her. They'd let first Mike stay and now her.

She pulled out her backpack from beneath a bay window, then decided to sneak back downstairs and find a blanket or an old towel to sleep on. If she hurried, she could take a shower before it got dark. She couldn't risk turning a light on.

Fifteen minutes later after she dried off and dressed, Melody began to explore the storage rooms on the second floor. From the looks of it, the Mackenzie family who owned this place never tossed anything away. Melody found boxes labeled *Grandma's rose dishes, 1975.* Mason jars filled other boxes. She discovered three bags of ladies' hats. They'd probably been beautiful sixty years ago, but now they looked a bit Halloween-y.

She had even found a wall of boxes labeled: *Jennifer*

Mackenzie. Will pick up. These fairly recently stored items might be useful.

Melody remembered Mike talking about how many Mackenzies there were in the valley. If Jessica was the owner, why had a Jennifer stored stuff here? Maybe they were sisters, or maybe she worked here. Maybe cousins. Maybe they'd started the café together.

Judging by the layer of dust on everything, this Jennifer person had left and probably wouldn't be back soon. No one would care if Melody borrowed a few things.

So, she went "shopping," promising she'd just use them, then pack them back.

First, a candle holder and three candles. Then a pair of jeans, two sweaters, socks, and a lightweight navy blue jacket.

When she leaned down to put on the jeans, she saw a plastic box under the frame of an old bed a few feet away. As she pulled the box out, Melody knew she'd found gold. Quilts. Old quilts, like people keep that are worn out and not in style, but were handmade by ancestors. Quilts no one used but they couldn't throw away.

These would work perfect. She carried the box up to the third floor and unpacked.

A yellow quilt with a sunflower pattern drew her attention. It was tattered in places. One side had ripped long ago and stitches, showing little skill, now held the pieces together. Though the red and blue materials were faded, the yellow patches were still bright. This would be her top blanket.

A quilt made of what looked like old overalls would be her mattress. There were two baby blankets in the box, but she left those alone.

The light was fading, so Melody tiptoed down to find matches for the candles.

No luck but she did find a flashlight by the back door.

She dressed in her borrowed blue jacket, jeans, and a baseball cap she'd found under the counter in a box labeled *lost and found*.

As the last light of day faded, she climbed out the dining room window and slipped into the cottonwoods.

It was time to look for Mike by the dock, just one more time. She'd learned to move in the night. Carefully, she weaved her way through the cottonwoods to the dock where Mike had told her to meet him.

She thought about how he'd told her she'd broken his heart for not agreeing to run away with him. With ketchup splattered over his heart, he'd played dead a moment before laughing.

She'd wanted to keep the shots of the roleplay she took with her new little camera, but the rain and the wind blew them away.

As she walked the empty dock tonight, a loneliness settled over her. Mike would come. Maybe not tonight, but he would come.

Melody might look younger, but she was almost eighteen now. She knew what she wanted. It wasn't so much that she wanted to leave her parents. It was simply she wanted and needed Michael in her life.

They'd had a hundred talks about everything, but that one day of freedom they'd shared in Honey Creek was enough to decide their future.

Chapter 35

McCoy's Inherited Enemies

Sunday

The old man was on the porch in his rocker when McCoy went to bed, and the next morning he was still there. The puppy that the fairy girl left behind was sleeping near Pop's feet. They seemed to be sharing one blanket.

Sadler's silver hair was wild, his eyes were even more bloodshot than usual, and his clothes had to be on their fourth day of wearing. Overall, he was starting to look like a Halloween decoration left out in the weather for years.

McCoy stepped outside with a cup of coffee in his hand. "You get any sleep, Pop?"

"Yeah, but I kept one eye open." Pop reached for the cup like he thought McCoy was room service. "I can feel it in my bones. They are coming back. I told the guys who wanted to dig that there was no treasure out there, but I could see it in their eyes that they didn't believe me. Some men will never stop being blinded by fool's gold. The developers are cut from the same cloth, I figure." Pop mumbled a few swear words. "The fortune hunters are dreamers chasing ghost stories, but the developers are businessmen. Far more dangerous. Last time I talked to them they hinted that my old donkeys might start dying. I think they thought I'd sell if I didn't have the herd. But, I'm not selling. Not ever."

"Don't you think it's time you told me the whole story of what is going on?"

The old man looked bothered. "Which one? This place has more stories than weeds."

"Start all the way back with the stagecoach one."

He leaned back in his chair, took a deep breath, and began. "A hundred years ago that pile of rocks wasn't nothing but a ten-by-ten rock house built for the station-master. Stage stopped just long enough to change horses."

Pop took a drink then continued, "Years ago there was a rumor that a strongbox was dropped off there. Legend was the driver feared there would be a holdup, so he left the box and the guard riding shotgun at the stone station. When the sheriff and his deputies rode out to get it two days after the stage got to town, they found a dead guard tied to a chair and the box was nowhere to be found. The guard had been tortured. They say his fingers were scattered around him and blood was on all four walls.

"It wasn't long before there were whispers that the robbers didn't get the box. Folks said one of the bandits went mad because he couldn't stop hearing the dead guard's screaming. Other stories popped up, but no one ever figured out what happened.

"Most folks believed the guard hid the box and died without telling where he hid it. The fellow who manned the station was found dead, tied to the corral gate with half a dozen bullets in him. Looked like he was killed when the bandits rode in."

McCoy leaned against the porch railing he'd fixed two days ago. "What a story, Pop. What happened next?"

"The story goes that men turned the station to rubble trying to find the strongbox. After a while people figured the bandits found the box and just killed the two men so there would be no witnesses. But back then outlaws tended to brag and there was never a word.

"The stage line changed the route because no drivers wanted to go past the remains of the station. My grandfather bought this place after World War One. Got it cheap because of the story. My dad grew up here. Both my folks were teachers here in the valley. They raised me here. About the time I was thinking of leaving home, they both died in a plane crash. After that, I just stayed."

This was the most Pop had ever talked. McCoy was finally piling up family stories. "Why did my dad leave?"

Pop shrugged. "Maybe he was bored. I knew he'd leave when he grew up, but I thought he'd come back. All the other Mason men have. I'm still thinking he will."

Pop stood and headed into the house, and the puppy followed. "I think me and the dog will have breakfast while you're here to keep guard."

"What are you going to feed him?"

"I'll have cereal and let him have the rest of the donuts. If we have takeout for lunch, get him a kid's meal. And don't forget the toy. The little girls like to play with them."

McCoy took Pop's place in the rocker and thought about the generations of Mason men who'd lived here. Pop stayed and married the girl next door. His dad couldn't leave fast enough, and now him. Would there be a next generation?

Picking up the rifle, McCoy rocked back in the porch chair. He'd always thought of himself as a drifter. It had always been his way of life growing up, part of his job since he was seventeen. Only now, would he stay, or run from this place like his father did?

This patch of land drew him somehow. If it came down to a fight, would he stand? Pieces of old movies drifted in his mind. He imagined a shoot-out, suddenly seeing himself in a Western. Maybe he was growing into the Stetson after all.

About the time McCoy was starting to doze off, Pop came back with a rain slicker. "You might need this. The sheriff said he's sending a deputy out to walk the spot where the donkeys were shot. Maybe we missed something. You might want to ride along with him."

McCoy limped into the house to get another coffee. His plan of daydreaming the day away was forgotten.

When he got back, the old man was watching the clouds. Pop didn't let McCoy get settled before he asked, "How you getting along with the vet?"

"Her name is Baylor, Pop, and since when did you get interested in me?"

"I'm not interested in you, boy. I'm interested in her. She's a good vet, and I don't want you breaking her heart."

McCoy laughed. He couldn't believe Pop, who hadn't asked how he was recovering, was worried about Baylor's heart.

"Now, McCoy, women ain't like us. They lead with their feelings. And they're smarter than us. Next time you get in an argument with a woman, give up quick. You'll be much happier."

"You an expert on women, Pop?"

Sadler must not have thought the question was funny. He turned and left saying he planned to take a nap.

McCoy relaxed back in the rocker. Pop didn't have to worry about the veterinarian. She wasn't likely to get involved with him.

An hour later the sheriff called and said they were not going to make it out to have one last look before the rain started. Apparently, some senior citizens were staging an all-night sit-in at the courthouse tonight. They were calling it a sleep-out for peace. To make sure everyone stayed awake, they were having pepperoni pizza every hour.

Evidently, grandparents going wild outranked donkeys being shot, but the sheriff did ask if McCoy had seen any more trouble or heard shots.

McCoy said he'd check on the herd before the rain moved in, but all was quiet.

They ended the call with the sheriff yelling for someone to stop swinging his protest sign.

To think he always believed small towns were peaceful.

McCoy decided to get out the ATV and go alone to check the herd. Pop needed some sleep.

The little donkey who was still alive after being grazed had been tame. How hard could it be to put a rope around her and slowly bring her back to the barn? He didn't like the idea of her being left out in the rain.

While he was out in the pasture, he took his time. He didn't expect to find anything, but it wouldn't hurt to look.

The story Pop had told whirled in his mind as he passed the pile of rocks left from the stage station. A strongbox filled with coins or gold. Outlaws willing to kill to get it. Two men dead. One shot and the other tortured.

It occurred to McCoy to wonder what could have been so important that they'd rather die than give away the hiding place? A million in gold?

One answer might be that there was no box. They couldn't have given up something they didn't have. They died because of a rumor.

Or maybe the stage driver left an empty box to get the outlaws off his tail. Or maybe another outlaw got there first, took the money so there was no box to find.

McCoy glanced at the rifle wrapped in a rain slicker on

the passenger seat of the ATV. He felt as if he was driving back in time.

Maybe he'd been reading too many of Pop's paperbacks.

As he drove over the rocky ground, thunder rolled far in the distance. Pop was right—in another hour it would be raining. The clouds made the colors of the land seem deeper. New grass was taking over where brown had been. For the first time he saw the true beauty of this place.

McCoy stopped the ATV and sat in the shelter of the trees, watching the slow rain. An hour passed, maybe more, and the sky turned even darker. But still, he waited.

Finally, he saw animals moving among the trees. The injured jenny was in with the small herd now. The bandage on her back made it easy to pick her out. The donkeys were calm around the ATV. These animals didn't spook like horses do, so moving slowly among them didn't send them running.

They reminded him of Pop. Old, stubborn, and a bit on the tattered side of life.

Cutting the engine, he climbed out and began to walk around them like he'd seen Pop do. They watched him and moved away when he neared but showed no fear. "Morning, guys. Just thought I'd come out and see how you're doing."

With Pop's old coat on, maybe McCoy didn't smell like a stranger. They began to let him into the herd.

He almost tumbled twice before he got close to the jenny but he kept going. He didn't come this far to give up on his mission. The bandage was waterproof so she'd probably be all right even if she stayed out of the barn. But McCoy would sleep better knowing she was warm and dry.

Darned if he wasn't turning into a mother hen.

Talking to her until he was close enough to loop a lead rope over her head, McCoy almost felt like a real cowboy.

As he stood near her and looked around trying to guess which way might be the easiest to take her back to the barn, he spotted a midnight-blue pickup parking at the fence line. It was too far away for the driver to see the house and his ATV was too close to the trees for whoever was in the pickup to notice it.

He stood perfectly still and watched the intruders.

Two men climbed out of the truck. McCoy realized that if he could see them, they could see him.

For a moment he thought they might be two deputies in an unmarked truck. But the sheriff had said his men weren't coming out.

McCoy leaned down, trying to blend with the herd.

One of the men yelled, "Let us on your land, Sadler. Talk to us and maybe we can make a deal. The money we're offering is twice what this rocky ground is worth. We need to wrap this deal up today. Time's running out."

Developers still wanting Pop's land. McCoy didn't know if they were better or worse than the treasure hunters.

"No," McCoy answered as he realized two facts. They were probably the men who'd shot at the donkeys, and Pop had faced them before because they called him by Pop's first name.

One more fact. They thought he was Pop. "Stay off my land!" McCoy yelled.

"You'll sell. They always do. In six months this land will be nothing but a road heading into our development. A hundred mini-ranches in the valley. You should be proud to be part of progress, not fighting it."

"No! Build your road to the highway somewhere else." This made no sense. Why would somebody be so determined? "Stay off my land."

One of the men yelled back. "We don't make that decision. We're just here to make sure you sell and my patience is wearing out. You're just another jackass in the way of progress."

McCoy stayed in the middle of the herd as the men turned back to the truck. As he began to pull the wounded donkey toward the ATV, she refused to move. He released the rope around her wishing he had time to walk her back to the barn, but he needed to get to his cell and call the sheriff.

These guys were playing hard ball. Millions might swing on this one piece of land. The old stagecoach route was still the only clear path. Rocky ground obstructed any other path to the land marked for developments.

He wondered how long these men had harassed Pop. How many months had the old man walked his land at night waiting for them to come? No wonder Pop had said this wasn't a good time for a visit.

Slowly, McCoy started limping toward the ATV. Over his years in construction, he'd heard of wars over one small piece of the pie. Two teams of developers with different visions who'd fight it out. Supplies being burned. Equipment damaged. Even a few fights. That was over one project, one building, but this might be a hundred times bigger.

A slow rain began to fall silently, turning everything around him gray.

McCoy thought the first shot was the pop of lightning. When he looked up, he saw the men had not been leaving. They'd been pulling their rifles.

Another shot sounded and one man yelled, "You're wasting our time, Sadler. How about I kill a few worthless donkeys?"

McCoy began swinging the rope toward the animals. They started to move as he herded them toward the trees.

One of the old donkeys fell a second before McCoy heard the shot. The animal tumbled, jerked once, then lay still.

Another shot.

Forgetting his broken leg, he ran for the ATV. Another donkey down. His death cry seemed to echo off the clouds.

The herd was moving faster now, into the trees. He reached for the rifle just as the last animals alive disappeared, hidden by branches and rain.

Just as he pulled Pop's old rifle to him, one more shot rang out. But it was too late to warn him. McCoy was already crumbling as pain sliced through his side and he landed hard on the rocky ground his family had owned for a hundred years.

The last Mason would spill his blood on Mason land.

He heard a pickup racing away, grinding gravel and sending rocks flying. The wounded donkey brayed a few feet from where McCoy lay. The earth settled into silence as the storm moved in and rain blanketed the land.

And then, he heard nothing.

Chapter 36

Mr. Winston and His Lilly

Winston heard the rain hitting the church roof, but he didn't care. Let it storm. Lilly was sitting beside him. She had on a spring dress with a full skirt. In the folds of her skirt, they were holding hands and no one noticed.

Each day he spent with her she became dearer to him. They had their own little jokes between them. Sometimes one word whispered would start them both laughing.

They were a couple now. People were getting used to them being together. The lady at the bakery even asked how Miss Lilly was doing when she bagged his scones. For years he'd bought one a week for his Sunday breakfast. Now he bought two because he knew Lilly would be waking up at his house.

They'd get up early, have coffee and a scone, then prepare for the Sunday dinner Winston often had for his friends. Lilly had worried that his friends might not welcome her, but he promised they would.

How could anyone not love Lilly? he asked himself. How was it possible that she'd walked through so many lives and never been seen?

There was only one thing to do about this oversight.

He'd just have to love her double time for the rest of her life.

This morning he'd driven her to church and parked close to the back door so she wouldn't get wet. Her whispered "thank you" made him smile.

When they entered, she turned toward the choir loft and he took his seat. He smiled and watched her organize the music, then she smiled as she walked toward him and sat so close, he could feel her warmth even though they weren't touching.

Winston didn't pay much attention to the sermon on heaven. He was already there.

Chapter 37

McCoy's Fall

The rain wasn't cold, but it seemed endless as McCoy lay in the mud. He drifted in and out of consciousness, and each time he came to it seemed colder. No, not just the rain. The whole world was getting colder.

Finally, he figured out it was because he was losing blood. The sky was almost black now and so was his world.

Using every ounce of his strength, he rolled to his side and crawled to the ATV. One hand's grip at a time he managed to climb in enough to reach Pop's old rifle. Slowly, as if the weapon weighed a hundred pounds, he finally pointed it at the midnight sky. He fired off three shots. SOS, he thought.

McCoy must have passed out after that, and when he woke again the rain had slowed and a slice of sunshine peeked between the clouds and the earth. He looked toward the house, but no one was headed his way. No one had heard. No one was coming.

Then, off in the distance, something was moving toward him.

A fox, a big rabbit.

McCoy tried to keep his eyes focused. After several minutes, he made out the animal coming at him. The puppy.

For a blink, he feared the men would come back and kill the dog. But, not even shots fired would have stopped the pup. He was running full out toward him.

McCoy slid down against the ATV and waited.

A moment later, the uncoordinated puppy slammed into his unharmed side and rolled several feet, then got back on his feet and seemed to shake off confusion.

The dog circled him a few times, picking up the scent of blood on his side, then crawled closer and licked McCoy's hand.

McCoy was getting colder, but the pain at his side seemed to be easing a bit. Closing his eyes, he tried to listen to the rain and ignore the pain.

The dog put his muddy paw on McCoy's face as if demanding his attention.

McCoy dug his fingers in the dog's fur and whispered, "I'm all right, pup. Don't worry about me."

"Like hell, McCoy. We're not going to stop worrying about you, boy. You look terrible." Pop's voice raged over the thunder. "We got to help you. Why else would I be out here in this damn rain?" Pop kept cussing as he poked around on McCoy. "Here I was just coming after my dog, and I happened to find you bleeding all over my slicker."

Pop pulled his jacket off and wrapped it tightly around McCoy's side. He used the sleeves to tie it in place.

McCoy gripped the ATV bar as Pop lifted him into the back, then Pop put the pup in beside him. "Hang on to that puppy. We don't want him falling out."

"Will do." McCoy tried to force away the pain.

Pop slapped McCoy's cell in his hand. "I found this on the rocker. Call the doc you're sweet on and tell her you're bleeding. Maybe she'll feel sorry for you and come out."

McCoy hit her number. When Baylor answered, he said in a forced calm way, "I'm at the farm. I'm shot."

He didn't have the energy to say more. The world was spinning as Pop drove toward home. Then, he gave into the pain.

He woke suddenly with lights flashing around him. He could hear Baylor yelling, but he couldn't move or put together her words. Shadows were circling him and Pop was ordering everyone to be careful of his boy's side.

Every time he tried to move, the doc yelled at him, but she never left him. If he recovered, he decided he'd kiss her. She was definitely a woman who needed to be kissed more. Of course, she probably wasn't interested in the dying guy who was bleeding all over her right now.

He not only had to get his life together, he had to find a life. Second plan, stop digging and start trying to get out of the hole he was in.

McCoy's last thoughts were of what he planned to do to Pop's house next. The fact that he was dying was too much to worry about.

Chapter 38

The Runaway

Melody Avendale figured out if she crawled to the far corner of the third floor above the Honey Creek Café, she could lean near a hole in the wall and hear people talking in the kitchen. The hole must have been a laundry chute or maybe a heating vent years ago.

She'd made her bed close to the small opening because hearing the voices made her feel less alone. Funny thing, her parents were always smothering her. No matter where she went after the age of ten, she'd always say, "I can go alone" and they'd answer, "We don't mind going with you, dear. We enjoy every minute with our only child."

Melody had been alone for a week now. She missed her parents saying good night every evening and asking if she'd eaten, like she might starve if they didn't remind her. She missed talking to someone. But the only person she ached for was Mike. The whole world just felt right with him nearby.

All the days in the library. All the lunches they shared. All the walks and talks. Light touches and warm kisses. All seemed scrapbooked in her mind. She could not picture a future without him in her life.

"I'll wait," she whispered. "I'll wait for as long as it takes." With no phone they had no way to talk. She just had to follow the plan. He'd show up.

Voices came up from below. Two men were talking about a shooting that had happened on the Mason farm. It wasn't that interesting to Melody. She liked it better when the staff laughed and joked, but since this was her only entertainment, she listened.

"Maybe it's me, brother," one man's voice downstairs said. "I swear nothing ever happened around here before I took over as sheriff. Just a quiet little town with a few speeders and kids drinking out in some farmer's field. Now I got old folks sleeping all over the first floor on the courthouse. A man shot on his own land. A runaway girl no one can find since you pulled her out of the river and pictures of a dead soldier spread out on the dock, who apparently jumped up and ran off. If it gets any worse, there'll be a *CSI: Honey Creek*."

Laughter came from the other man in a deep voice. Melody thought he sounded like the soldier who'd pulled her from the water a few days ago. It hadn't occurred to him to look for her one floor up from where he'd left her.

"Pecos, I can't help you much. In a few days I'll be leaving," the deeper voice answered. "How about we finish our coffee and start with trying to find the men who shot McCoy? He's the only friend I got in this town, and I don't want to lose him."

The sheriff's voice lowered, and Melody could barely hear. "I'll meet you at the clinic. McCoy should be out of surgery by now. He is young and strong. He'll pull through. While I check on him, you head over to Clifton to talk to a recruiter at the college."

Melody heard them moving around. Then, the one the sheriff had called "brother," added, "Don't worry about the senior citizens. It'll get cold tonight and that floor in City Hall will get icy. They'll all be gone by morning. The runaway probably went home and the soldier on the dock will still be dead tomorrow."

Suddenly all was silent. She heard a door close below.

The last words they'd said sank in. 'The soldier will still be dead in the morning."

She leaned back and closed her eyes as silent tears slid down her cheeks. She'd heard them talk about a soldier they'd called O-Positive, but she hadn't heard about him being left on the dock.

What if the dead soldier was Mike? Maybe something terrible had happened to him.

If he never showed up, she had no idea what to do. Melody didn't want to face life without him. He was kind and listened to every word she said. He cared about her and a few times he'd whispered that he loved her.

Melody loved her parents, but they lived in the world of museums and concerts. Any time the house was quiet, one of them would start a lecture. Most of the time she felt like she was living in the echo hall with dueling life lessons. She wanted to see the world. She wanted Mike. She might be seventeen, but Melody felt like she'd been old all her life.

She didn't want to go home, but she couldn't stay hidden forever. She'd search for Mike one more night. If he was nowhere, she'd have to find help. "He isn't dead," she told herself. "He can't be or my heart would have stopped beating."

But who could she turn to?

Only one person came to mind. Jam. Mike's almost-mother.

She'd know what to do.

Chapter 39

McCoy Broken Again

McCoy slowly came awake with a round five-feet-nothing of a nurse telling him he was in a clinic and he was lucky to be alive.

Since he felt like death warmed over, he didn't believe her. He'd heard the same talk a month ago when he woke up from the wreck. He felt like he was tied to one bucket on a Ferris wheel and every time it circled, his seat hit the side of a building.

Since he was awake, he decided to take inventory of what worked and what didn't. It might not be a bad idea to count his body parts to see if they were all there.

The little bowling ball of a nurse yelled as if his ears might have been damaged. "You've just been through surgery, Mr. Mason, to remove a bullet from your left side!" Then, like an angry mother, she added, "If you don't stay still, I'll strap you to the bed."

Not surprising, she asked if he knew what day it was, and he decided to go back under. Someone had stuffed cotton balls in his head. His brain was swinging on a cloud about a foot above his body and machines were beeping out the worst tune ever played.

He'd been here before and there was nothing worth seeing.

When he finally got the energy to open one eye, Baylor was sitting beside him reading what looked like a patient chart.

"Did you stitch me up, Doc?"

She grinned that half smile that was growing on him. "I wanted to, but Dr. Hudson said he needed the practice."

To his surprise, she took his hand. "Sadler had no trouble finding you, that pup was yelping like he was the one shot. I followed the ambulance in and met you guys at the house. While the EMTs loaded you, the old guy told me about five times that you were not going to die. As the ambulance pulled off, your pop ordered me to climb in and take care of his grandson because he had to stay behind on the land. He said you'd understand."

"I do understand. I would have done the same. Pop would be nothing but trouble here and someone needs to stay on guard. If no one was on the land, I have a feeling all the old donkeys would be dead by morning."

"You care about those donkeys?"

"Sure. They're Pop's first cousins." McCoy tried to smile. "I come from a long line of stubborn jackasses."

She picked up her phone. "I'll call and tell Sadler that you came through the surgery just fine, but you look terrible."

"Pop doesn't have a cell or an answering machine. If he's out on the porch, he won't hear the house phone."

"He's got your cell." She smiled. "He said you wouldn't need it. I showed him how to call me and answer if it rang. He said that's all he needed to know."

Then, the doc surprised McCoy by kissing him on the

cheek before she dialed Pop. He decided not to get his hopes up. Maybe the vet kissed all her patients.

McCoy listened while Baylor answered all of Pop's questions. This was the second time he'd been in a hospital this year and February wasn't even over. At this rate he didn't see any chance of making it alive much past June.

His brain was probably dead already. All he could think about was that if he got one dying wish, he wouldn't mind another kiss. Maybe her aim would be better the second time.

With all his problems circling around him, McCoy could only wonder about what Baylor's lips might taste like.

She dropped her phone back in her pocket and smiled at him. "Sadler said he's calling John."

"John who?" McCoy really didn't care who Pop called. All he wanted to do was drift beyond the pain.

"John, his son. John, your father." She looked at him as if she thought he had brain damage.

Before her words made sense, Tucson stormed into the room and started firing questions like McCoy needed to testify to his own death before he drifted off.

"What did the men who shot you look like, McCoy?" Tucson moved closer. "Come on, McCoy, stay awake. I got questions. Have you ever seen them before? What was the make of the pickup? Color? Year? Anything you remember, like a 'baby-on-board' sticker on the back or a cracked taillight?" Tucson stopped to swear then asked, "What did they say exactly? Did they mention who they were working for?"

This was reminding McCoy of school. All he had to do was make a seventy to pass. Besides, Tucson was asking questions without offering much break for McCoy to answer, so eventually he closed his eyes figuring it was nap time.

Evidently, Tucson was looking for a higher score. The big sergeant leaned closer and yelled louder, repeating the questions.

Mini-nurse rushed in and started yelling for Tucson to be quiet. He shouted back that this was police business and she needed to stand down.

He bent to her level and they faced off for a fight. McCoy had to open one eye to watch.

Despite the pain, McCoy smiled. The sergeant looked huge next to the nurse, but McCoy's money was on her.

Tucson stood his ground and kept firing questions as she yelled.

Finally, McCoy snapped and said, "I don't know any more, Sergeant. They were shooting at the animals and I must have looked like one. I don't think they were trying to kill me because when I was tumbling, I saw them running. Seems to me if I was their target, they would have stayed around a minute to make sure I was dead. I guess I took a bullet for one of the donkeys."

Both Baylor and Tucson laughed and agreed with him. Mini-nurse huffed and left, obviously deciding they were all crazy.

McCoy moaned, "I'm starting to sound like Pop."

To his surprise no one was listening to him.

Tucson was leaning down to kiss the doc on her forehead like they were friends, then whispered just loud enough for McCoy to hear, "Take care of him, Bay."

Baylor kissed Tucson on the cheek as they hugged goodbye at the door. "I'll watch over him, Tuc. When we got there, he was all blood and mud, but he was fighting.

Once he settled down, I gave him a sponge bath as they were prepping him for surgery."

"If he doesn't behave let me know," Tucson said. "I'll beat him up for you. He may be my only friend in town, but you've been my partner since grade school."

"I'll watch over the cowboy, Tucson. But I hope you'll stay around for a few days so we can catch up. I've missed our talks when I was in grad school and you were on assignments all over the world. Midnight talks about everything that lasted until dawn."

"Will do," the sergeant said a moment before he vanished.

McCoy stared as she walked back to his bedside. He didn't know which question to ask first. The doc was a total mystery to him. "You gave me a bath and I missed it?"

She laughed. "I enjoyed it. You are one good-looking man, all over. It was a change from most of my hairier patients."

"You are kidding, right?"

"You'll never know."

He stared at her. "I don't care what you did to me. After all you are a doctor and I'm more animal than man most days. Anyway, you're miles out of my league so don't tease me with a fantasy that will never happen."

She sat on the corner of his bed. "Why do you say that? We're about the same age and I thought we had a lot of things in common. We both love animals. You even took a bullet for one."

"But that's as far as it goes, Doc." McCoy had just enough drugs to be honest. "First of all, you probably have twice the education I have. Second, you've got a job. Third, I'm guessing you've got a home. And last, I've developed a tendency to break. The only way I'd get to hang around you, lady, is if you adopted me as a pet."

Baylor laughed as if she thought he was kidding. "I have a feeling that little fairy girl of yours will be giving you a lecture as soon as you get back. She worried over your leg and now you've given her bullet holes to fret over." Baylor patted his hand. "You think we could work on being friends? If we both have Sergeant Tucson Smith as a friend, we might be more alike than you think."

"I'd like that, Doc."

She smiled. "Call me Baylor, McCoy."

"Will do."

She moved near the window. "I'd better call Sadler again. I'd bet you Tucson is headed out that way to ask more questions. I should probably warn the old guy."

"Tucson will have to follow Pop around as he's patrolling his land. It's all he's got or cares about."

"No, McCoy." She looked directly at him with those pale blue eyes. "Since he figured out your phone, he's been calling me every twenty minutes. He's got you to worry about."

McCoy closed his eyes. "I don't like the idea of Pop being out there alone."

She patted his hand again. "He's not. Pecos assigned two deputies to stay with him. Their cruisers are parked by the gate. Last I heard, they were planning to play poker all night. Your grandfather will be fine tonight, and with luck you'll be back home in a few days."

He hurt all over and now worry was washing over his brain. "I know he'll be okay. He's tough." Caring about someone, really caring, was new to McCoy and he wasn't wearing it well.

"Your pop said the same thing about you."

When she started the patting again, something made him push her hand away. "I don't like to be pampered," he said, suddenly irritated. "Good news or bad, give it to me straight."

She moved away. "Sorry about that, McCoy. I'll remember. No touching. No sugarcoating."

Before he could apologize to her for snapping at her, a white-haired man rushed in. There was no doubt he was Dr. Hudson.

"You're one lucky man, McCoy. Bullet went in and came out without hitting anything vital," the doctor announced as if nothing was happening in the room. "Pretty much all I had to do was stop the dripping and my job was done."

McCoy knew it couldn't be that easy if the surgery took two hours, but he didn't ask questions. He'd learned from the Houston hospital that he wouldn't understand the answer anyway.

Dr. Hudson checked the charts, then the machines, and finally the patient.

"You're my tenth shooting patient, you know. I wanted to keep the bullet, but the sheriff says I have to turn it over. I've delivered almost a hundred babies and believe me it is far bloodier than a gunshot. Unless it's a shotgun fired against a head. Brains fly everywhere." The doc shook his head. "Never want to see that again."

He kept talking as he checked the bandage. "The last bullets I removed were from the Winford brothers. They were out hunting and Van was swinging his rifle and accidently shot himself in the leg. His brother, Tad, carried Van back to the house, and while Tad was showing his mother how it happened, he shot his own leg. The mother was so mad, she begged the sheriff to keep them in jail until the desire to kill her offspring subsided."

McCoy had no idea if the doctor was crazy or brilliant, but the seasoned professional made him laugh, which eased his pain and his irritation. He'd forgotten what he and Baylor had been arguing about, but he did remember she suggested they be friends.

That would be great.

He was almost asleep an hour later when Baylor walked back in. She looked tired as she settled into a chair as if she'd been ordered to stay the night.

"You don't have to stay, Baylor. I'll be fine."

"I promised Sadler I would watch over you, but don't worry, I won't pat on you."

He silently called himself every name he could think of, then whispered, "I didn't mean to be a bear. I'm sorry. My problem, not yours. I grew up with a dad who never hugged me or even spanked me for that matter. A pat on my arm seemed more an insult than comfort. Like I'm a kid, or one of your hairy patients."

She glared at him for a while, then moved closer, more interested than angry now. "I didn't mean it that way and you are an idiot. I meant it as comfort, as affection. I thought we were becoming friends."

Baylor shrugged and folded her arms over her chest as if protecting her heart. "Maybe I'm the idiot. Maybe I should have had a few more dates in college and not studied all the time. You read me wrong and I was way off on understanding you. From now on we'll be friends with six feet of boundary between us. Eventually, I might warm up enough to shorten the distance to five feet."

"We'll be friends . . . like you and Tucson are? What's

going on between you two?" McCoy hated the way he was acting. "Forget I asked. None of my business."

"Ah," Baylor said. "Tucson . . . He and I were in grade school together. Both quiet but somehow we liked talking to each other."

She smiled. "We had a few classes together and liked to pair up on projects. He was the only friend I had really until I got to college. I remember once he parked out front of my house until I came out. He got out of his old pickup and asked if we could talk. He wanted to know what I thought about him going into the service as soon as he graduated.

"I told him about my dream of going to vet school and we decided to keep up with each other.

"He was my first Facebook friend. While I was in vet school, he was traveling the world but we always kept in touch."

The third time she brushed McCoy's forehead with a cool towel, his eyes crossed. "Want to tell me what you're doing?"

"Just making sure you don't have a fever. Are you on Facebook?"

"I keep meaning to be, but I've never got around to it. I'm a bit of a workaholic." It crossed his mind that she was asking questions to keep him awake. "I rarely keep up with guys I work with unless they show up on another site."

"What about keeping up with school friends or meeting online and getting to know someone you might want to date? Everyone does that these days."

"If I need a date, I go to the nearest bar."

"How is that working out for you?"

"Not great."

She moved away, walked the few feet to her chair, and sat down.

He dropped his head back and stared at the ceiling. Anger and frustration fought over the pain in his side to control his mind. She had no right to judge him. He was doing all right. "I get it. You're one of those women who wants to hold hands, cuddle on the couch while you watch a movie no guy would watch. You like candlelight dinners and long walks in the rain. Passion has to come one drop at a time until the poor man goes mad."

She leaned the chair back and pulled her blanket around her as if it might protect her. "And you are the man who walks into a bar, picks out the woman you're going home with before you even talk to her. No romance. Just something like, 'How about we get out of here and get naked?'"

"You guessed it, Doc. Sometimes I don't even ask their names." He was exaggerating, but at the moment he couldn't remember the name of his fiancée with the soft hair.

"What is going on?" The question was meant for her but he could ask himself the same questions. Maybe they were both tired and worried about Pop. Maybe he needed to be mad at the world right now.

His life was a mess and now, somehow, he'd dropped into Pop's life and that was falling apart.

McCoy looked over at Baylor. She was curled up in a ball in the big recliner, her hands clutching a blanket. She looked so small. He saw where his blood had stained her shirt. Her hair was a mess and her clothes were wrinkled. She had no makeup on and freckles spotted her cheeks and the bridge of her nose.

Damn she was cute but she'd already typed him. Fat chance of them being friends. If he had any brains left, he'd keep it strictly professional.

But, he watched her. At first, he thought she'd gone to sleep. Her eyes were closed and she wasn't moving.

Then McCoy realized she was crying. This gentle soul who thought she had men figured out. This workaholic with angel eyes was crying and McCoy guessed he was to blame.

He decided to join the crowd wishing he was dead.

Chapter 40

Sergeant Tucson Smith

Tucson drove the thirty miles to Clifton College, parked, and wandered around the small campus until he found Captain Baden Puller in a third-floor recruiting office. He might be fifty years old with gray hair, but he was solidly built and looked combat ready.

Puller stood. "I've been expecting you, Sergeant Smith. How may I help you?"

They talked for a few minutes over a cup of coffee, telling each other where they'd been stationed, as soldiers do. Tucson figured the ritual was a way of establishing a bond, a brotherhood.

Tucson then lifted a folder and pulled out the blown-up copies of the photos from the dock. Blood all over his heart. Dog tags. O-positive blood type showing on his tags. All other information blocked by blood.

Captain Puller was immediately totally engaged in the mystery.

"We're guessing they were taken a week or less ago. We matched the background of the trees and the water level. Probably last Saturday or Sunday."

Tucson began his full report. "The dock was completely

cleaned before anyone saw anything. We roped it off as soon as we saw the photos but found nothing. It was probably too cold for kids to swim. I did find a footprint at the river's edge. It could have been our supposedly dead soldier rushing away.

"The damaged photos were found scattered over the dock. No man has been reported missing that matches this man on the dock. It might have been a prank, but if not, I need to find this guy, dead or alive."

The recruiter studied the shots as Tucson answered questions.

When the captain finally looked up, he asked, "How old are you guessing he is, Sergeant?"

"Young. Not more than twenty."

"How did you come to that conclusion?"

"No chest hair. No scars. Soldiers tend to collect scars and tattoos the longer they're in."

"I agree." Captain Puller glanced once more at the photos. "He looks familiar. I'll check my records. If he came to the valley to die, maybe he was coming back home. Give me an hour."

"Will do. The sheriff in Honey Creek wants me to drop off a set of photos with the campus police. Maybe one of them might know the kid. Like you, I've got a feeling he's from around here just because he knew about the dock and that no one would be there on a cold dawn. It was far enough from town to be abandoned, yet close enough to walk back to a parked car if he faked his death, or float down the river and climb out wherever he stashed his car.

"I don't think he swam, Captain. How would he keep the photos and camera dry? Of course, if someone carried off his body, he might have had a boat waiting. But why stage the whole scene, photograph it, then carry the body off? If it was a murder, why take trophy shots and not leave the body?

"The bare footprint and type O-positive blood splattered by it, suggests to me that he is alive, Captain Puller, but I have no proof."

As Tucson stood, the recruiter admitted, "Something's not right about the shots. He might have blood on his chest, but he just doesn't look dead. I'm not an expert, but this crime scene looks too clean. How'd you find these shots, exactly?"

"They were scattered on the dock. Most were ruined by the rain and wind."

Puller asked, "Maybe we should question the deputy first on the scene again. Maybe he forgot one little detail."

Tucson couldn't believe he hadn't asked Pecos. It was routine to take the facts down twice.

"It's worth looking into." Captain Puller lined the photos on his desk. "The army is not going to be happy if they find out he was trying to fake his death just to get out of the service. It'll mean more paperwork for Uncle Sam. I'll do what I can to find an ID."

"See you in an hour."

After leaving Puller, Tucson walked across campus and handed over the other set of photos to the college policeman on desk duty.

The middle-aged officer looked too tired even to answer a phone.

"Hard day?" Tucson asked.

"Every time I work the weekend shift, I swear I'll never have any more kids. You spend eighteen years raising them, then send them off to college where they spend all your money while they're going crazy." The campus cop glared at him. "You got any kids?"

"No, I guess I was lucky. I raised my little brother. You might know him, Sheriff Smith."

The guy seemed to wake up. "Of course, I know Pecos. He went to school here. He's a hero, you know."

"I know." Tucson mentally patted himself on the back. He was suddenly in with the campus police, one of the family. This office would give him all the help he needed. The sleepy policeman was now a part of Tucson's team.

Now he studied the photos.

The cop didn't recognize the soldier in the photos, but he said he'd pass the file to the chief. "Right now, he's got his hands full. Parents of a missing girl are in his office. Since they are both professors, they think it's only fair all the campus cops in the state start searching. I tried to tell them that she's a teenager. Running away is what they do. Run away. Get drunk. Wreck your van with half a dozen of their friends inside."

Tucson grinned. "How many kids do you have?"

The desk clerk frowned. "Got four and this youngest one may be the death of me. He calls me 'old man' and never answers any questions. I swear if I asked him if he was alive, he'd just glare at me."

"I know how you feel, pal. I fished a girl out of the river a few days ago and she disappeared before we could get any information. We don't know if she was a runaway, or trying to commit suicide, or just an embarrassed local kid who walked too close to the water."

"What did she look like?"

"About five foot five with reddish hair, but that may have been the mud she was covered with. We thought she might have been looking around the dock for our dead soldier, but that's a long shot. But why look after dark?"

Tucson and the clerk shook hands, then Tucson added, "I need to get back to the recruiter. That's my best chance of a lead, but keep in touch. You might just be the one to find the missing piece of the puzzle."

Twenty minutes later, Tucson stopped at the coffee shop before heading back to the recruiter. He needed to wash down the taste of the recruiter's weak coffee. After he downed a few of the shop's muffins, he started missing Jam's cooking.

Trying not to keep smiling over midnight memories, Tucson stepped into the army office.

Captain Puller was frowning. Before Tucson could say a word, the captain said, "Very funny, Sergeant. I don't have time for games."

"What games?"

"A boy just turning eighteen enlisted last year. Michael Wes Alderton. I swore him in myself. Nice kid who didn't look the least bit frightened. I remember him because he had no one with him. Sometimes we get the whole family in this office."

The captain pushed a file over. "That's him in your pictures, but he's very much alive."

Puller tossed the bag of photos back across his desk. "I made one call. Michael Alderton had reported for duty, on time, every morning last week. He even pulled an extra guard shift this weekend. You have no dead soldier. In fact, Michael will be deployed within a month with his team. The soldier has a perfect record." The captain ran his fingers through his gray hair. "All I can think is he must have been messing around or very drunk when he took these but he tossed them and reported to work. I see no crime here."

Tucson wasn't ready to give up yet. "Did Alderton have O-positive?"

"He did, but, Sergeant, it's the most common blood type."

There was nothing left for Tucson to do but thank the

captain for his time, pick up the photos, and head for the door. Apparently, he and Pecos had worried over nothing. The young soldier was manning his post.

At the door, he turned. "Captain, may I ask how sure you are that those pictures are of Michael? There was blood on his face in all but one shot and in that one he is not facing the camera."

"I'm ninety-five percent sure. See the bridge of his nose. I remember him asking me if the bump from a break would keep him out of the service. Same build. Same light brown hair. Same nose. No clue why he wasted his time taking pictures, but as far as I know it's not illegal.

"And another thing, the kid was bright. Asked me questions I had to look up. I remembered him saying he planned to make the army a career."

"Thanks," Tucson answered. "Sorry to bother you, Captain."

Puller had settled down. "It was just some kind of prank. It's my guess he never meant for anyone to see the pics. He tossed them or accidentally dropped them. A prank is far better than a real dead body."

"Can't argue with that." Tucson saluted and left.

As he walked back to his car, it bothered him that this Michael might have wanted the pictures to be found. Had he planned to fake his death and backed out, or had he planted the photos because he knew deputies routinely checked the dock?

The kid was from this valley. He probably knew that the deputies circled the dock for any evidence of drugs. Maybe he just wanted to worry the new sheriff.

Only problem was the captain's Michael didn't seem the type to cause trouble.

Tucson drove back with more questions than answers.

When he walked back into Honey Creek's sheriff's

office, he realized he was starting to feel like the station had become his new home. He was even thinking like a local. He wanted to know what was going on.

He didn't have to wait long. By the time he poured his third cup of coffee for the morning, every phone in the place was ringing.

The news that McCoy Mason was in the clinic recovering from a gunshot wound had spread.

Tucson swore Sadler Mason's grandson was suddenly everyone's best friend. McCoy had not set foot in Honey Creek until a week ago, and now everyone knew him and they all thought they should check up on him.

Betty, the dispatcher, must have decided she had the power to assign Tucson to the information desk. Since they didn't have one, he just wandered around picking up phones. All he had to do was man the phones Betty relayed to him and handle any walk-ins.

Two drunks came over from the pool hall claiming they remembered McCoy from their high school football days and wanted a report on how he was doing.

The grocer came in to ask if he should deliver a week's worth of supplies to the Mason farm. He claimed he knew what Sadler bought every week.

The Baptist "Onward Christian Soldiers" group offered to sit with McCoy and sing.

Tucson figured that if McCoy knew how many people were worried about him, he'd run full out back to Houston, even with a broken leg and a few bullet holes in him.

About eleven o'clock Betty put her tenth call through to Tucson. She'd given up on explaining who was calling. She just yelled, "Phone, Sergeant! Call coming in from Alaska."

Tucson took the call, and immediately said, "McCoy is recovering. Probably will be out of the clinic soon."

"Good," a gravelly male voice answer. "I need more details. I'm his father. Name is Johnathan David Mason. I go by J.D. or John to everyone but my father."

"Yes, sir, Mr. Mason." Tucson decided the middle Mason was no more friendly than the older or younger one.

J.D. was all business. "Now it's my turn to ask the questions. Where was he shot? When will he get out of the hospital? Give it to me straight, Sergeant."

Tucson knew how to give the facts. "He was shot on your father's land. One shot, entry and exit wounds. We have two deputies at the farm with Sadler, in case the men who shot McCoy come back. The doctor wants to keep McCoy in the clinic for twenty-four hours. If any trouble appears from the wounds, they'll take him to the hospital fifty miles away. If he's doing well, I'll be riding home with him in the ambulance tomorrow. I'm a friend of McCoy. It is my understanding that your son came to Honey Creek to recover from a car wreck. Head injury and broken leg. Because of that broken leg, he wasn't running full speed when he was shot."

There was a long pause, then McCoy's father asked, "How is the old man?"

"Sadler Mason is fine. Mad as hell. He wants to be with his grandson, but he thinks he has to guard the farm. So, he stayed to walk his land but the old man calls into the hospital every twenty minutes to check on McCoy, then he calls me and lets me know how 'the boy' is." Tucson barked a laugh. "Then the old guy cusses me out for not finding the shooters yet."

There was another long pause. "When I got home from work last night, I had a call from my son's number. It was Sadler. He simply said, 'Come home, son.' I've booked my flight but I wanted to know what I'm walking into. I'll rent a car and be in town by noon tomorrow."

Tucson told the truth. "You'll be walking into a hell of a mess."

"Then I'm needed."

The phone went dead. Tucson had just encountered his third generation of Mason men and none seemed friendly enough to talk to. He could hardly wait to see the family reunion.

Hours later and more calls than he could count, Tucson called it a night. He wasn't on the clock so what did it matter? For once he had somewhere else he'd rather be.

On Sunday night the café usually closed early and he planned to be alone with Jam. He wanted to talk about how they'd make love and then spend half the night opening up to one another. Even when she fell asleep, he'd hold her close, knowing that he'd found a rare treasure.

She was open to his touch, but he knew she was holding back. He knew she didn't trust him completely. Maybe she'd been hurt. He'd tell her she was safe with him. He'd never hurt her, but he wasn't sure she believed him.

It made no sense. When they made love, she wanted him near. It was almost as if she wanted a lover but not a friend.

One more question had been worrying at him. Why had she been hidden away in the cottonwoods when he'd stumbled on her? Jam had it all together. She'd reached one goal of starting the café and now she was dreaming of starting another business.

Was she crying because she was missing something in her life? No children. No marriage. Why had she looked so broken?

He'd let her know that for the first time he wanted to build something lasting with a woman. Since he'd left home Tucson had been a soldier, but now he was starting to see a life beyond the military. It might just be seeing each other every few months, or it might be much more.

She'd let him come easy to her bed, but he doubted she'd let him come into her heart.

Could he be with her, knowing he was falling in love with her, if she only allowed less?

This leap he was about to make frightened him more than any assignment he'd ever had.

Chapter 41

McCoy's Recovery

Monday

McCoy had no idea what time it was. Near dawn Monday, he guessed. The beeping machines had kept him awake most of the night.

Baylor was still asleep in the big recliner by his bed. She looked younger than thirty. More like a teenager than a veterinarian who owned her own clinic. Her black slacks had dirt stains, probably from when she'd knelt in the mud over him. Her shirt was spotted with his blood.

She'd been the one he'd called for help. She was the one who'd stayed through the night.

And how had he repaid her? He'd teased her about being a dreamer, a romantic. It occurred to him that she might someday find a man who loved her enough to play that role. Some guy who would remember to bring her flowers on her birthday and every anniversary. Someone who'd know how to say he was sorry and mean every word.

Not anyone like him or Sergeant Tucson Smith, but maybe a poet or a writer. Most of them lived in fantasy

even after they put their pens down. Or a singer who'd
write her a song. Or maybe one of the firemen he'd met the
night he'd fixed the elevator. They all seemed like nice
guys and none of them cussed much. Everyone knew
firemen cared about people. She cared about animals.
They'd make a great pair.

Yeah, a fireman. A man who'd never make her cry.

He almost laughed at himself. Since when had he
become a matchmaker?

McCoy felt irritated just thinking about her with someone else, but he wasn't the kind of man for her. They were
just two different people who happened to pass one another by accident. They were both attracted to each other,
but they would never be a match.

She'd lived a sheltered life. He'd even heard her say that
she should have dated more in college and studied less.
McCoy could almost see her at every age. Always kind,
helpful, caring, but never wild or even sexy. She was cute
and maybe she was right about them being friends.

He lay still, pretending to be asleep, but inside he decided the car wreck and the bullets were slowly draining
what sense he had left. He'd be so dumb when he got back
to the farm, Pop would probably plant him in the ground
and see if he'd grow.

He leaned back and tried to remember what Baylor had
talked about last night. He'd described her as a woman who
wanted to be courted with flowers and candlelight.

How could that be so hurtful? Those kinds of women
are just romantics at heart. He might not like to play that
game, but she could if she wanted to. There were plenty of
men willing to send flowers and write love letters, he
guessed. How was it possible that she hadn't found one?

There he went again, trying to help her find a man.
McCoy decided he need to get out of this town and go

back to only talking to women in bars. He never wanted to be tied down with a wife.

McCoy studied her. She'd made it pretty plain she didn't like him, but yet, she'd stayed last night to watch over him.

In the stillness of the room, a truth came to him as he watched her. Dr. Baylor Blanton might be a dreamer, but no man had ever written her love letters or brought her flowers. He'd bet on it.

She had a big heart without anyone to share it with.

All McCoy had ever wanted from a woman was someone to spend a little time with, but with Baylor it would have to be love.

McCoy wasn't sure what love was like. He'd used the word a few times before. Sort of like, "Of course I love you, baby. What's not to love?"

Love was something he knew nothing about and probably never would.

He tried to go back to sleep, but dawn was shining in his window and he had never been one to waste daylight by sleeping.

Mini-nurse stormed in with a breakfast tray in one hand and a portable urinal in the other. "I brought your breakfast, cowboy. You'll be heading home after Dr. Hudson checks you out. Meanwhile we want samples of everything."

"Give my breakfast to my friend, and I'm not giving out any samples."

Before she could argue, a thud hit the door and a man who looked very much like McCoy stormed in.

The first thing McCoy saw was a bulky coat way too thick for the weather in Texas.

The intruder was tall, thin. His salt-and-pepper beard must have taken all winter to grow. With his graying hair and deep wrinkles, he looked like an older version of McCoy, or a younger copy of Pop.

A mountain man emoji come to life.

"Morning, Dad," McCoy said calmly as if it hadn't been ten years since he'd seen his father. "Who called you? By the way, I'm doing just fine. You didn't need to come."

"You're obviously not 'just fine.'" Three steps and Dad was six inches from McCoy's nose. "Pop said you were shot and some guy at the sheriff's office said you'd been in and out of the hospital lately. When I left home thirty years ago, I told Pop to call if he ever needed me. Every time I changed numbers or addresses, I mailed him the update. I called every holiday and he always said he was doing fine. Over the years he never called, not once. Not a word. Then he calls on your cell phone to tell me to come home."

"I'm fine, Dad," McCoy said again. "But Pop's got trouble. A big development outfit wants his land. He's the only holdout left. You know how these things sometimes work. The big guys hire lawyers first, and if that doesn't work they hire a gang to make things happen and the gang tries to cut corners. They've started shooting Pop's donkeys to get his attention."

John Mason dropped his coat on a cart. "And they thought you were one of the donkeys?"

"Something like that." This was definitely not one of those stories he'd ever tell anyone.

"How can I help?" His dad didn't need details. He was in.

"Get me out of here. We need to be at the farm with Pop. I don't like the idea of him being out there alone."

His dad leaned over and sniffed McCoy's head as if he was smelling to see if rot was moving in.

McCoy closed his eyes and silently cussed. Pop was

crazy and his father had turned into a mountain man. He wouldn't be surprised if Dad had a hatchet on his belt and made wolf calls in his sleep.

"Did you pass out?" John shook McCoy's shoulder. "Maybe I should get a doctor. Surely they got one in this birdhouse of a hospital."

McCoy glanced over toward Baylor. All he saw was blanket. "Baylor?"

She pulled the blanket just low enough for her to see. "It's too early to be yelling, gentlemen."

Dad moved closer. "Who is she, son?"

When she didn't answer, Dad moved in front of her chair. "Hello, little lady. I'm J.D. Mason but around here most folks call me John."

Watching her come awake, McCoy forgot to join the conversation. The lady was adorable at dawn. In a low voice, he answered his father, "She's my vet. Dr. Baylor Blanton. She's been treating me for a broken leg. She may have saved my life last night. Don't yell at her, Dad, or I swear . . ."

"Yell at her!" J.D. yelled. "I'd never do that to a lady." Dad walked slowly toward her and offered his hand. "A pleasure to meet you, miss. Thanks for watching over my son. I would say he's the stray dog of our family, but to tell the truth we're all mutts."

Baylor shook his hand and smiled. "You know something, Mr. Mason, I see both your father and your son in you."

"Sorry to hear that, Miss Blanton. Any chance you might be kin to the vet I met one winter in Honey Creek? I was just a kid hanging around the horse clinic. Dr. Blanton was a great old guy. I did some work for him after we settled here. The old doc never stopped talking about the animals."

"He is my grandfather. He had three sons and six grandsons. Not one became a vet, but me, his only girl. He turned the clinic over to me two years ago, but he comes around regularly to tell me what I'm doing wrong."

McCoy had heard enough. He needed answers. "Dad, you came all the way from Alaska to help. Well, get me out of here. We can catch up on family trees when we get back to the farm."

His dad smiled at Baylor. "Is he always so gripy these days? I remember him as quiet, always a busy kid. He used to take things apart and try to put them back together. If he tries that with you, just let me know. I'll yell at him and then replace the things that he can't reassemble. I must have bought half a dozen toasters, three lawnmowers. I lost count of the watches he took apart."

"I will keep an eye on him, but we've got to cut McCoy some slack. After all, he's hurting. Totaled a car. Broke his head and leg. Sadler told me he lost his job and his fiancée in one day. Collateral damage from the wreck. He's not an easy man to be around. I'm here more to protect the hospital staff than watch over him."

They were both having a grand time picking on him, McCoy decided.

She leaned close to Dad and added, "He did take a bullet for a donkey. That should count for something."

"You're right. I'll go talk to the doctor on duty and see if I can take him home. Somebody has to. Once he's mobile, all these machines are in danger of being disassembled."

McCoy had never seen his dad like this. Friendly. Funny. McCoy remembered the man as serious. Always fair but never comical. Dad rarely helped him with his homework or came to anything McCoy had at school, but there was always food in the fridge and money in a jar if he needed lunch money. McCoy got his tinkering gene from his dad. Every time they moved, he'd rebuild the next house, then overhaul his truck so they'd be ready when they moved again.

Dad had told him once that Pop may have settled down, but he never would. McCoy thought that was just the way most people lived. Always on the move.

When J.D. left, Baylor crawled up on McCoy's bed and brushed his hair out of his eyes. "Your dad is a sweetheart," she said as if she was letting McCoy in on a secret.

When he didn't agree, Baylor reached for his chart and began checking McCoy. Nothing personal. All professional.

She was touching him, like doctors do, nothing more.

Only, he was aware of her so near.

"Doc, you're growing on me."

Her eyes darkened slightly but she didn't say a word.

McCoy thought about telling her to run as far away from him as she could, but he couldn't get the words out. For some reason she seemed to want to be his friend. No, not just that. She wanted to understand him.

They were like two different species watching each other through the zoo fence. She probably didn't understand him any better than he understood her.

But this morning he couldn't turn away. She'd been kind to him.

Very slowly, he leaned toward her and kissed her gently. When she didn't move away, he whispered, "Thank you."

"You're welcome," she said as she turned to watch the machines.

If the world were different. If he'd learned how to understand a woman like her. If happiness could be measured in acres instead of inches.

McCoy knew he wasn't for her. Two different worlds.

But, if there was a chance she could put up with him around, it would be worth it to try to make her happy.

She moved a few inches away from him as he said, "You know, my dad is right. I do take things apart trying to figure out how they work. Maybe a part of me is trying to figure you out. I've always been easygoing when it comes to relationships. Never letting it get too complicated. But I don't think it would ever be like that with you."

He shrugged. "I'm a kind of a 'stick my toe in the ocean' kind of guy and you're more like a 'dive into the waves' kind of girl. I'm not sure I'd even know how to do things differently."

"I have no idea what you are talking about," she answered, but her blue eyes gave away her lie.

He wanted to make a joke about how he had brain damage, but he couldn't. He'd seen her in the blink of an eye and he knew she felt the pull toward him just as he felt the pull toward her.

He almost added that it would be better to hurt her a little now than wait until they both walked away shattered. But it was only a blink, nothing more. He was on meds. Maybe it was nothing, but for a moment he felt they saw each other. Really saw.

She opened her mouth to say something, but noise outside in the hallway stopped all talk.

Baylor slipped off the bed and stood back as what sounded like a herd of stampeding cattle headed toward them.

He'd never thought that discharging a patient was a team event.

McCoy wasn't sure what was happening. Everyone who worked in the clinic stormed in the room. The doctor, mini-nurse, two nursing students, and the ambulance drivers. Everyone seemed to have a job but him. McCoy just watched as they rolled him on a gurney, packed up his things while the nurse unplugged him from the machines, and the old doctor checked his wounds.

McCoy glared at his father standing by the door with his arms folded. "What did you do, Dad?"

"Nothing. I just told them what the sergeant said. You are in danger of your life and you'll be safer on the farm." J.D. picked up his coat. "The sergeant and the sheriff will be riding with you. I'll head out in my rental car as soon as I know you're loaded."

McCoy reached for Baylor's hand. "She goes with me."

"No, she goes with me. If bullets rain, it'll be at the ambulance. Your girl will be safe with me."

McCoy didn't have time to correct his father about Baylor being his girl. He agreed with his father's plan to get back to the farm. "But the men who were shooting at me thought I was Pop. They didn't even get a good look at me."

Sheriff Smith stepped into the already crowded room. His big brother followed, taking up the rest of the space. "They now know it was you, not Pop. I issued a statement about an hour ago. I also told the paper that you would be able to identify both men."

McCoy's mind was still trying to make sense of what was going on. "Maybe I should stay here. Thanks to you I might as well put a target on my back."

Pecos grinned. "I may have mentioned it to a few people online, too. We'll be ready when they come to shoot you again. I'm setting a trap that they'll walk right into."

McCoy dropped his head back so hard on the gurney, he saw stars. "I'm the bait."

His father actually patted McCoy's arm. "Somebody had to be, son. You said you had to get out of here, and it was the only plan we could think of fast."

When McCoy just glared at his father, Dad added, "If this plan doesn't work, we'll find another way."

It was a wild shot, but McCoy decided to inject reason. "If this crazy plan doesn't work, I'll be dead. There is no plan B."

J.D. looked disappointed. "Darn, I figured you'd come up with one."

McCoy heard a calming tone in his Dad's joking words, but when he looked in J.D.'s eyes he saw fear seesawing on panic.

McCoy raised his hand and his dad caught his grip. They were both men who worked with their hands and the hold was solid.

"We have to draw them out if we want this to be over," Dad whispered. "I'll be right with you, son."

McCoy did not loosen his grip but he lowered his voice. "In that case, take care of my girl. Make sure she's safe. I'm crazy about the doc."

J.D. whispered, "Does she know it?"

"Nope."

"Well, you might want to tell her when this is over."

There was no time left to talk. The staff moved out of the room as the EMTs loaded him for transport.

McCoy had a bedside seat to it all. His gaze never left Baylor until his dad drove away. They'd get to the farm first and be waiting when the ambulance arrived, but McCoy didn't like the idea that she wasn't with him.

As they rattled along in the ambulance, McCoy closed his eyes. He hurt all over, his head was cloudy, and he could feel trouble rushing toward him.

"Hell of a time to fall in love," he almost said aloud.

Everyone was organized. Both Tucson and his brother had weapons ready to return fire if the ambulance was attacked. Half a dozen lawmen were watching from the tree line along the county road. Two troopers were driving back and forth from the farm on alert. Everyone had their jobs.

Even McCoy. His job was to be the target.

Chapter 42

McCoy's Long Ride

The whole world seemed silent as the ambulance drove out of Honey Creek.

Inside, McCoy, the sheriff, and Tucson were quiet for a time as if they were listening for a shot to be fired at them.

Pecos whispered, "They might have the county road blocked. I can think of a dozen places where it wouldn't be hard. The bend about a mile before we turn on Sunflower Lane would be a logical place. Thanks to the trees, they'd have plenty of cover and we'd have to slow down to make the curve. Or they might catch us at the crossroad. They could ram the ambulance hard enough to knock us in the ditch. Or they might shoot out the tires. We're most vulnerable at the gate."

"Stop trying to cheer us up, little brother." Tucson's voice was low.

"What's our plan for each of the scenarios?" McCoy's question seemed to bounce off the inside walls of the ambulance. "Unstrap me from this gurney so I can help."

Pecos patted McCoy's shoulder. "You're hurt. It's our job to protect you."

McCoy fought down a scream of cuss words. "Give me a rifle or one of your Colts. Hell, give me a hammer and I'll take care of myself. I've fought my way through a few construction site fights and held my own."

He was starting to feel like he was headed to the O.K. Corral without a gun.

The Smith brothers were looking out the small windows of the ambulance and ignoring him.

He bumped his head against the board they had him strapped to, hoping to knock himself out. Forget the bad guys trying to kill him; if one more of the locals patted on him, McCoy decided he'd go nuts.

He stared at the sheriff. "You do have a plan, right?"

Pecos shrugged. "All I've thought of so far is when bullets fly, I'll order Tucson to fall on you. Two hundred pounds of muscle is bound to stop a bullet."

"I see a few flaws in that plan." McCoy figured talking was better than worrying. "First, if he fell on me, I'd probably be crushed. At the least the two holes I just got stitched closed will pop open and I'll start leaking again. Second, if he's on top of me, he can't return fire."

Pecos sounded irritated. "Hey, man, what do you want me to do? I've only had this job a week. We had to think of something. There were a dozen doors into the clinic and they don't even have a guard. I agreed with your dad that you being at the farm is safer. Only trouble is getting you there."

"Slight problem, Sheriff. The farm was where I was shot. So, you're telling me that returning to the scene of the crime is my best chance of survival?"

When Pecos looked like he might throw up, Tucson slapped his brother on the back. "We've got a plan B, right?"

"Right." Pecos straightened. "But it's a secret."

McCoy relaxed a bit. Bugging the sheriff gave him a way to pass the time. Now that he realized Pecos had another plan, McCoy calmed.

"At least you got a job, Sheriff. If I die the paper will say, 'McCoy Mason died for no reason. He had no job, no address, no woman to cry over his grave. The good news is he might have saved an old donkey.'"

For a moment both Smith brothers looked like they felt sorry for him, then they laughed.

Tucson went first. "You got a cute little vet who slept next to you last night. And, just as a reference, if you hurt her, I'll kill you."

McCoy pointed at the sheriff. "Did you hear that, Pecos? Your brother just threatened me."

"I heard and I'm not happy about it. I'll have to help him bury your body if you mess up with Baylor, so I'd suggest you treat her right."

"No matter where I go around here people seem to want to kill me. And you can stop worrying about Baylor and me getting together. I think I'm more of her new pet than her boyfriend."

"Your life is not all bad, McCoy. You got a relative you can stay with. And you got land you'll inherit in fifty years or so." Pecos added, "A man who has land is a rich man."

"No, it's Pop's land and he plans to live forever. Besides, my occupation is building strip malls and ten-floor office buildings. Not much need for my skills in this valley."

They heard a tap from one of the two men in the front seat.

"We're halfway to the farm." All talking stopped as Pecos and Tucson moved to the edge of the windows.

McCoy had never felt so helpless. Who knew being the "sitting duck" was such a hard job?

Suddenly the driver sped up, making everything in

the ambulance rattle. McCoy forced his mind to start listing all the projects he still had to do at Pop's place to distract himself from trying to guess which body part would be shot next.

He could be of no help in the fight sure to come. He was strapped on a gurney. He had no weapon. He didn't even have clothes or a cell. He felt like the raw meat left hanging from a tree to attract bigger game.

"Fire trucks coming alongside us with their lights and sirens blaring," the driver yelled.

Pecos relayed what he saw from the window. "One truck pulled in front of us. One alongside so close I can see their smiles. The fire chief is bringing up the tail in his pickup."

"Why?" both Tucson and McCoy asked at the same time.

Pecos laughed. "Because, now no one can get near us. Or even see us for that matter. If anyone out there fires off one shot, every lawman, fireman, and Texas Ranger will be hunting for them. Even the town folks will get involved. They might think of it as part of the job for lawmen to have shootouts, but no one is allowed to shoot at a fire truck. Everyone loves firemen, you know."

"Why are they protecting me?" McCoy asked.

"I don't know, McCoy. Maybe because you fixed the elevator in the courthouse. The fire chief's daughter is big pregnant and she works there. Or Betty told them what was going down. You're Sadler's only grandson." Pecos lowered his voice. "You're one of us, McCoy."

Tucson interrupted, "I wish I'd thought of the trucks. There was no way an ambulance could go anywhere unnoticed. So why not have a parade?"

A few minutes later, the caravan slowed. One of the firemen in the first engine must have opened the gate.

To McCoy's surprise the trucks pulled in and followed all the way to Pop's house.

No sign of a dark pickup. They'd wasted worrying.

The old man stood on the newly painted porch. He waved everyone in for coffee. Then he nodded at McCoy once and disappeared in the house. Apparently, speaking to his grandson wasn't necessary.

The two ambulance drivers lifted him out and started in. Both looked disappointed that nothing had happened.

One of the volunteer firemen waited at the bottom of the steps.

McCoy raised his hand signaling for the men carrying him to stop.

As the ambulance drivers waited, the short, redheaded volunteer fireman moved closer.

McCoy said, "Let me guess. You've tasted my pop's coffee and are hoping he'll run out before you get inside?"

The fireman shook his head. "No, it's not that. I just don't know if I'm welcome."

McCoy studied the stranger. "Look, man, I know my pop is a grumpy old man, but he's going to welcome someone who helped get his kin home."

"I'm Harvey. He threatens me every time he sees me. He thinks I should get hitched to his neighbor, but she won't marry me." Harvey hung his head. "Sadler said he'd kill me if I didn't have a ring in my pocket the next time he lays eyes on me."

"Pop's got other problems right now. You're safe." McCoy hoped he was right. "Do you love my second cousin once removed and her three little girls?"

"I do. I know I don't have much to offer, but I'm a hard worker, go to church every Sunday, and I volunteer to fight fires. That should count for something. She says we're having an affair. Says that's more exciting. But after six years and neither of us being married, I think we should call it marriage. She'll be the only woman I'll ever love and I don't think she wants anyone but me."

Harvey looked like he might cry.

"You're a good man, Harvey. I can tell. I'll stand up for you, and I've only known you a few minutes." McCoy knew how the man felt. Only Harvey was way ahead of him. McCoy didn't work or go to church or volunteer. No wonder his fiancée had left with the moving truck.

"Me too," Pecos said as he held the screen door open. "I've known you all my life, Harvey. You'd be a good father to them girls."

Harvey puffed up. "I am their father and I'll fight anyone who says I'm not."

Tucson stomped up the steps and motioned the men to carry McCoy in the house. "Can we talk about this later, boys? We need to get the target undercover."

Inside, McCoy noticed Baylor was helping Pop hand out cups of coffee, and the sheriff and Tucson were assigning a man at every window. All McCoy could do was try to not pass out. Even the air seemed still as they waited.

Nothing. No blue pickup even passed the gate. Not a sound.

Eventually they finished their coffee and began to head out.

First the volunteer fire chief and a few firefighters pulled one fire truck away to handle a grass fire over by the feed lot. Then Pecos was called back to the office to meet with a couple looking for their lost girl. The ambulance went back to town in case they were needed. Even Baylor said she had work to do. She left with only a nod toward McCoy.

When he dozed off, the farm seemed peaceful. The only sounds were the two deputies talking.

Just before dark, McCoy saw his dad lift Sadler's jacket off the hook by the door and slip it on as he walked out of the kitchen door.

McCoy tried to call his father back, but then reconsidered. Dad was going outside in the direction of where the donkeys were. He was taking long steps like Pop always did. The hood covered his head.

If he didn't know better, he would think it was Pop.

Chapter 43

The Sergeant's Longing

Since the day Tucson Smith enlisted in the army, he'd never wanted more than what he had. He figured any life was better than what his parents had planned for him. They seemed to think they were raising farmhands to work for free.

Everything about the army was exciting and Tucson was always learning, and growing. He'd even had a few girl-friends over the years but never anyone serious. He had no doubt that he was living the perfect life for himself.

Then, he met Jam. No. That was not right. He found her.

As he walked the streets of Honey Creek, he turned toward the edge of town. He didn't head to the café, but to the cottonwoods where he'd found her that first night. Her lean body blended with the branches. Her eyes were wide open and filled with tears.

He was fascinated with her before she said a word.

He stopped at the river's edge and listened to the night. If she was still up, he knew she'd offer him something to eat. She'd invite him to spend the night.

She always came so easy to him, as if they both knew

they were meant to be lovers. A woman easy to love but hard to know.

She'd told him during one of their midnight talks that she'd once been engaged. When she'd learned she would never have children, her fiancé had ended things, saying he couldn't settle for a part of his dreams.

Tucson held her all night thinking even a small part of Jam in his world would be enough happiness to last a lifetime.

When he turned from the river, Tucson saw Jam standing in the open doorway. He knew every curve of her body, but he might never know her completely.

She held out her hand. Without a word she led him upstairs.

Chapter 44

Mr. Winston's First Love

As was becoming his habit nowadays, Winston only walked the streets of Honey Creek on the nights he wasn't with his lady. He knew she loved sleeping next to him, but she needed her time alone. Miss Lilly had been alone all her adult life and needed her quiet time.

So did he. There was an odd kind of calmness knowing that you can be content with your own company and that somehow made their nights together even more precious.

As he moved around the sleeping town, his only company the tap of his cane, his thoughts were turned to the future. He'd never worried much about tomorrow or even the years to come, but now that he had someone, each day mattered. At their age, he knew it wouldn't be long before one of them would fall ill or die. It was the way of life.

If they married, they wouldn't count anniversaries in years but in months. They'd already passed the building and dreaming time of life. All that was left were the quiet years, the slowly growing weaker in mind and body. He wouldn't get to take her hand and run into life; he'd only get to hold her when it came time for one of them to step toward death.

The thought of it made him sad and also made him treasure their time even more.

And what would happen when this time ended? One of them would be alone again.

All he, or Miss Lilly, would have were memories.

Winston smiled, thinking they were building some unusual memories in the small time they had. He loved their talks and dinners out. He loved holding her hand while they watched TV. He loved sleeping against her, knowing he was keeping her warm.

And, Winston almost laughed aloud, he loved their lovemaking. Lilly was a bit of a surprise. A bit frisky. She wanted to do things until they got them just right, and he didn't mind practicing until she was satisfied.

She was playing "catch-up" on all she'd missed over the years. He feared she was wearing him out, but then, what a way to go.

Winston shattered the night air with his bark of laughter. He'd always said he wanted to die in bed, and Miss Lilly might see that it happened.

A pickup's engine raced through the dark street as it passed him.

As Winston stood among the trees, he watched with a frown. When the pickup turned the corner, it cut too sharp and bounced over the curb and murdered a dozen poppies.

"Strange," Winston said aloud as he walked over to examine the flowerbed. "I should report this crime."

After forty years of reading mysteries, he played a game sometimes in his mind. He pretended it was important he remembered details. Blue ten-year-old pickup, left fender with a dent, mud now caked around the tires.

And the license RC 112.

He knew the tricks. Noticed patterns, linked letters

to words. In his mind he noted: RC, a cola. One and one is two.

Winston filed the information in his brain. The folks of Honey Creek would be surprised to know that he knew most of the makes, models, and plates in town. This pickup was not a local.

He slowly turned back toward home and his thoughts filled with tomorrow. They'd have an early dinner at the Honey Creek Café and then go back to her place to watch the news. She'd turn off the TV when it was over, and he'd hold his hand out to her and ask if he might stay the night.

She'd smile and say, "Of course, dear."

Miss Lilly always wore her blue nightgown on Tuesday morning even though she'd gone to bed in a white gown. He figured she did so because she thought her robe went best with the blue gown. He wondered if she knew he didn't care what color she wore.

He smiled again, thinking about how they always slept late and ate breakfast before they got dressed. He loved that time.

Chapter 45

Melody's Tears

Tuesday

The third floor of the café smelled of mahogany, and age, and dust. Melody had cried so many silent tears that the front of her wrinkled shirt was wet. Every day for two weeks she'd tried to find Michael.

They'd talked of someday running away if her parents learned about Saturdays. If she was eighteen, they'd get married and spend the rest of their lives together. If trouble came before her birthday, they'd find a way. Maybe her parents would be so angry they'd let her stay with her grandmother. Or Michael had said he had married friends who might let her stay with them.

But, she'd had only seconds to call before her phone was taken away. Three times, she'd let it ring once, before she hung up and erased the number. No time to talk to Mike before she followed the plan they'd laid out. He had no opportunity to talk to her.

Maybe something horrible had happened. Or, he'd changed his mind. Maybe he figured she wasn't strong enough to leave her parents. Maybe the army had needed him and he had to wait to come.

The dream of living together forever was beginning to fade. She had no way to contact him and she must be lost to him as well.

Thanks to her hiding place on the third floor of the café, she'd been warm and dry at night and the huge kitchen always had food she could borrow. She'd made up her mind that when she was older and had a job and was settled, she'd return to the Honey Creek Café and pay the owner back for all her meals.

But as the days went on, she felt trapped. She couldn't go out to look for Mike in the daylight. Someone might see her. In a big city no one would notice her, but in a small town they might.

She'd heard Jam and Tucson talking about her a few times. Wondering where she was. Worrying that she might not be safe. Melody almost laughed. The couple sounded almost like parents.

She'd also heard the big man everyone but Jam called Sergeant mention pictures of a dead body—a soldier.

Melody remembered one rainy day at the library, Mike had talked about how he could leave the army. It wouldn't be easy, but maybe they could disappear to California.

But, he'd also said he loved the army. He'd told her if they could wait until she was eighteen, no one could stop them from being together. If he stayed in the army, they could travel the world.

Melody didn't believe that. She might be old enough to be an adult at eighteen, but her folks would never let her go. They were already planning her college years. First two years at Clifton College, then if they thought she was ready, going away to a university would be the next step. Mike, or any other man, was not in the plan. No high school dates. They said there would be time for dates later. No serious boyfriends in college. Definitely no soldier.

Another thought worried in her mind. Mike liked the army. He was studying and planning his life with his army training as his base. She didn't want to take his dreams away.

In her hiding place on the third floor, the whole world seemed to grow darker as thunder rolled in. Hope was dying inside her.

She'd go out one more time tonight and look for Mike. If she didn't find him, she'd have to make other plans. She couldn't live forever on the third floor with the other mice.

Opening her hand, she remembered how Mike had touched her. A brush of his knee against hers beneath the library table. How gently he'd hold her hand. The way he kissed her the few times when they were alone. How he tickled her ear with his words when he whispered that he loved her.

If she had to go home, she'd never get to see him again. Her parents would have him arrested if he tried to get to her.

Tears dripped from her chin. There was no happy ending to her story.

A knock on the kitchen door suddenly drew her to the corner where she could listen. It was too early for customers. Maybe a delivery or maybe the sergeant who'd saved her was dropping over to talk to Jam.

They sometimes whispered when they talked. Melody liked that. Somehow it made her think that the café owner and the sergeant were happy.

Melody liked listening when the two of them were alone downstairs. She usually couldn't make out the words, but she heard laughter. When she got back from her nightly searches of all the places Mike could be hiding, waiting for her, Jam and Tucson were usually asleep in the one bedroom on the second floor.

They were lovers, this big man who helped out at the sheriff's office and the lady who owned the café. It seemed a very nice thing to be. Lots of laughter drifted from the bedroom.

But as Melody heard Jam rushing across the floor to answer the knock, Melody guessed whoever was outside was not coming in until invited.

"May I help you?" Jam's greeting drifted upstairs. "The café door is out front. We're open at five, but you are welcome to sit on the porch until then."

A voice Melody knew well rattled up from the main floor. "We've come to ask you a few questions, if you don't mind, Miss Mackenzie." There was a slight cough her father did when he was nervous. "We may be the parents of a girl pulled from the river a few days ago. We've been searching for her for days and any lead is a hope."

Melody couldn't breathe. All her dreams of being with Mike were silently crumbling around her. They'd found her hiding place. It was only a matter of time before they climbed the stairs to the third floor.

She pressed her cheek next to the opening and silently cried as she listened.

After Jam welcomed them in and offered coffee, Melody heard her mother say, "We brought a picture. If you could look at it."

"I will be glad to look, but the girl my friend pulled from the water disappeared the next morning. I don't know where she is."

Melody heard tears in her mother's weak voice. "But, if it was our Melody, it will give us hope."

In the silence, Melody could see her parents below in her mind. Dad would be standing straight and tall. Her mother would be slowly wilting into a ball. Dad faced things straight on. Mom tended to hide like Melody was doing now.

She heard the rattle of cups and paper. Then the world below went silent for a while.

Melody hugged her knees to her chest and fought not to make a sound. She hated that she was hurting her parents. That was never her plan. She just wanted to be with Mike. She loved him. She always would. She couldn't give him up.

"It's her," Jam's voice came strong and clear. "She was muddy and afraid, but this is the girl my friend pulled out of the river."

Melody heard her mother cry out, "Thank God."

Her father's tone was logical. "Can you tell us what she was doing here? She's never been to this town. She knows no one here. Did she tell you why she came to Honey Creek?"

"No. I wanted to let her rest once we got her warm and dry. After she recovered a bit, I thought we'd talk, but she ran. She did tell us she was eighteen. My friend from Fort Hood thinks she might be here to meet a soldier who took pictures on the dock near where she fell in the water."

"Impossible," her father barked. "Our daughter does not know any soldier. She doesn't even date. We decided there would be time for that sort of thing once she gets established in college."

Her mother interrupted her father. "We do know that she talked to a boy at the library before she disappeared, but he wasn't a soldier."

"He was probably a student at Clifton College," her father added. "But we have not been able to find him. If we do find him, the young man will never see her again."

Melody laced her fingers as her arms pulled her knees

closer. She couldn't move. She wouldn't go downstairs no matter how much her mother cried. If she didn't find Mike tonight, she'd keep looking.

She had to fight for the first time in her life if she wanted a chance of ever having a future of her own.

Rolling away from the kitchen talk below, she moved to the other end of the hallway. Now she could cry, no one would hear her this far away. No one was downstairs on this side of the big old house. The café wouldn't open for another hour.

"Mike," she whispered as she cried. "Mike, come get me."

Chapter 46

McCoy's Awakening

McCoy woke early the next morning. After little sleep in the hospital, one night in his bed at Pop's place made him feel like a new man. He didn't know how it happened, but he'd gotten used to the quiet of the country and having the sunrise be his alarm.

Then he made the mistake of moving. A tsunami of pain washed over him.

When he groaned, his father appeared in the doorway. "I see you didn't die in your sleep."

"I see you didn't get shot last night during your walk." McCoy had meant to stay awake and worry about his dad out wandering around the field, but sleep had got the better of him.

His dad grinned. "You worrying about me, son?"

"Nope."

"I needed to get the feel of the land again." Dad walked into McCoy's room and stood by the window, as if on duty. "Your girl, Baylor, told me to call her when you were awake. She said she'd come over and change the bandage."

"Forget the call. I can do it myself. If she comes over,

she'll either give me a sponge bath or yell at me for still bleeding."

"Suit yourself. You've got another visitor. She showed up with sopapillas about half an hour ago. If Pop didn't eat them all, I'll bring you a few." Dad turned and sauntered out without another word. Lack of communication seemed to be a family trait.

McCoy glanced over at the open door and there stood his fairy. "Morning, Sunshine."

The tiny little five-year-old put her tiny little fists on her hips and said, "So, you're broken again, McCoy."

"Afraid so." He noticed she had cinnamon sugar and honey on her cheek.

"Harvey told me you got shot. He came over to tell my mother a bedtime story. He said he was your friend. He told me to tell you he'd help out if you need him."

As she came closer, he asked, "You like Harvey?"

"I sure double do. He's always nice to me. He's a fixer and that kind of man is rare, my momma says. He fixes stuff around the house and brings Momma a freezer full of beef in the fall and vegetables all summer. He built us a fort out back that looks like a tree so we'd have shade and branches for swings. He said redhead little girls are very rare and he's got to watch over us."

"Does your mother really, really like him?"

"I guess so. After they put us to bed, they go in Momma's room and giggle. She says she's not going to marry him because that's what makes women grow old. She also says Harvey is too poor to buy her a ring."

That was enough for McCoy. He talked the fairy girl into pulling his duffel bag to the bed and told her they were going on a treasure hunt.

Ten minutes later she found a tiny box with a ring in it. What's-her-name in Houston, with the hair that smelled so good, didn't want the ring. He might as well give it to someone who was about six years behind in popping the question.

"Take this box to Harvey and tell him to get down on one knee. He'll know what I'm talking about."

She frowned as she slipped the box in her pouch over the chest of her overalls. "Is this a magic ring, McCoy?"

"It might just be. Tell Harvey I'm not giving it to him. It'll cost him a dollar. That's all it's worth to me, but to him it might be worth a great deal more."

She danced out of the room as if someone had just struck up a band and, as always, she was gone before he had time to say goodbye.

McCoy leaned back on his pillows and wished he'd be around to watch her grow up. Olivia Whatever-Harvey's-last-name-was would grow up to be a beauty. She'd sell flowers like her mother, and he hoped his little Sunshine would always be dancing through life.

He was almost asleep when Baylor came in with her arms loaded down with supplies.

"I don't need anything, Doc. I'm fine."

When she kept spreading bandages and tape out on his bed, he gave up and rolled to his side. She might not want to talk to him, but worry lines crossed her forehead and he knew he was the cause.

If he was guessing, she'd already talked to Dad or Pop and gotten all the facts. He'd had a good night but was in pain this morning.

Her gentle hands pulled off the old bandage and washed away the dried blood.

"You've got a soft touch," McCoy said.

"Thanks. You're the first patient who has ever said that to me. But most of my patients can't talk."

"You think you would ever touch me when you're not

doctoring me, I mean? I had a dream last night that you put your hand over my heart and smiled."

She didn't say anything for a while, then she admitted, "Maybe, if you ever figure out what a good guy you are."

"You want a saint, or maybe a rich guy, or a genius, I'm guessing?"

Baylor began taping his side. "No, I want a kind man. A man who knows how to love. My grandfather told me once that if you have love you don't much need anything else."

McCoy looked straight into her eyes. "I don't know much about love. It was missing when I was growing up. My mother left. My dad never said a word about even liking to have me around, and my grandfather never called or wrote. Not everyone is surrounded with love like you probably were. Not everyone gets a pony."

"You're wrong."

"About what, the pony?"

The doc laughed. "No. I got the pony. You're wrong about no one loving you. Your dad flew home from Alaska when he heard you were hurt and your grandfather took you in. He frets over you."

She finished her care and walked to the door. "I see something in you too, McCoy. Maybe something you don't even know is there. You're a special man."

"You're such a dreamer. I live in reality, and in my world love is a lousy glue to hold people together. There is nothing special about me."

"Maybe so. But if you ever find something worth caring about, let me know. I'd like to get to know *that* McCoy."

"What man? One who carries his heart on his sleeve, Doc?"

"Yes, *that* McCoy."

Chapter 47

The Café

Jam talked the Avendales into waiting in the dining room with Mr. Winston and his lady who'd dropped by earlier, while she called Tucson. Jam promised them Sergeant Smith would answer all their questions, which seemed endless.

When she saw Mr. Winston and Miss Lilly return for coffee and a muffin midway through their midmorning walk, Jam introduced them to the professors.

Mr. Winston nodded once to Jam. He seemed to understand.

To Jam's relief Mr. Winston played host to the couple and Miss Lilly comforted them as if she'd known them for years.

As Jam walked back into the kitchen, she couldn't help but smile. Somehow, since Winston called Miss Lilly his fiancée, the town seemed to have adopted the practice. In an odd way the couple had become Honey Creek's royalty. Everyone watched them. Everyone spoke or tipped a hat when they saw them. Neither of them had a single relative, but they seemed to belong to everyone in the valley.

As she called Tucson, Jam remembered that he'd told her when he was leaving before six this morning, that he had a hunch about the soldier.

Then he'd stormed back to her bed to kiss her one last time. He might not say much about how he felt, but he showed it.

Tucson didn't pick up.

Walking around the kitchen Jam thought about how he made love. Completely, like there might not be another time for them, like what they had was too perfect to last.

She checked on the pies in the oven, then tried to call Tucson again.

Maybe after he talked to the Avendales, he would have a moment to spend a few minutes alone with her. He might whisper like he had in the night, "Again?"

And she'd giggle as she had twice last night and whisper, "Please."

But Tucson still didn't pick up his cell.

Thirty minutes later, still no answer.

An hour later Jam noticed the Avendales were still talking to Winston and his lady. Jam offered lunch to the parents of the missing girl. Winston and Lilly stayed to keep them company. The old couple were good listeners and Melody's parents were talkers. They often talked over one another.

She guessed the old couple might want a quiet lunch alone, but they were too polite to not welcome the two professors.

By the time they'd finished their salads, the two couples were talking like friends, as Jam knew they would.

As the lunch crowd dwindled, she insisted they have dessert on the porch. When she returned to the busy kitchen,

Jam couldn't miss Tucson standing near the stairs as if he was on guard. At his side was a young soldier, who stood tall even though he looked worried.

She handed off a tray of dirty dishes to one of the kitchen crew and moved to Tucson. "What's wrong?"

"Jam, I'd like you to meet PFC Michael Alderton. I drove over to Fort Hood this morning and asked if he could help me today. His commanding officer gave him a two-day leave because he's had guard duty all weekend."

The young soldier looked barely old enough to shave. Jam thought he looked familiar.

Tucson continued, "The private will be leaving the States within the month, but he wants to help us find the girl who almost drowned." Tucson put his hand on the soldier's shoulder, more like a hold than a pat.

Amid all the racket of the lunch run, PFC Michael Alderton offered his hand. "Do you have any idea where she is, Miss Mackenzie? I am a friend of hers. I told her about this town. I told her I used to hide out here when I was a kid. I never caused any trouble. I just hid here when I couldn't go home."

She smiled as a memory flashed in her mind. A boy who'd saved her one night.

Jam chose her words carefully. "Private Michael Alderton, you are welcome any time, upstairs or down." She waved her hand as if opening a door. "Make yourself at home. The muffins are just out of the oven. Perhaps you'll remember them."

Michael nodded politely, then met her eyes. There was no need for more words.

Jam saw Tucson's surprise as she stepped forward to give the boy a hug. In a low tone, she added, "Of course I remember you, Michael. You saved my life when I was attacked several years ago. I looked for you when I got back from giving my statement. I never got to thank you for what you did for me. You just disappeared that night. Sometimes I thought I heard you upstairs, and I'd leave out extra food for you. Whenever you are near Honey Creek, this is your home."

The young soldier smiled. "I know. I thought of you as my almost-mother. I was only about twelve then, but I collected a few rocks and sticks to use as weapons if that guy ever came back."

Her eyes were wet as she hugged him again. A boy had saved her that night, but a man stood before her now.

"I will be your almost-mother anytime, Michael, and you'll never have to pay for a meal in my café." She swatted Tucson's hand off Michael's shoulder. Whatever you're thinking he did, just forget it. Michael is my guardian angel."

Anger fired in the sergeant. "Wait a minute, Jam, this is the soldier who may have tried to fake his death. I've spent two weeks investigating. He's wasted a lot of my time."

Jam looked to see if steam really did come out of people's ears. Tucson looked furious at being pushed away.

She held on to Mike's shoulder as she turned into a warrior-mother defending her child. "You said the photos were found blowing in the wind. He obviously didn't go through with faking his death, and if you found him at the fort, he didn't go AWOL."

Tucson didn't give up. "He was making a scene on a public dock."

Jam grinned. "So was the bridge club."

"Right," Tucson almost growled, and Jam fought the urge to hug the bear of a man.

Tucson wasn't ready to give up. "Obviously he's the

reason the girl came here. Somehow, he's linked to the girl I fished out of the river. She's underage, and after talking to her parents, they will press charges on him if the private had anything to do with her disappearance."

"I just talked to them too. In fact, I was trying to get in touch with you while you were out hunting my Michael."

"Oh, he's your Michael now? A minute ago, you didn't even know the kid's name and suddenly you're his mother."

Jam saw it then, the big, strong, intelligent sergeant was hurt, maybe a bit jealous for the first time in his life. All at once she saw Tucson's heart. He was trying to help his brother, solve a crime, and take care of her.

"Excuse me for a moment, Michael. I need to talk to my friend." Jam pushed Tucson with her body.

It wasn't easy getting the sergeant to move, but she pulled him to the center of the room and faced him straight on. "Before we get too far into this argument, I need to make one thing perfectly clear."

She could see every muscle in his body tightening. He'd never raise a hand to her, but he might explode, she thought.

Leaning close, she whispered, "I love you, Sergeant Tucson Smith. I love you for a thousand reasons, but right now I want you to understand that no matter what happens I'm going to love you after we finish arguing."

Jam lowered her forehead to his chest, ready to stand between him and Melody's parents to defend Michael. "No matter how or when we fight, I don't see any way I'll stop loving you. You got that, Sergeant?"

When she looked up into Tucson's eyes, she saw no anger, just a smile.

He circled her with his arms and rocked her onto his chest as he kissed her full out.

The noisy room fell silent, but Jam barely noticed. The sergeant was showing her he felt the same way. He loved her.

Before anyone could make a sound, a cry came from the second-floor landing.

Jam and Tucson looked up, but Mike darted around them and was on the landing a moment later, greeting their lost girl.

She jumped into the private's arms. The boy twirled her around as if they were dancing on the landing.

Jam kissed Tucson's cheek. "I think you're right, Sergeant. They just might know each other."

"She's not eighteen," Tucson said. "He may be committing a crime."

"And I'll bet he's not twenty yet." She cuddled close to the wall of muscle. "I want to help Mike and you want to help her. Somehow, we've got to meet in the middle."

The entire kitchen staff had stopped to watch the two kids on the landing. With their arms still holding each other they were whispering as if they were the only two people in the world. Mike kissed her lightly twice. "I had to stay at the fort. I couldn't leave my team. The army is our future, Mel. But, in my mind I was fighting my way here. I knew you were waiting."

Jam saw all she needed to see. They were in love. Michael wasn't talking her into anything.

"He ships out for the Middle East in less than a month," Tucson said. "We've got to get this mess straightened out. If the parents file charges, he could go to jail or have to face a dishonorable discharge. He told me he loved the army. It was the only home he'd really ever had. I understand that."

"He loves that girl too." Jam fought down tears.

Jam slipped her arm around Tucson's waist. "We've got to help them. I'm his almost-mother."

"I agree. And speaking of love, did you just say what I think you said a minute ago, or were you just trying to stop the argument?" Tucson stared down at her. "Which worked by the way."

"I said it, Tucson, and I meant it. I know they say women fall in love over candlelight dinners, long talks, and time, but with you I fell over bed."

He hugged her. "I may need a few of those talks and dinners before I say the words. I'm a hard man, Jam. I fire fast and yell to the roof. But, I swear if I rant, all you'll ever have to do is whisper those words and I'll settle down."

She raised an eyebrow. "So you need more courting before you make up your mind."

"I've never heard those words and I've never said them. If I say them, I'll never take them back."

She kissed his cheek. "I guess I best get to courting you fast. Slow floats down the river. Picnics on the grass. Long strolls in the moonlight. Holding hands at the movies. No sex until you make up your mind."

"What?"

For a moment she saw the bear again, then he relaxed. "I'm leaning toward making up my mind fast. Probably before nightfall."

Jam looked at the crew watching the young couple half a flight away. The cook was letting the grilled chicken burn. The dishwasher was dripping soap as he watched. Two of the waitresses were smiling and crying at the same time.

As long as they were distracted, Jam decided to give the sergeant an all-out kiss.

When he whispered, "Again," she pulled away and said, "After our candlelight dinner, and our moonlight walk, and our long talk."

Her bear growled again but she just patted his chest.

After all, he was her bear and she planned to keep him.

Chapter 48

McCoy's Plan

McCoy watched as Harvey stepped up onto Pop's porch, looking like he had a hundred-pound weight in his pocket instead of an engagement ring.

"Sarah-Jane left a note on her door that she and the girls would be over here. She even said I was invited to join them for dinner here, but I don't know. Sarah-Jane and I have never gone anywhere together. I used to ask her out on dates, but she'd say we shouldn't be seen together or folks might think we were a couple."

McCoy laughed. "I think people know you two are a couple. We'd be glad if you'd join us for supper." He had to ask. "If she invites you to come over and read her a bedtime story, why won't she go out with you?"

"I don't know, but I'm guessing it's because I'm downstream river trash, or maybe it's my red hair. She don't like it, but she says it's not so bad in the dark."

The littlest fairy girl toddled out. She couldn't walk straight, but she made it to Harvey and held her hands up.

He lifted her up and kissed the top of her red head.

"Bring your daughter in, Harvey. We're about ready to eat."

The shy man managed to eat with at least one of his girls on his knee the entire meal. When Sarah-Jane served pie, Harvey didn't seem to care that tiny chocolate handprints were on the white shirt he wore.

After everyone finished, Harvey asked Sarah-Jane to sit down for a minute.

She looked irritated, but she sat.

To everyone's surprise except McCoy's, Harvey knelt on one knee. He seemed too choked up to say anything, but he held out an open box with a diamond shining inside.

Sarah-Jane covered her face for a minute, then looked again at Harvey still on one knee. Without a word, she offered her left hand and Harvey fumbled to put the ring on her before she changed her mind.

He kissed her so tenderly, he might have thought she was made of glass.

McCoy grinned, happy for them both as the fairies danced around them.

At that moment, McCoy saw something he'd never witnessed. Pure love.

She was a poor farmer and Harvey might be downstream river trash, but McCoy envied them.

Harvey might not know the words to say, but he was wearing his heart on his chocolate-spotted sleeve.

Chapter 49

Melody

All the tears were forgotten as Melody sat beside Mike on the stairs of the café that led up to her hiding place. The days of worry washed away, and she knew she was finally where she was meant to be—in Mike's arms.

"I thought I'd never find you," she whispered guessing no one would hear her in the kitchen below.

"I felt the same." His forehead was almost touching hers. "I want you at my side forever, but I felt like something was wrong with our plan. I must have called your cell a hundred times. We've got to get this right, Mel."

"We will." She rubbed her cheek against his shoulder now covered by a uniform. They'd talked at the library on Saturdays for months, but she'd only seen him in civilian clothes. Somehow, he looked older today.

"I drove over to Honey Creek after I heard the rings on my phone. I searched most of the night but had to report back at the fort by dawn."

"I didn't come until the next day."

"I realized we only had to disappear for three months until you are eighteen. But, if I ran with you I'd let my team down. The army wouldn't take me back. We'd have no future. If I kept my job in the army, we'd see the world. I knew, if you managed to get away from your parents, you'd wait for me in Honey Creek. Only you didn't call back and I had no idea what was happening. I almost went mad. Just a few days, I thought. Then I'd ask for a day off and I'd come find you. Only I was needed. I had to work days and I couldn't sleep nights for worrying about you. This wasn't the way we planned it. I thought you'd leave home after your birthday. We'd meet on the dock at midnight and start our new life."

"I guess I was dreaming too," she answered. "I thought when I found you, I'd talk you into staying in the army. It just made me too sad to think you were giving up so much."

Melody continued, "I messed up our plans. A friend of my mother saw us at the library. When Mom asked me about you, I couldn't lie. I knew they wouldn't understand. 'No dates until college,' my father kept yelling. When they demanded my phone, I only had time to call you and let it ring once each time. Then I erased you from my phone as I walked toward my mother and handed over my only way to contact you."

Tears were rolling down her face, but she didn't care. She'd almost given up hope and she would never, ever do that again.

"The rest of the evening my parents talked and I tried not to listen. What they wanted for me was not what I wanted. I wanted you, Mike. That night I packed my backpack and wrote a note saying I was stopping off at my grandmother's place after church. I left the next morning with my head down. They thought they'd won. After my dad dropped me off at church, I walked the two miles to the bus station. The bored clerk didn't even look up at me when I paid in cash. I bought a ticket to Waco knowing I'd be getting off at Honey Creek."

Mike laughed. "Remind me to always let you plan our trips. You're much better than me."

She kissed him quickly before she continued, "I thought the rest would be easy. When you weren't at the dock, I looked all the places you'd told me you used to hang out when you were hiding as a kid. When I made it to the third floor of the café, I finally felt safe."

He laced his fingers in hers. No one in the busy kitchen was paying them any attention as they sat in the shadows halfway up the stairs.

No one but the big man who'd pulled her from the water. He stood at the bottom of the stairs, his back to them, as if he was on guard.

"I have to tell you something, Melody, but first you've got to promise you will not cry. Soldiers' wives have to be strong."

She held him tight as he said he was about to be deployed to a place she couldn't go, but in a year he promised to be back.

A cry came from deep inside, but she straightened trying to be brave.

Several people in the kitchen glanced in her direction.

Melody saw that the big sergeant no longer looked angry.

The people working in the kitchen went back to work and stopped staring. Melody guessed they, like the man called Sergeant, were giving them time.

Finally, Jam climbed halfway up to them. "Dear," she began, looking straight at Melody. "Your parents are in the dining room. They're worried sick about you. If this mess is ever going to be resolved, the best chance might just be here. You two need to face them and tell them how you feel."

Jam turned to Michael. "I know you love her and if

you two want to be together, you will be. But remember, they've loved her for almost eighteen years. And I bet after they meet you, they'll know they'll lose this argument. So, Private, be kind to them."

Mike nodded. "Thanks for letting us have a little time."

Jam smiled. "I'm in your corner, Mike. I always will be. After all, I'm your almost-mother."

While Jam walked away to get the parents, Mike and Melody whispered and hugged. By the time Jam returned, they looked prepared. They stood a few inches apart on the landing, calmly holding hands. Neither made a move down the last half of the stairs leading to the kitchen floor.

Her parents might have tried to get her away from him if Melody stood too far away. She didn't plan to budge, not even if they ordered her down, and the two professors were not the kind of people to make a scene.

"You are never going to see this boy again. Never, Melody, never. As of this minute you are grounded forever." Her dad kept shouting while her mother just cried. Everyone in the room could tell there was no real bite in her father's words.

"Marriage never works at your age," he added. "You don't know enough about life. Soon he'll be halfway around the world."

She and Mike listened without comment, but their grip on each other's hands never relaxed.

Mike looked at Melody and whispered, "We'll figure it out."

When Dr. Avendale took a step toward the stairs, the sergeant blocked his way. He was a few steps away from his daughter but it might as well be a canyon between them.

Jam pulled up a few stools and suggested the parents sit down. The kids came down two steps and sat on the steps at eye level with her parents.

The lectures began, as Melody knew they would. She was tossing all her dreams of becoming educated and finding a challenging career.

But she just sat on the stairs leading up to her hideout, her fingers laced tightly in Mike's hand. All the worry and fear had melted away when she saw him. Her parents no longer held power over her.

She was with Mike. He was alive and he looked as glad to see her as she was to see him. This was the beginning of her future and the ending of her childhood.

Finally, her father lost a bit of his polished air.

First, he tried to get the big sergeant to take Mike away. "He's a child molester. You should lock him up immediately."

The sergeant ignored the professor for a few minutes and finally said, "Near as I can tell, she's holding on to him. Maybe I should arrest her for tampering with government property. I also doubt there was any molesting going on. He told me they met at the library and talked. Unless you count sharing a sandwich on the library steps, these two haven't even had a date."

Her dad then raised his voice. "He's brainwashed our child."

Tucson shrugged. "I don't know about that. Seems your daughter is the one taking action and she ran away from home, your home. Mike, on the other hand, stood his post last week, even took a weekend duty. He didn't even know your daughter was in Honey Creek."

The sergeant's voice was calm. "Apparently, she was running away from you, Professor. All the private seems to be doing is letting her hold his hand. Besides, if he hadn't been helping me out, you would have never found your daughter."

Melody's father seemed to contemplate this for a

moment. Tucson added, "After raising three little brothers, I pretty much figured out that talking a teenager into something is almost impossible."

Melody noticed that Mike looked surprised that the sergeant was taking his side. From their seats halfway up the stairs, Melody felt like they were in the stands watching a drama play out.

Tucson continued, "I'll call the sheriff. I think I'll let him figure this one out. After the riot at the courthouse, he needs the rest." Tucson smiled. "I should warn you, the sheriff met his bride in high school, married her a few days after graduation, and now has two beautiful babies. I think he believes in young love."

Dr. Avendale frowned. "You people had a riot in this little town? What kind of place did this boy drag my daughter to?"

The sergeant frowned. "That's all you got out of my talk? The riot."

No one but Melody seemed to notice an elderly couple stepping into the kitchen. The crew cleaning up from the lunch run flowed around them, politely nodding at the couple, but didn't seem surprised that the lunch guests were walking into the kitchen-turned-courtroom.

Tucson's voice played above all the clanking and footsteps of the café kitchen. "First, at the chance of repeating myself, I need to say, this soldier didn't drag your daughter anywhere, and second, the riot was all senior citizens deciding to have a sleep-in at the courthouse. The sheriff finally arrested the leaders, half a dozen women wearing red hats and one guy who said he had no idea what was going on. He claimed he must have got on the wrong bus. After the leaders were loaded up in the town's three cruisers and taken to jail, all the other rioters came along to visit. I swear the whole sheriff's office reminded me of Congress on a bad day."

Tucson added, "The judge said, since it was after eight a.m. by the time the sheriff got around to arresting them, that legally the courthouse was open. He also claimed there was no law against sitting down in public.

"I heard them talking about holding their next riot in the library, but it will be a lot quieter since the seniors will respect the posted signs."

Melody almost giggled. The sergeant knew what he was doing. He was giving her parents a chance to calm down. Smart battle plan. Her father looked like his eyes might cross at any moment.

Jam finally stepped into the conversation. "Dr. Avendale, don't you think we should all calm down? Your daughter is safe and sound as far as I can see, and less than three months from being eighteen. You can take her home, but you can't keep her away from Michael forever. Please think of what you are doing. If you're not careful, you'll damage your relationship with your daughter forever."

"She's too young to be in love. She'll forget about him." Her father blew up. "She's our child!"

Tucson put his arm around the foot shorter professor and suggested they cool off on the porch. Jam offered Melody's mother tea and Mr. Winston and his lady joined her at the prep bar. The old guy said he was Michael's unofficial grandfather.

While everyone's attention was elsewhere, Mike slipped his high school ring onto Melody's thumb. "Will you be my girl until I get back? I can think of nothing grander than knowing you'll wait for me."

As she stared at the ring, she promised, "I'll email you every day. I'll send pictures."

"You will not," her father demanded as Tucson pulled him out the door.

Mike agreed with her father. "Pictures seemed to cause a bit of trouble. Maybe we should just FaceTime."

Melody watched her mother messing over her tea as she always did. Tea had to be just the right amount of sugar and milk. Just like she'd made it the year she'd spent in England decades ago when she'd been eighteen.

In her mother's world all had to be balanced. Melody had the feeling it might never be that way with her life.

Finally, Melody's mom turned to her. "Do you know his mother?" she asked calmly.

"Of course I know her. She took care of me when I fell in the river. The sergeant saved me. I've been staying with her for a while now. She just didn't know it." Melody looked at Jam. "If you'll let me stay upstairs a little longer, I'll help out in the café for free."

Her mother was always reasonable. "That will not be necessary, Melody. Surely we can work this out. You have to finish high school or they might not let you in college come fall. You'll have to plan, dear." A tiny smile lifted her mother's lips. "At eighteen a woman can know her own mind."

Suddenly the argument changed to a negotiation between Melody and her mother. Her father might think she was his little girl, but her mother knew better.

They began to talk of options. Marriage right now was off the table, but letting Melody stay on weekends in Honey Creek until Mike left might be arranged. Maybe they could still meet at the library, her mother gave in, then added, "But he'll have to go to dinner with us afterward. You'll not be alone with him. And we'll need to get to know him."

Her mother lifted her chin. "A year is a long time to be

apart. You'll grow. You'll change. After writing for a year, you might be closer friends."

Melody almost laughed. "We are friends now, Mom."

Tucson came in with her father, telling him that Mike was a near perfect soldier. He was taking classes in his off time and planned to be a traffic controller by the time he finished serving two more years.

Her father couldn't settle into the idea that his daughter had a boyfriend who was a grown man, but Melody knew her mother was more reasonable. Maybe she knew a great deal more about compromising than her husband did.

As the lunch crew disappeared, Jam invited everyone to coffee and pie on the porch. People drifted outside, but Mike held Melody in place.

She watched the older couple, who'd just dropped in to watch, take her parents in hand like lifetime friends sometimes do. Her father was telling the whole story of how frightened they'd been when Melody disappeared, and surprisingly, the old man in a fedora was asking questions as they headed out.

Mike stood and gently pulled her up beside him. With his arm around her waist, the two of them began to walk backward up the stairs, a step at a time.

As soon as he reached the second floor, they turned and ran up to the third floor, laughing.

In the silence of the dusty hallway, Mike pulled her to him and just held her for a long while, then he kissed her.

She pulled back and stared at him wishing she could remember everything about him. "Don't grow any taller while you're gone. Don't gain a pound. Don't get hurt or shot or even fall and don't do anything that might leave a scar. I want you to come back just the way you are now."

Mike laughed. "I can't promise I'll be exactly the same. You'll grow too, you know. You'll have a year of college when I come back. You might get fat or turn skinny. You might fall down and get a scar. But, Melody, it doesn't matter. I'll still love you."

She kissed him back and he held her so close she could barely breathe. They spent time learning how to kiss and how to hold one another.

Finally, he whispered, "Be happy every day while I'm gone because every day will be one day closer to when I come home."

"Sorry about my parents."

"Don't be. They love you. Eventually, in thirty years or so, they'll figure out I have something in common with them. A love for you too."

He held her face in his hands. "One more moment. I have to remember everything about you."

"We have a little time. I don't want to just look at you. I want a hundred kisses before you leave."

"I'll work on that," he laughed as he picked up her backpack.

Two rag dolls tumbled out.

"Dolls?"

She smiled. "My father asked my grandparents to give me a savings bond for my birthday and Christmas every year." She showed him a slit in the back of one of the dolls. "I think I'll have enough to put down on a house when we settle down."

Mike studied both dolls. "Any idea where this house might be?"

"How about Honey Creek?"

"I'll be there if that's where you are."

Chapter 50

McCoy's Battle

Thursday

McCoy woke the next morning still thinking of how much fun it was to watch Harvey's family come together. The couple would probably never see a Broadway show or travel to another country, but they had something very special right here in the valley.

Sarah-Jane said she'd loved Harvey for a long time, but she didn't want him to think she was easy to get. She had land and that meant something. Of course, Harvey had a good job, and that meant something too. They'd be fine.

McCoy stared at the sunrise and thought about how a place shifts your way of thinking. What seemed so important in the city didn't matter here. He knew when he healed, he'd have to make some choices.

Jam Mackenzie, who owned the Honey Creek Café, had mentioned she wanted to remodel an old house on a property that bordered Pop's land. Like Pop, she'd refused to sell to the developers, but her land wasn't essential to their plan. She had rolling hills and acreage grand for short hikes and long walks. The sunrise and sunset on her land was almost as wonderful to watch as the view he saw from Pop's porch. Jam's few acres were spotted with sunflowers, though, and that made it seem like the whole world was smiling.

In the back of his mind, McCoy had been thinking, if he could get the remodeling job, he might stay around for six months. By then he'd know if small-town living was meant for him, and Pop's place would be in great shape. Maybe, with his dad here, they might build a second floor just in case they decided to come visit now and then. His dad had mentioned a few times that his joints had started acting up during Alaska's hard winters.

McCoy played out the good and bad about staying around. He could help Pop. He might lose some contacts in Houston. He could maybe get a real date with Baylor. She might not be the girl of his dreams, but she could be the woman for a lifetime. There was something about her that made him want to be a better man.

Thinking of the doc, McCoy slowly climbed out of bed and slipped on a lightweight, mud-colored jogging suit his dad had picked up for him at Walmart. The good news was the clothes were a size too big so they went on easy and the cotton felt soft against his skin after wearing the hospital gown. The bad news was they looked like a poor choice in pajamas. A homeless person would have to dress down to meet McCoy's standards.

He slipped into his tennis shoe, knowing he'd never be able to lean over to tie it.

When he walked out into the living area, he almost felt normal. Except, now he was dressed in the same color as everything in the big room.

His dad was cooking breakfast. He looked up and

smiled. "Glad to see you up, son. I'll have breakfast ready in five. Omelets and French toast."

McCoy remembered growing up on cereal for breakfast. "When did you learn to cook?"

"I don't remember the date, but one morning I just woke up and couldn't face another bowl of Wheaties. After that morning, I ate out until the first snow. In Alaska folks stay in after that. So, I learned to cook."

McCoy moved very slowly, but he made it to the table.

"Need any help?" Dad asked as McCoy lowered into the nearest chair.

"I could use a little help tying my shoes."

Dad laughed. "I've done that a few hundred times for you. I thought you'd never learn." As he knelt to tie the sneaker, he added, "You were a fast learner on most things. You could pick up how to fix things fast and you wouldn't leave a project until you'd finished. I was always proud of you."

McCoy stared at his dad, trying to understand the man before him. Dad somehow had found feelings along with his cooking skills and sense of humor.

Suddenly, McCoy heard the echoes of every girlfriend he'd ever had. They'd all said he never talked about his feelings, never said "I love you."

If he blamed that on his dad never talking about feelings, then Dad could blame Pop and, who knows, Pop might blame his father. McCoy was from generations of men who never talked of their emotions. It was hereditary.

Somehow, just knowing that one fact helped McCoy forgive his dad. J.D. had loved him in his own way, in the only way he knew how.

It stops here, McCoy almost said aloud as his dad served breakfast.

They ate in silence for a few minutes, then McCoy said

calmly, "You do know that I love you, Dad. You raised me all by yourself. You always saw that I had what I needed and you taught me to work. You didn't just do as good as you could. You did great."

His dad didn't say a word; he just kept eating. But when McCoy looked up, he saw a single tear sliding down his dad's weathered face.

The silence was shattered as Pop rushed in from the porch. "Car's coming up the road."

The old man pulled the rifle propped behind the door and headed back out as if no further explanation was necessary. Dad grabbed his phone and followed.

McCoy slowly stood, nursing his side as he limped out the door. Without a word, he lowered himself into the rocker.

He was once again at his post as target.

They didn't have to wait long before two men climbed out of a limo. Both were dressed in expensive suits and the younger carried a thick folder.

When they saw the rifle resting across Pop's arm, they slowed.

McCoy didn't move. He felt like he'd been living in an action movie for weeks and it was about time to yell, "Bring it on, guys. I'll take whatever you've got." If the suits turned into armor and their heads popped off to allow room for horns, he wouldn't flinch.

"We mean you no harm, Mr. Mason," the younger man said as he rested one foot on the first step as if staking a claim.

Pop shifted the rifle. "State your business."

The older man moved forward. "Robert Harold with Norris, Mays and Harold, Attorneys-at-Law. I'm here to tell you the investors on the Lone Star Country Living Project are very upset about the trouble you're having.

They hired men to talk you into selling, not shoot your stock. I want you to be aware that those men have been fired."

"They shot my grandson," Pop said.

McCoy didn't appreciate Pop pointing at him with his rifle.

The older suit looked surprised for a blink. "I'm sure that was an accident. We are here to offer you twice the value of your land. That should more than cover any bills you've encountered from the trouble."

"Not interested," Pop said in a low voice.

The older lawyer fought to hide his anger. "Are you aware, sir, that this entire project will have to be scratched if you don't sell? We'll have to start over somewhere else. This is the perfect location and your land is vital to our success."

Pop smiled. "I know. This land has one of the first trails running through it. If you look close, you can still see the line of stagecoach tracks. No one has ever thought this land was worth anything except for just passing through. That's why my grandfather bought it so cheap."

The men in suits kept talking, but the Mason men had quit listening.

Eventually, the strangers climbed back in their car and drove away.

The last words McCoy heard from the lawyer was something about "who cares about a stagecoach trail."

Chapter 51

Breaking Ground
on the Sunflower Inn

Friday

Tucson stood on the porch of an old rundown house out in the middle of land that had never seen a plow.

Jam wanted to show him her mother's childhood home. Her grandfather had built it for nine children and Jam swore she could almost hear the echoes of laughter. Mackenzie had built the house to live in, not farm. Jam's grandfather had owned the mercantile.

"I'll never have children," she whispered as she brushed the wood of a door that had stood for almost a hundred years. "But I can build a place where people can come to relax or heal from the sadness life sometimes brings. This won't be a bed and breakfast or vacation spot. It will be calm waters amid the storms of life."

She scrubbed tears away. "It's my next dream, Tucson. I have to build it."

The sergeant stood behind her and circled his arms around her. "Mike said you were the only mother he's ever had. It was nice of you to invite him to stay with you until he's deployed. The kid surprised me. He stood up to

Melody's parents, never raising his voice. Even in their anger, they could see his nature."

She laughed. "I'm going to treat him like he's mine, but I'm guessing he'll be visiting Melody often for the next few weeks. Her parents finally agreed to let him see her. He's a good man, even if he is young. I heard Dr. Avendale telling Mr. Winston how much money traffic controllers make. He claimed Mike would make twice a professor's salary by the time he gets out of the army."

Tucson laughed. "I'll be surprised if he gets out in two years. He might just stay in. It's not a bad life and Melody said they planned to see the world before they settle down."

Tucson kissed her neck as he turned Jam in his arms. "I have to leave at dawn. My time in Honey Creek is over. Little brother doesn't need me anymore. When Mike told me the photos were just pictures of their day and the blood was ketchup, I considered stopping the car to show him what real blood looked like. But then I'd lose time with you because I'd probably have to take him to the hospital."

He stopped laughing. "I don't want to miss an hour of being with you."

"Don't leave," she whispered as he kissed a tear away. "Even with all the things happening, I've never known a time in my life like these few weeks."

"I can't stay. Come with me, Jam. We could travel."

"I can't go. My roots are here."

"I do love you, Jam. That is never going to change. Sleeping next to you seems to be where I belong. I feel wholly alive for the first time in my life. Marry me. Travel with me. Sleep with me every night."

"I love you too," she whispered. "I could never move. My life, my dreams are here."

For a long while they just held each other. They'd spent

almost every night wrapped up together since she'd met him by the river. They'd made love more times than she could count, but they both knew they were not meant to be a couple.

Finally, he whispered, "If I asked you to, would you meet me somewhere, anywhere when I have leave? You'd only be away a few weeks. A month at the most."

"I would." She smiled. "Will you come home when you're in the States for holidays? I'd love to cook for you." She winked. "Among other things."

He kissed the tip of her nose. "Who knows. Mike and Melody might join us."

"I would like that but best of all, I'd love to sleep beside you on a cold night. You might not know it, Sergeant, but you're a very cuddly man."

"I will come see you in every season and, if it's possible, I plan to be standing right here every February fourteenth to kiss my one love on Valentine's Day. We may not be with each other every day, but you'll know I'm loving you wherever I am."

He lifted her up and swung her around. "We'll make this work. I'll call you every night we're not together. And, when we are together, we'll store up enough memories to last us until we meet again."

Jam kissed him. They might love their jobs, but somehow they'd figure out a way to love each other as well.

Epilogue

McCoy's Revelation

Three Months Later

McCoy watched the sunset. Pure gold. He sat in one of the new rocking chairs Pop had brought home from his weekly trip to town. He watched as Pop came in from his walk around the land. The dog was bouncing along beside him.

Pop put his rifle inside and said, "I went over to see the remodel on Jam's new Sunflower Inn. It looks real good, boy."

"I've got some inside work." McCoy frowned. "I'm not a boy, Pop."

"You are to me. You're not dry behind the ears before you're forty." Pop took a seat. "Did John call? It's about time he comes home."

"He called. Said he'd be back in Texas before the first storm hits Alaska."

Pop nodded as he rocked.

They'd just had one of the longest conversations they'd shared in days, but McCoy wasn't finished. "Pop, that day the men in suits came, you said your grandfather bought this place. Didn't it bother him that something terrible happened here? At the little stage station, two men died in a botched robbery. I read the account in a copy of one of the early newspapers. One man was tortured, his fingers cut off, and the other was tied to the fence and used for target practice."

"I've heard the story. My grandfather told it to me when I was a kid. He was almost a hundred and I was six. The two men who died were his uncle and his father."

"What!" McCoy almost tumbled out of the rocker.

"Grandpa said his uncle often rode shotgun when the stage was carrying gold, and Grandpa's father operated the station."

McCoy tried to make sense of the story. "You're telling me my ancestors were tortured and killed over a box of gold."

Pop stopped rocking. "No, they didn't care about the box. I'm guessing they knew the outlaws would kill them no matter what they said."

"Then why didn't they give them the strongbox? They might have had a slim chance of living."

"Because the strongbox was buried in the ground surrounded by a thick stand of trees. My six-year-old grandfather was hidden there. If they'd told the outlaws where the box was, the kid might have died with them.

"My grandfather must have helped bury the box and waited in the trees for the bad guys to leave.

"Neighbors, the first Mackenzies to settle here, took him in and helped raised him. When he was grown, he bought this land no one else wanted."

McCoy raised one eyebrow suspecting Pop was pulling

his leg. "I guess you're going to tell me next that he gave you the strongbox."

"No. He gave me the key and told me the box was over there under that big elm that forks just like a giant pitchfork. I put the key in the mortar of the fireplace so I wouldn't lose it. I guess I should've told you, McCoy, in case you ever need money."

McCoy rocked back in his chair. "No, Pop, I'm good right now."

He'd just realized two Mason men, almost a hundred and fifty years ago, went through torture to save a kid. Now that's love.

He came from a long line of men who might not know how to talk about love, but they lived and died for it.

That night McCoy decided when Baylor picked him up for their second real date, he planned to love the doc whether he was good enough for her or not. Maybe if he kept it up, she'd finally break and take him home.

She grew more beautiful every day. Somehow she completed his world.

He could see the whole future. They'd get married and have a few kids who would, of course, get ponies. He'd help her out in her work while he restored some of the beautiful old houses in Honey Creek. After looking around town, he figured he could spend fifty years remodeling.

Then they'd retire on the farm and drive over to Jam's Sunflower Inn and have dinner like all longtime lovers do in the valley.

Then one day, when he was old, he'd show his grandson the key in Pop's old fireplace and tell him the story of the strongbox.

McCoy didn't plan to ever dig up the strongbox.

After all, he was rich already. He had all the gold he needed in the sunset.

STRAWBERRY LANE

**Set in the charming small town of Honey Creek,
Texas, *New York Times* bestselling author Jodi
Thomas's latest novel tells the heartwarming,
tenderly romantic tale of a man
who drives his car off a cliff—
straight into a life he never imagined . . .**

Starri Knight is a big believer in fate. How else to
explain the compelling connection she feels to the
stranger she pulls out of a wrecked car on the very same
road where her parents died twenty years earlier?
Alongside Auntie Ona-May, the only mother she's ever
known, Starri saves Rusty O'Sullivan's life—just as
Ona-May once did when Starri was an orphaned babe.
But convincing Rusty he has something to live for is
going to take all of Starri's faith in miracles . . .

Like a wish he hadn't even known to make, Starri landed
in Rusty's life, filling him with a longing for a family. . . .
Then Jackson Landry, a new lawyer, turns up to present
a surprise that will change the direction of his life:
An inheritance from the father Rusty never knew—
and the promise of the family he'd never had.
It's a lot for the hard-bitten loner to
accept as love rushes into his life . . .

A sense of duty has Rusty heading to Honey Creek to
deal with his father's estate—and find his lost siblings.
But having family is one thing;
learning to love them is another.
Good thing new friends are by his side
to help him along the way.

The Will

"The bed is too hard. I thought hospital beds were supposed to be comfortable," Joey Morrel complained to Jackson Willington in a half-drunk whine.

"Mr. Morrell, I'm not involved in hospital furnishings. I'm your lawyer." Jackson lifted his briefcase as if showing proof of his new title. "Now, we need to get down to the topic of your will. You may not have much time left."

Jackson kept his voice low, hoping to sound older.

Joey reached for his cigarettes. Camels, no filter.

"I didn't know they still made Camels. Never mind. Irrelevant. You can't smoke in here, Mr. Morrell. I don't think Dr. Henton would approve, and I saw the no smoking sign when I ran through the emergency entrance."

"Jackson, you're no more fun than your dad. The SOB up and died on me before I got my affairs organized. I'd just finished listing my heirs from a few of those affairs years ago, when they tossed me in the ambulance, and now, I find out I've got a wet-behind-the-ears lawyer."

"You were having a heart attack, Mr. Morrell. The bartender called 911, then you told him to call me." Jackson noticed the old guy wasn't listening. If sins showed on a man's face, Joey Morrell was the bad side of Dorian Grey.

Joey coughed. "I did love those women I found in my

younger days, but I never wanted to do the paperwork. Every darling I slept with cussed me out for not marrying her. They all said I didn't have a heart, so that's proof I can't die of a heart attack. But you, being my lawyer, are going to make it right, Jackson, just in case? I'm keeping my word to your old man to sign a will. I plan to pay for my folly."

"I'll do my best to help you, sir." Jackson thought of cussing. He should have been an accountant. His dad left him every crazy old goat in the valley to deal with. Joey Morrell was as bad as the lady who came in every Monday to change her will. Every time one of her cats died or peed on the rug, the feline was disinherited.

"Good. Make it fast, boy. I'm not feeling so good." Morrell coughed again. "About time to roll the dice on whether I walk out of this place one more time. The women I attract nowadays are drunks, mean and ugly even with my glasses off. Might as well head down to Hell. The pickings couldn't be much worse."

Jackson leaned over the bed. "That why you're refusing the heart surgery, Morrell? You want to leave it to chance?"

Joey smiled. "I may have done a hell of a lot of bad things, but I swear I'm not a liar. I've spent sixty years gambling and I ain't stopping now. I like women, but I wasn't born with enough heart to love one. Strange little creatures if you ask me. Nesters. And me, I was born to ride the open roads." He stopped long enough to push the call button again.

"I've already cheated death three times. I got out of that hospital in New Orleans after I was left for dead in an alley for two days. Ten years ago, I was in a bad wreck, they said no one could walk away from and at twenty a medic took four bullets out of my chest.

"Jackson, it'll be another thirty years and another dozen

women before I wear out, but I promised your daddy I'd make a will if I ever ended up in a hospital again."

"Then, let's get started. How about we begin with your assets, Mr. Morrell. I know you have an old Camaro, a little piece of land along the north rim, and an eighteen-wheeler truck. You never married. No living relatives."

Waving the lawyer away, Joey leaned back on a stack of pillows. "I'm tired, boy, and I'll miss the news if you stay any longer. I wrote down all you need to know." Joey handed him a folded piece of paper. "Draw it up all legal like. Don't come back until after breakfast. The nurse said she has to spoon-feed me if I'm weak come morning." A wicked smiled crossed his pasty face. "There ain't nothing nicer that a big-busted woman with short arms feeding a man."

Jackson had enough of Joey Morrell. The drunk was as worthless as his father used to say he was. "I'll take care of everything, Mr. Morrell." Just for spite, he added, "Anyone you want to notify to come to your funeral?"

"No. I'll go it alone. Cremate my body and spread my ashes out on Eagle's Peak."

Jackson put the folded paper in his empty briefcase and walked out of Joey's room. As he passed Dr. Paul Henton, Jackson shook his head. "The old man thinks you're too young to be a doc and I'm too dumb to be his lawyer."

Paul took the time to look up from a chart. The doc nodded. "He won't let me operate or move him to a big hospital for surgery. Claimed he'd chosen option number three. Get over it. He told me he plans to be out of this place before happy hour tomorrow."

"What are his chances?" Jackson asked.

The doctor, whom Jackson had played football with through high school, was honest as always. "Not good. You might want to get that will done."

"I'm heading home before the rain gets worse. I'll work on it tonight and have it ready by morning." Jackson hesitated, then added, "Call if you need me."

The doctor turned back to his charts as he added, "I will. Same for you."

Jackson turned his collar up and ran for his pickup, thinking if he ever made any money in this small town, he'd buy a proper car. Maybe a Lincoln, or a BMW. Lawyers should drive something better than a twenty-year-old, handed-down beat-up farm truck.

Half an hour later Jackson was holding the square of paper Joey had given him in his hand when the hospital called. As the nurse explained how Mr. Morrell died yelling for his supper, the lawyer read the note below four names with birthdays beside each. It read: Give it all to my offspring.

Morrell's signature was clear. Dated an hour ago. Witnessed by a nurse and some guy who wrote "janitor" under his name.

"Damn," Jackson said as he stared at the names. "The old guy knew he was dying. Probably didn't mention it just to irritate the hell out of me."

Joey died leaving all he owned to four names on a piece of paper.

Four sons he'd probably never met. All with different last names and none of them Morrell.

ANDY DELANE—30—FORT SILL

RUSTY MACAMISH—34—SOMEDAY VALLEY

ZACHARY HOLMES—25—AUSTIN

GRIFFITH LAURENT—27—FRENCH QUARTER
NEW ORLEANS

Joey lived within a day's drive of one of his sons. Another son lived thirty miles away on the other side of the valley, but Jackson would bet not one of them had ever seen Joey. That could be a good thing. Joey wasn't much of a man or a father. Not one carried his name was proof.

Jackson had taken over his father's practice in Honey Creek two months ago and his first client left this world without paying.

But Jackson would do his duty and hope none of Joey's boys took after their sperm donor. He'd find the boys, now men, but he doubted they'd be glad to see him.

Chapter 1

Someday Valley

Midnight

Rusty MacAmish gunned the old Ford's engine just before he swung left and headed up the hill toward Someday Valley. There was always a chance the car wouldn't make the incline on the dirt road, but he'd had a hell of a day and figured bad luck had to run out sometime.

Mud moving downhill like lava on his left. A ten-feet drop was on his right. Bald tires didn't put up much of a fight to hold on to the two-lane road.

In the midnight rain Rusty felt the Fairlane began to slide sideways. Then like a slow-motion rerun, the Ford tilted left as the road disappeared and three thousand pounds of steel began to roll. Rusty tightened his grip on the steering wheel as if he still had some control of the car or his life.

He didn't bother to scream or cuss. He simply braced for a crash.

The ground slammed into the passenger side shattering glass and metal. Then, as the roof hit the incline, he felt the cut of his seatbelt and it seemed to be snowing glass.

The Ford rolled again and the driver's door pushed against Rusty's shoulder. He clenched as it rolled again and the inside of what had once been a car was now a coffin of flying glass and metal.

Something hit his head and the night went completely black, but for a moment, the sounds remained in his head as if echoing what had been his life.

One last echo whispered through the bedlam. One word he'd heard for as long as he could remember.

Worthless.

Chapter 2

Starri Knight lay on the hardwood floor of her aunt's hundred-year-old cabin as she watched rain slide down the huge picture window. If she didn't move, maybe she'd feel closer to nature as she had when she was a child. Maybe the moon would play peek-a-boo with her in the storm clouds. She was almost positive the man in the moon had once when she was small.

When she was a kid, stars winked at her and the moon smiled. She'd tell her Aunt Ona-May and they'd laugh.

But tonight, all Starri saw was car lights making their way up the hill and lightning running across the sky like a tidal wave igniting.

All her life pretty much everyone who took the back trail in rain got stuck. Her Aunt Ona-May would wait until morning to back the tracker out of the barn and go pull them out of the mud. For thirty bucks, of course.

Starri watched the rain as she remembered the story of the night her aunt took her in as if she were really kin. Her aunt said one dark night a young couple, not out of their teens, took the road to Someday Valley way too fast.

They collided with a pickup coming down hauling hay. The crash killed both the teenagers instantly, but the baby in the back didn't have a scratch.

While the two farmers to the north heard the crash and came running to help the driver pinned inside his truck, Ona-May crawled in the window and pulled out a baby in the backseat of the young couple's car. She said the minute she pushed the blanket away the baby reached up trying to touch the stars.

No one came to take the baby that night. Ona-May decided to call the tiny child Starri until kin came. But, no one came. No one wanted the tiny baby.

Since Ona-May Jones was a nurse in her younger days, the county let her foster the child.

Starri smiled, remembering the beginning of her story. She couldn't miss parents she'd never known, but she was thankful Aunt Ona-May found her. Auntie might never have a family of her own, but she poured all her love on a tiny baby.

Starri watched as the car on the incline began to roll sideways down the hill. For a moment it seemed no more than an awkward falling star.

Then the sounds of glass and metal snapping blending with the rain, and Starri screamed.

Someone was dying in the same spot her parents had twenty years ago. She closed her eyes reliving a memory that had formed before words.

As always her auntie's arms surrounded her. "Starri, it's all right." As the old woman saw the car rolling, she added calmly. "Get on your boots. We've work to do."

Auntie's old body straightened into the nurse she'd been in Vietnam, fifty years ago.

As she collected supplies, Starri dialed 911 and was told

the road between Honey Creek and Someday Valley was closed. One of the bridges was out. The only ambulance in the valley was on the other side of the bridge.

"We'll take care of it, Starri. Don't worry. Doctoring humans is pretty much like doctoring the other animals around here."

Starri nodded, but she wasn't sure she believed her aunt.

As they marched up the hill, the lights on the car went out but the rattling continued as if the auto was dying a slow death. The engine was still sputtering when they reached the wreck. Their flashlights swept the ground like lightning bugs hopping in the night.

"Here," Ona-May yelled as she moved a few feet below the car.

Starri ventured closer making out the outline of a body. A tall man dressed all in black. Rain seemed to be pounding on the body as if determined to push him in the ground.

Auntie pulled off her raincoat and covered him. "I can't see where he's hurt, but he's breathing. We'll roll him on your raincoat and pull him to the cabin. If he makes the journey back to the house, I'd say he's got a chance."

Starri followed orders. She'd seen her aunt set a broken leg and stitch up a cowboy who refused to go to the doctor. Auntie delivered babies before the doctor could come out. The people in the valley were mostly poor and didn't go to a doctor unless they had to. They knew Ona-May would take care of what she could and often loan them money if she recommended the doctor.

As they pulled the unconscious stranger over the wet grass, Starri thought of another talent her aunt had. She loved people. Not just the good ones or the righteous ones like the preacher counted. She loved them all, even the sinners and the drunks.

Starri figured Ona-May overlooked folk's shortcomings because she had a few herself. She wasn't beyond stealing the neighbor's apples or corn and she cussed when she was frustrated. And, every New Year's eve she'd drink and tell stories of her days in the Army.

As they reached the cabin, her aunt started issuing orders as if she had troops and not just Starri.

"We'll put him on the floor by the fireplace. Get me towels and warm water. Start cleaning him up while I collect supplies and call the doctor over in Honey Creek. I can already see our patient has an arm broke so cut off his shirt. I'm guessing he's got internal injuries. Oh, add logs to the fire, girl."

Starri stared down at the muddy man with hard times showing in worry lines. "You'll have to help me, mister. I can't even remember all the orders. Ona-May gets like that sometimes when she's excited but my ears still listen slow. She was an emergency nurse for thirty years. You're in good hands."

"Starri, get moving," Ona-May yelled from the kitchen. "We got to keep him alive until the ambulance gets here."

She handed her aunt the phone as she ran for towels and a pan of hot water. When she returned, the stranger's eyes were open. She saw pain, but not fear.

"You an angel, sweetheart?" he whispered.

"No," she answered. "I'm a star that fell out of the sky twenty years ago. Kids at school said I'm as strange as they come, but I'm not. I'm just different."

"Me too," he said. "I'm Rusty MacAmish. Folks say I'm worthless. You're wasting your time fixing me up. I'll just scatter again."

He closed his eyes as she gently washed his face. She didn't know if he fell asleep or passed out, but the worry lines faded on his face. She barely heard him whisper, "Watch over me, little star."

"I will. You just rest. Don't worry about that windshield wiper sticking out of your side. My aunt can fix that."

Chapter 3

Jackson ran through his parents' house stripping off his clothes as fast as he could with one hand as he held his cell in the other.

"Slow down, Paul. I can meet you at the bridge with two mounts. I've got Raymond saddling two horses and loading them in the trailer now. I can be there by the time you can drive to and from the hospital to that old bridge heading into Someday Valley." Jackson hit speaker as he pulled on jeans. "Any idea who the injured man is?"

"Yeah," Paul answered. "He's your client's son. He's Joey Morrell's oldest son."

Visit our website at
KensingtonBooks.com
to sign up for our newsletters, read
more from your favorite authors, see
books by series, view reading group
guides, and more!

Become a Part of Our
Between the Chapters Book Club
Community and Join the Conversation

When she didn't say anything, he finally added, "I was fishing and flipped my boat after a water moccasin crawled in with me. I grew up in this valley, but I've been gone a dozen years, and apparently I've forgotten all I ever knew about fishing."

He sounded angry, not at her but maybe at the world. Jam wished she'd brought out a flashlight so she could see him better and, if needed, to use as a weapon. "What's your name?"

"What do you care?"

"I own this land you flopped up on."

His words were no more friendly than hers. "You want me to jump back in? It seems I'm in hostile territory."

He reminded her of a wild animal. Powerful. Primeval. Ready for battle. She had no doubt he'd dive back in the water if she ordered him off her property.

"No. You can stay. I've got towels in the kitchen. You can borrow a few. I might get arrested for letting you walk back to town naked." Jam couldn't resist looking, just to make sure he was totally naked.

He didn't seem to notice or care. "Thanks. I'm Sergeant Tucson Smith, by the way. My younger brother is getting sworn in as sheriff tomorrow. If you want to file charges on me for trespassing, call him."

She relaxed a bit. Her mud monster was becoming human.

"I know your brother. I'm proud to call Pecos a friend. I'm Jessica Ann Mackenzie. Everyone calls me Jam." She didn't say more. They knew one another's families. That was enough of an introduction.

Jam headed to the house. He followed.

As they reached the porch light's glow, she looked back. Mud man had Pecos Smith's coloring, brown eyes and hair, but this older brother was twice the deputy's weight and looked solid as a tree trunk. Even naked, he marched like a soldier.

"Where are you staying, Sergeant Smith?"

"Nowhere. Pecos said I could borrow the mayor's boat if I wanted to fish, but to tell the truth, I didn't even bother to buy bait. I just wanted to drift on the water for a while. I figured I'd just sleep out here, but I'm guessing my gear and the mayor's boat are both at the bottom of the river."

She opened the back door, reached in, and handed him a towel that barely went halfway around his waist. "Drop your things in the washer under the stairs. You can shower upstairs while you wait for your uniform. I can at least offer that to our new sheriff's brother. He may be young, but most folks in this county look up to him."

"Good to hear," Tucson said as he walked into the shadows of the stairs.

It crossed her mind that he could have gone to the farm where he grew up, but Pecos never talked about his parents. Maybe they'd moved years ago or didn't speak to their sons.

She heard Tucson follow orders. He dropped his clothes in one of the café's washers. "It won't take long," she said.

The only answer was the sound of the washer lid dropping.

Jam forced herself not to look at him as she turned on the prep table's light in the big kitchen. "You hungry? I could scramble you up some eggs and make toast."

Halfway up the stairs, he turned. "I don't want to be a bother. I'll be on my way as soon as my clothes are ready. I got a rental car up the road a few miles. I can sleep in it. Come morning I'll buy something to wear to the ceremony."

She nodded and added, "Shower is the second door on the left. I'll watch your clothes. How many?"

He was on the landing. "How many what?"

"Eggs. I'll have them ready by the time you clean up."

"A dozen if you've got them." Then wearing only a towel, he disappeared.

"I've got them," she murmured. It occurred to her that the valentine wish she always made might have finally come true. A lover for a night with no strings attached came wrapped in a towel.

Only the soldier seemed about as cuddly as a cactus, and he looked like he never bothered to smile.

She made him ranch eggs with sausage and peppers, then heated several pieces of homemade bread with butter and cinnamon sugar on top. By the time he came down, wearing a bigger towel, she'd switched his clothes to the dryer.

Jam handed him the biggest T-shirt she had with the café's logo on it. It stretched over his chest like a second skin.

They sat on stools pulled up to the prep table. When she passed him a heaping plate, he managed a quick smile. "Thanks, I'm starving."

"I hope it's good."

He grabbed another fork from the rack and handed it to her. "Join me."

When he took his first bite, he closed his eyes. "Perfect."

Then he stared at her, and whispered again, "Perfect," as if he were no longer talking about the food.

She reached over and stabbed a morsel, and nibbled on it while he ate a meal big enough to feed a family of four.

No longer covered in mud and almost smiling, Tucson Smith was an attractive man, and Jam had to fight the urge to touch him. Somehow, he still didn't seem real. But, since she'd found him, she decided he was hers, at least for Valentine's Day.

"I was told never to trust a slender cook, but you are a master." He winked at her. "And I am not saying that because I've been living on army food for a dozen years."

He ate and she watched him enjoy the meal. They didn't know one another well enough to make conversation. She refilled his milk twice, and he thanked her both times.

As he finished the plate, the buzzer went off on the dryer. He stood and moved to the shadows under the stairs. With no hesitation, he dropped the towel, pulled out his wrinkled uniform, and began to dress.

Without hesitation, she watched.

"How can I repay you, lovely cook?" His back was to her as he buttoned his trousers.

Jam stepped closer, almost near enough to touch the muscles on his back.

When he turned, she saw surprise in his eyes, then a silent question, and then definite interest.

For one long moment their gazes locked. Two people truly seeing one another. His words came so low it seemed a thought passing between them. "Name it, Jam. What's on your mind? Name how I can repay you."

Lowering her eyes, she whispered, "My café was full of lovers tonight, and I can't even remember the last real kiss I've had."

He frowned as if he didn't believe her. "You're sure?" He seemed to breathe the question in as he halved the space between them.

"I'm sure."

Slowly, like a man approaching a mirage, he moved his hand to the side of her face. She felt the warmth of his palm and closed her eyes, pretending he was real. Pretending he wanted her.

His arm circled her waist and pulled her against him gently, but his lips brushed her ear, not her mouth.